"Something altogether d_____
for a lush style . . . Wit_____
it delivers on heat and emotion and a__
well-earned happily ever after."
—*The New York Times Book Review*

"ONE OF THE RISING STARS OF
HISTORICAL ROMANCE."
—*Booklist*

"THOMAS . . . HAS MADE A NAME FOR HERSELF
WITH HER EXQUISITE USE OF LANGUAGE."
—*Library Journal*

PRAISE FOR THE NOVELS OF SHERRY THOMAS

"Ravishingly sinful, intelligent, and addictive. An amazing
debut."   —Eloisa James, *New York Times* bestselling author

"Enchanting . . . An extraordinary, unputdownable love
story."   —Jane Feather, *New York Times* bestselling author

"Sublime . . . An irresistible literary treat."   —*Chicago Tribune*

"A masterpiece . . . A beautifully written, exquisitely seductive,
powerfully romantic gem of a romance."
                                    —*Kirkus Reviews* (starred review)

"Sherry Thomas's captivating debut novel will leave readers
breathless. Intelligent, witty, sexy, and peopled with wonderful
characters . . . and sh_____

Berkley Sensation titles by Sherry Thomas

BEGUILING THE BEAUTY

RAVISHING THE HEIRESS

TEMPTING THE BRIDE

THE LUCKIEST LADY IN LONDON

MY BEAUTIFUL ENEMY

My Beautiful Enemy

SHERRY THOMAS

BERKLEY SENSATION, NEW YORK

THE BERKLEY PUBLISHING GROUP
Published by the Penguin Group
Penguin Group (USA) LLC
375 Hudson Street, New York, New York 10014

USA • Canada • UK • Ireland • Australia • New Zealand • India • South Africa • China

penguin.com

A Penguin Random House Company

MY BEAUTIFUL ENEMY

A Berkley Sensation Book / published by arrangement with the author

Berkley Sensation Books are published by The Berkley Publishing Group.
BERKLEY SENSATION® is a registered trademark of Penguin Group (USA) LLC.
The "B" design is a trademark of Penguin Group (USA) LLC.

For information, address: The Berkley Publishing Group,
a division of Penguin Group (USA) LLC,
375 Hudson Street, New York, New York 10014.

ISBN: 978-0-425-26889-6

PUBLISHING HISTORY
Berkley Sensation mass-market edition / August 2014

PRINTED IN THE UNITED STATES OF AMERICA

10 9 8 7 6 5 4 3 2

Cover art by Gregg Gulbronson.
Cover design by George Long.
Interior text design by Laura K. Corless.

To Louis Cha and Gu Long,
for making my childhood magical

ACKNOWLEDGMENTS

Wendy McCurdy, for the wonderful creative freedom I enjoy.

Kristin Nelson and everyone at the Nelson Literary Agency, for always being there.

Janine Ballard, for her invaluable guidance in shaping the final draft of this book.

Samantha Whiting, for answering my questions about display cases in the British Museum. Her answer did not make it into this version of the story but I am no less grateful.

My friends, for being the best friends ever.

My family, for handling my deadlines with panache.

And you, dear reader, thank you. Thank you from the bottom of my heart.

PROLOGUE

On a storm-whipped sea, some prayed, some puked. Catherine Blade wedged herself between the bed and the bulkhead of her stateroom and went on with her breathing exercises, ignoring fifty-foot swells of the North Atlantic and the teetering of the steamship.

A muffled shriek, faint but entirely unexpected, nearly caused her pooled chi to scatter. Really, she'd expected more reserve from members of the British upper class.

Then a blunt sound, that of an object striking the human body. She frowned. Was it a passenger banging into the furniture or had she heard an act of violence? She checked for the box of matches she carried inside her blouse.

There was no light in the corridor—the electricity had been cut off. She braced her feet apart, held on to the doorknob, and listened, diving beneath the unholy lashing of the waves, the heroic, if desperate, roar of the ship's engines, and the fearful moans in staterooms all along the corridor—the abundant dinner from earlier now tossing in stomachs as turbulent as the sea.

The shriek came again, all but lost in the howl of the storm. It came from the outside this time, farther fore along the port promenade.

She walked on soft, cloth-soled shoes that made no sounds. The air in the passage was colder and damper than it ought to have been—someone had opened a door to the outside. She suspected a domestic squabble. The English were a stern people in outward appearance, but they did not lack for passion and injudiciousness in private.

A cross-corridor interrupted the rows of first-class state-rooms. At the two ends of the cross-corridor were doors leading onto the promenade. She stopped at the scent of blood. "Who's there?"

"Help . . ."

She recognized the voice, though she'd never heard it so weak. "Mrs. Reynolds, are you all right?"

The light of a match showed that Mrs. Reynolds was not all right. She bled from her head. Blood smeared her face and her white dressing gown. Next to her on the carpet sprawled a large, leather-bound Bible, likely her own—and likely the weapon with which she had been assaulted.

The ship plunged. Catherine leaped and stayed Mrs. Reynolds before the latter's temple slammed into the bulkhead. She gripped Mrs. Reynolds's wrist. The older woman's skin was cold and clammy, but her pulse was strong enough and she was in no immediate danger of bleeding to death.

"Althea . . . outside . . . save her . . ."

Althea was Mrs. Reynolds's sister Mrs. Chase. Mrs. Chase could rot.

"Let's stop your bleeding," she said to Mrs. Reynolds, ripping a strip of silk from the latter's dressing gown.

"No!" Mrs. Reynolds pushed away the makeshift bandage. "Please . . . Althea first."

Catherine sighed. She would comply—that was what came of a lifetime of deference to one's elders. "Hold this," she said, pressing the matchbox and the strip of silk into Mrs. Reynolds's hands.

She was soaked the moment she stepped outside. The ship slanted up. She grabbed a handrail. A blue-white streak of lightning tore across the black sky, illuminating needles of rain that pummeled the ankle-deep water sloshing along the walkway. Illuminating a drenched Mrs. Chase, nightgown clinging to her ripe flesh, abdomen balanced on the rail, body flexed like a bow—as if she were an aerialist in midflight. Her arms flailed, her eyes screwed shut, her mouth issued gargles of incoherent terror.

A more distant flash of lightning briefly revealed the silhouette of a man standing behind Mrs. Chase, holding on to her feet. Then the heavens erupted in pale fire. Thunderbolts spiked and interwove, a chandelier of the gods that would set the entire ocean ablaze. And she saw the man's face.

Lin.

A numb shock singed every last one of her nerve endings, so that she was cold and burning at once.

The man should be dead. He had been beheaded years ago, hadn't he? She wiped the rain from her eyes. But he was still there, the murderer of her child. He was still there.

Sometimes she could no longer recall her infant daughter's exact features, but always she remembered the warmth of holding the baby close—the awe that she should have been given such a wonderful child. Until she was sobbing over the baby's lifeless body, with nothing in her heart but despair and hatred.

A dagger from her vambrace hissed through the air, the sound of its flight lost in the thunder that rent her ears. But he heard. He jerked his head back at the last possible second, the knife barely missing his nose.

Darkness. The ship listed sharply starboard. Mrs. Chase's copious flesh hit the deck with a thud and a splash. Catherine threw herself down as two sleeve arrows shot past her.

The steamer crested a swell and plunged into the hollow between waves. She allowed herself to slide forward on the smooth planks of the walkway. A weak lightning at the edge of the horizon offered a fleeting glow, enough for her to see his outline.

She pushed off the deck and, borrowing the ship's own downward momentum, leaped toward him, one knife in each hand. He threw a large object at her. She couldn't see, but it had to be Mrs. Chase; there was nothing else of comparable size nearby.

She flipped the knives around in her palms and caught Mrs. Chase, staggering backward. The ship began its laborious climb up another huge swell. She set Mrs. Chase down and let the small river on deck wash them both toward the door. She had to get Mrs. Chase out of the way to kill him properly.

More sleeve arrows skimmed the air currents. She ducked one and deflected another from the back of Mrs. Chase's head with the blade of a knife.

She kicked open the door. Sending both of her knives his way to buy a little time, she dragged Mrs. Chase's inert, uncooperative body inside. A match flared before Mrs. Reynolds's face, a stark chiaroscuro of anxious eyes and bloodied cheeks. As Catherine set Mrs. Chase down on the wet carpet, Mrs. Reynolds, who should have stayed in her corner, docilely suffering, found the strength to get up, push the door shut, and bolt it.

"No!" shouted Catherine.

She preferred to fight outside, where there were no helpless women underfoot.

Almost immediately the door thudded. Mrs. Reynolds yelped and dropped the match, which fizzled on the sodden carpet. Catherine grabbed the matchbox from her, lit another one, stuck it in Mrs. Reynolds's hand, and wrapped a long scrap of dressing gown around her head. "Don't worry about

Mrs. Chase. She'll have bumps and bruises, but she'll be all right."

Mrs. Reynolds gripped Catherine's hand. "Thank you. Thank you for saving her."

The match burned out. Another heavy thump came at the door. The mooring of the dead bolt must be tearing loose from the bulkhead. She tried to pull away from Mrs. Reynolds, but the latter would not let go of her. "I cannot allow you to put yourself in danger for us again, Miss Blade. We will pray and throw ourselves on God's mercy."

Crack. Thump. Crack.

Impatiently, she stabbed her index finger into the back of Mrs. Reynolds's wrist. The woman's fingers fell slack. Catherine rushed forward and kicked the door—it was in such a poor state now that it could be forced out as well as in.

As she drew back to gather momentum, he rammed the door once more. A flash of lightning lit the crooked edges of the door—it was already hanging loose.

She slammed her entire body into it. Her skeleton jarred as if she had thrown herself at a careening carriage. The door gave outward, enough of an opening that she slipped through.

His poisoned palm slashed down at her. She ducked. And too late realized it had been a ruse, that he'd always meant to hit her from the other side. She screamed, the pain like a red-hot brand searing into her skin.

The ship plunged bow first. She used its motion to get away from him. A section of handrail flew at her. She smashed herself against the bulkhead, barely avoiding it.

The steamer rose to meet a new, nauseatingly high wave. She slipped, stopping herself with the door, stressing its one remaining hinge. He surprised her by skating aft quite some distance, his motion a smooth, long glide through water.

Then, as the ship dove down, he ran toward her. She recognized it as the prelude to a monstrous leap. On flat ground, she'd do the same, running toward him, springing, meeting him in midair. But she'd be running uphill now, and against the torrent of water on deck. She'd never generate enough momentum to counter him properly.

In desperation, she wrenched at the door with a strength that should have been beyond her. It came loose as his feet left the deck. She screamed and heaved it at him.

The door met him flat on at the height of his trajectory, nearly twelve feet up in the air, and knocked him sideways. He went over the rail, over the rail of the deck below, and plunged into the sea. The door ricocheted into the bulkhead, bounced on the rail, and finally, it, too, hit the roiling waters.

The steamer tilted precariously. She stumbled aft, grasping for a handrail. By the time the vessel crested the wave and another flash of lightning split the sky, he had disappeared.

She began to laugh wildly—vengeance was hers.

Her laughter turned to a violent fit of coughing. She clutched at her chest and vomited, black blood into the black night.

CHAPTER 1

The Lover

England
1891

For someone who had lived her entire life thousands of miles away, Catherine Blade knew a great deal about London.

By memory she could produce a map of its thoroughfares and landmarks, from Hyde Park in the west to the City of London in the east, Highgate in the north to Greenwich in the south. On this map, she could pinpoint the locations of fashionable squares and shops, good places for picnics and rowing, even churches where everyone who was anyone went to get married.

The London of formal dinners and grand balls. The London of great public parks in spring and men in gleaming riding boots galloping along Rotten Row toward the rising sun. The London of gaslight, fabled fogs, and smoky gentlemen's clubs where fates of nations were decided between leisurely sips of whiskey and genteel flipping of the *Times*.

The London of an English exile's wistful memory of his gilded youth.

Those memories had molded her expectations once, in

distant days when she'd believed that England could be her answer, her freedom. When she'd painstakingly made her way through Master Gordon's copy of *Pride and Prejudice*, amazed at the audacity and independence of English women-enfolk, the liberty and openness of their lives.

She'd given up on those dreams years ago. Still London disappointed. What she had seen of it thus far was sensationally ugly, like a kitchen that had never been cleaned. Soot coated every surface. The grime on the exterior walls of houses and shops ran in streaks, where rain, unable to wash off the encrusted filth, rearranged it in such a way as to recall the tear-smudged face of a dirty child.

"I wouldn't judge London just yet," said kindly Mrs. Reynolds.

Catherine smiled at her. It was not London she judged, but the foolishness of her own heart. That after so much disappointment, she still hoped—and doomed herself to even more disappointment.

In any case, she had not come to make a home for herself in England. Her task was to retrieve a pair of small jade tablets and deliver them to Da-ren, Manchu prince of the first rank, uncle to the Ch'ing emperor, and her stepfather.

The jade tablets, three in all, were said to contain clues to the location of a legendary treasure. Da-ren was in possession of one of the tablets, but the other two had been taken out of China following the First Opium War.

"There they are," cried Mrs. Chase. "Annabel and the Atwood boys."

It was impossible to know Mrs. Chase for more than five minutes—and Catherine had known her five weeks, ever since Bombay—without hearing about her beautiful daughter Miss Chase, engaged to the most superior Captain Atwood.

Such boastfulness was alien to Catherine, both in its delivery—did Mrs. Chase not fear that her wanton pride would invoke the ill will of Fate?—and in its very existence.

Parental pride in a mere girl was something Catherine had never experienced firsthand.

At her birth, there had been a tub of water on hand—to drown her, in case she turned out to be a girl. In the end, neither her mother nor her amah had been able to go through with it, and she'd lived, the illegitimate daughter of a Chinese courtesan and an English adventurer who had died before she was born.

She'd been a burden to her mother, a source of anxiety and, sometimes, anguish. She'd never heard a word of praise from her amah, the woman responsible for her secret training in the martial arts. And Da-ren, the true father figure in her life, the man who'd brought her mother to Peking and given the latter a life of security and luxury, Catherine had no idea what he thought of her.

And that was why she was in England, wasn't it, yet another attempt to win his approval?

Someday, she used to think, someday he would invite her to take a seat in his presence, and she would know for certain that she wasn't simply an obligation her mother had left him with. But that someday kept receding and he was no longer a young man. She tried not to imagine the very great likelihood that on his deathbed he would glance at her and sigh with a mixture of exasperation and disappointment.

On the rail platform, a handsomely attired trio advanced, a young woman in a violet mantle flanked by a pair of tall men in long, black overcoats. Catherine's attention was drawn to the man on the young woman's left. He had an interesting walk. To the undisciplined eye, his gait would seem as natural as those of his companions. But Catherine had spent her entire life in the study of muscular movements, and she had no doubt that he was concealing an infirmity in his left leg—the strain in his back and arms all part of a mindful effort to not favor that particular limb.

He spoke to the young woman. A strange curiosity made Catherine listen, her ears filtering away the rumble of the engines, the drumming of the rain on the rafters, the clamor of the crowd.

". . . you must not believe everything Marland says, Annabel," he said. His head was turned toward the others, the brim of his hat and the high collar of his greatcoat obscuring much of his profile. "My stay on the Subcontinent was entirely uneventful. The most excitement I had was in trying to keep a friend out of trouble when he fell in love with a superior's wife."

She shivered. The timbre of that quiet voice was like the caress of a ghost. No, she was imagining things. He was dead. A pile of bones in the Takla Makan Desert, bleached and picked clean.

The other man, who spoke with a slight American accent, was adamant. "Then explain why your letters came only in spurts. Where were you all those months when we hadn't the least news of you?"

Miss Chase, however, was more interested in the love triangle. "Oh, how tragic. Whatever happened to your friend? Was he heartbroken?"

"Of course he was heartbroken," said the man who refused to limp. "A man always convinces himself that there is something special about his affections when he fancies the wrong woman."

Catherine shivered again. An Englishman who'd spent time in India, whose brother suspected that he'd been further afield than Darjeeling, and who had a lingering injury to his left leg—no, it couldn't be. She had to have been a more capable killer than that.

"You wouldn't be speaking from experience, would you, Leighton?" said Miss Chase, a note of flirtation in her voice.

"Only in the sense that every woman before you was a wrong woman," answered the man who must be her fiancé, the most superior Captain Atwood.

A shrill whistle blew. Catherine lost the conversation. Mrs.

Reynolds reminded her that she was to entirely comply with Mrs. Reynolds's desire to put her up at Brown's Hotel. Catherine suspected that Mrs. Reynolds, out of gratitude, planned to find Catherine a respectable husband. A tall task: Catherine had never come across a man willing to marry a woman capable of killing him with her bare hands—and easily, too.

Except *him*.

Until he changed his mind, that was.

The welcome party was upon them. Greetings erupted, along with eager embraces. Miss Chase's fiancé stood slightly apart, a cool presence at the periphery of this sphere of familial warmth.

His brother, golden and gregarious, should be more noticeable. *Was* more noticeable. But Captain Atwood was the man Catherine would immediately single out from a horde of a hundred for the danger he presented.

Latent danger. The danger of a man who knew how to handle himself. Who, like a predator of the jungle, was perfectly aware of his surroundings.

Her heart beat fast: This was how she had first noticed her lover, by his aura of control and perceptiveness.

She expelled a breath and, at last, looked directly at him.

A tall, dark, handsome man—remarkably handsome, one might say. Yet there was something extraordinarily understated about his person, something meant to deflect attention from himself, so that he could pass through the crowd like a shadow, little noticed except by those who had trained for years to be alert to just such hidden peril.

Catherine had never seen this man before.

Of course. What could she have been thinking? That not only would the lover who had betrayed her, and whom she had punished in turn, be miraculously alive after all these years, but that her friendship with Mrs. Reynolds, largely a product of chance, would lead her to him, on the other side of the world from where they had said their farewells?

No, such hopes were only for moments of weakness, moments of desperation, moments when she would rather lie to herself than submit to the bleakness of reality.

Now that the initial hugs and handshakes were out of the way, Mrs. Chase fussed over Captain Atwood. Mrs. Reynolds spoke to him eagerly. Miss Chase had her gloved hand on his arm. Even his brother tapped him on the shoulder, wanting a quick answer to some question.

Yet Catherine had the feeling that it was she, the stranger, who commanded the bulk of his attention—he was as keenly aware of her as she was of him, though he had not even looked in her direction.

But now he turned partly toward her—and she gazed into the green eyes from her nightmares.

If shock were a physical force like typhoons or earthquakes, Waterloo station would be nothing but rubble and broken glass. When remorse had come, impaling her soul, she'd gone looking for him, barely sleeping and eating, until she'd come across his horse for sale in Kashgar.

It had been found wandering on the caravan route, without a rider. She had collapsed to the ground, overcome by the absolute irreversibility of her action.

But he wasn't dead. He was alive, staring at her with the same shock, a shock that was slowly giving way to anger.

Somebody was saying something to her. ". . . Mr. Atwood. Mr. Atwood, Miss Blade. This is Miss Blade's very first trip to England. She has lived her entire life in the Far East. Mr. Atwood is on his grand tour after finishing his studies at Harvard University."

"Please tell me that I did not overlook your society while I was in Hong Kong, Miss Blade. I would be devastated," said Marland Atwood, with an eagerness to please that seemed to arise not from a need to be noticed but from an innate happiness.

She made herself smile. "No need for premature devastation,

Mr. Atwood. I rarely ventured that far south. Most of my life has been spent in the north of China."

"And may I present Captain Atwood?" Mrs. Reynolds went on with the introductions. "Captain Atwood, Miss Blade."

Leighton Atwood bowed. Leighton Atwood—a real name, after all these years. There was no more of either shock or anger in his eyes, eyes as cool as water under ice. "Welcome to England, Miss Blade."

"Thank you, Captain." Words creaked past her dry throat.

Then she was being introduced to Annabel Chase. Miss Chase was young and very, very pretty. Wide eyes, a sweet nubbin of a nose, soft pink cheeks, with a head full of shiny golden curls and a palm as pliant as a newborn chick.

"Welcome to England, Miss Blade. I do hope you will like it here," Miss Chase said warmly. Then she laughed in good-natured mirth. "Though at this time of the year I always long for Italy myself."

Something gnawed at the periphery of Catherine's heart. After a disoriented moment she recognized it as jealousy. Miss Chase was not only beautiful, but wholesome and adorable.

What had Leighton Atwood said to her? *Every woman before you was a wrong woman.*

Of course. A woman such as Catherine was always a wrong woman, anywhere in the world.

"Thank you," she said. "It has been a remarkable experience already, my first day in England."

*C*atherine could not stop looking at her erstwhile lover. She glanced out of the corner of her eyes, or from below the sweep of her lashes. She pretended to examine the interior of the private dining room at Brown's Hotel: the crimson-and-saffron wallpaper, the moss-green curtains, the large painting above the fireplace—two young women in white stolas frolicking against an dizzyingly blue sea that reminded her of Lake Kanas in the Altai Mountains—and then she would dip her gaze and let it skim over him.

Without the thick beard that had obscured the lower half of his face, he looked quite different. Not to mention, his black hair was cut short, leaving no hint of the curls through which she'd run her hands. The lobes of his ears still showed indentations of piercings, but the gold hoops he'd worn were long gone. And the deep tan that had fooled her so completely as to his origins had disappeared, too: Compared to the milk-white ladies at the table, he would still be considered bronzed, but to her he appeared pale. Pallid, almost.

He did not return her scrutiny, except once, when his brother seated himself next to her. He had glanced at her then, a hard, swift stare that made her feel as if someone had pushed her head underwater.

"Tell us about your life in China, Miss Blade," said Marland Atwood. "And what finally brought you home to England?"

"My mother died when I was very young." At least this part was true. Her next few sentences would be well-rehearsed lies. "I lived with my father at various localities in China, until he passed away several years ago. I suppose some would call him idiosyncratic—he did not seek the company of other English expatriates and rarely spoke of his life before China."

Leighton Atwood did not roll his eyes, but the twist of his lips was eloquent enough.

She made herself continue. "Sometimes I, too, wonder why I didn't venture out of China sooner—I'd always wished to see England, and in China I will always remain a foreigner. But the familiar does have a powerful hold. And part of me was afraid that perhaps in England, too, I would always be a foreigner."

There was the faintest movement to his left brow. She could not interpret whether it expressed further scorn or something else.

"But that is nonsense!" exclaimed Marland Atwood. "You

are home now. And we shall all of us endeavor to make you *feel* at home, too."

She smiled at her former lover's brother. "Thank you, Mr. Atwood."

"I quite agree with Mr. Atwood," declared Miss Chase. "I think it's marvelous that you have come. You must not hesitate to let me know if there is anything I can do to help you become better settled."

The girl was so fresh, so unsullied, a lovely, innocent Snow White—with Catherine very close to becoming the fading, malicious Queen. When she smiled this time, her face felt as if it were made of stone. "Thank you, Miss Chase. You are too kind."

She glanced at Leighton Atwood. He appeared so . . . very English, so very proper and buttoned up. She could not imagine this man riding across the length and breadth of Chinese Turkestan in a turban and a flowing robe, sleeping under the stars, and hunting her suppers with a slingshot.

"Mrs. Reynolds, I understand that you and Miss Blade"—did she detect a slight hesitation, the space of a heartbeat, before he said her name?—"met in Bombay?"

"That is correct," said Mrs. Reynolds. "We were introduced by Dr. Rigby, an old family friend."

"Oh, I remember him—such a dear old man," said Miss Chase. "How did the two of you meet, Miss Blade?"

Catherine supposed there was nothing for it, since Mrs. Reynolds and Mrs. Chase both already knew. "In Shanghai. Outside the ticket agent's at Mortimer hong. I found Dr. Rigby's wallet on the pavement."

Miss Chase leaned back an inch. Mrs. Chase wore a look of sly satisfaction. Now it was out in the open: Catherine had not been introduced to Dr. Rigby by a known third party; therefore, what everyone knew of her was only what she chose to tell them. Leighton Atwood looked meaningfully at his brother.

"It sounds like a wonderful coincidence," Marland Atwood said in oblivious cheerfulness.

"It was a stroke of luck for the rest of us, too," said Mrs. Reynolds firmly. "Miss Blade kept us alive when we were set upon at sea."

"Set upon?" exclaimed Miss Chase. "Surely not by pirates?"

"Only the most awful Chinaman," answered Mrs. Chase. "Oh, darling, forgive us for not telling you sooner. It was a terrible ordeal. We thought we'd spare you the knowledge, if we could."

That said, Mrs. Chase launched into a luridly detailed account: her first glimpse of the insolent Chinaman during a shore excursion to Gibraltar, his aggressive pursuit of her, her virtuous attempts to avoid his distressing attention.

Miss Chase listened with wide eyes. Marland Atwood abandoned his lunch entirely. Mrs. Reynolds looked more than once toward Leighton Atwood and seemed discomfited by his carefully neutral expression—so Catherine was not the only one to suspect there might have been a reciprocal sexual interest on Mrs. Chase's part, at least initially.

Mrs. Chase was now vividly recreating the night of the storm off the coast of Portugal. The ocean that had the ship in its hungry maw. The hapless vessel, pitching and bobbing like a piece of refuse at high tide. The intruder in her cabin, subduing her, hauling her outside to set her on the railing, above the roiling black waters, tormenting her with visions of her own death.

She ended with a coy, "Then I knew no more."

"But what happened?" Miss Chase and Marland Atwood cried in unison.

"Miss Blade saved us," said Mrs. Reynolds quietly. "I couldn't. But she ventured out into the storm and brought back my sister. And when the man almost broke down the door, Miss Blade saved us once again."

"Did you bring him to justice, Miss Blade?" asked Marland Atwood, his eyes bright with an astonished admiration.

Catherine shook her head. "He fell overboard."

"That's justice enough for me," said Mrs. Reynolds.

"Hear, hear," said Marland Atwood.

"And were *you* all right, Miss Blade?" asked Miss Chase. She had one hand over her heart, the other clutching at Leighton Atwood's sleeve.

He had been gazing into his water goblet, but he looked at Catherine now. Pain suffused her, pain that had nothing to do with her injury—pain complicated with a twist of pleasure, like a drop of blood whirling and expanding in a glass of water.

"I was fine," she said. "Mrs. Reynolds was the one who suffered injuries."

When Mrs. Reynolds had satisfied everyone that despite the bandages under her turban, she was quite all right, Marland Atwood turned to Catherine. "But to single-handedly fight off a villain, Miss Blade, how did you manage it?"

For once, Catherine was happy that Mrs. Chase, even if she had seen something beyond her own misery, would not come forth with details of Catherine's strength and dexterity. "I had the advantage of surprise on my side, a great deal of luck, and the experience of taking a pot to a miscreant's head once in a while."

Marland Atwood laughed. "My goodness, Miss Blade. Do remind me to remain in your good grace at all cost."

Leighton Atwood's lips curled in a sardonic smile. "Yes, indeed. Do remind us."

Marland Atwood leaned forward. "Do you know what? Miss Blade's bravery made me remember the time Leighton faced down a lethal beast."

"What is that?" Miss Chase turned toward her fiancé. "I've never heard you mention any such deed."

"You never told her?!" Marland Atwood exclaimed in disbelief. He grinned at his brother. "You must have become quite a catch if Miss Chase accepted you without ever hearing that stirring tale."

"Well?" Miss Chase prompted, eager admiration in her eyes. "Won't you tell us, Leighton?"

"There isn't much to tell. A boy got too close to a tiger and I pulled him back."

Marland Atwood shook his head. "And if you listen to him, you'd have thought that our men in India daily ran in front of full-grown tigers. Allow me to tell it better. Sir Randolph Clive was a nabob who lived like a maharaja. He kept elephants and pet tigers. And one day, in the middle of a garden party, one of the tigers got loose."

"My goodness gracious," said Miss Chase.

Leighton Atwood turned the base of his water goblet a few degrees. There was no expression of modesty on his face, only detachment, as if he himself played not the least role in the tale.

He did not like being talked about, it struck Catherine. He did not like being the center of attention.

"Pandemonium ensued, of course, when the guests realized that a wild beast was in their midst," Marland Atwood continued. "The panicky ones climbed trees; the more sensible ones made for the house. And in all this commotion, no one realized that Sir Randolph's toddler son had left the house to pet the tiger, thinking it a big cat. The boy walked until he was no more than two feet away from the tiger."

"Oh no," Miss Chase whispered.

"The situation was precarious indeed. The tiger growled, a rumble full of menace. The boy stopped—but only for a moment." Marland Atwood paused dramatically. "Then he began advancing again. Women fainted. Men stood paralyzed. The servants came with Sir Randolph's rifles. But Sir

Randolph, that ass—pardon my language, ladies—would not allow anyone to shoot it."

"Then what happened?" demanded Miss Chase, her hand on Leighton Atwood's shoulder.

"Then Leighton, cool as a cucumber, strolled up to the child, took him by the hand, bid the tiger to 'Stay where you are,' and delivered the boy to his eternally grateful mother."

"What valor!" gushed Mrs. Chase.

"Most impressive," declared Mrs. Reynolds.

"Most impressive indeed," Catherine murmured—not that she wasn't impressed, but of course he would have been the one to take charge when everyone else lost their heads. "And when was this, if I may ask?"

"Six or seven years ago," answered Marland Atwood. "But nobody has forgotten it."

How strange to think that in the eight years since their parting, Leighton Atwood had not merely survived, but had led a normal life, a life that included such things as attending garden parties, traveling on trains and ocean liners, and finding himself a suitable woman to marry.

"Ladies," said Leighton Atwood, "you should know my brother was not present in person."

"But I've heard it from a dozen eyewitnesses," Marland Atwood retorted gleefully. "Of course, wouldn't you know it, everyone who related the tale to me had been on the verge of doing something heroic, but Leighton beat him to it."

"What a story." Miss Chase beamed. She leaned into Leighton Atwood. "You should have told me. Are there any other harrowing tales you are keeping secret from me, Captain?"

His eyes met Catherine's for the briefest second, an opaque, almost serene gaze. "No, my dear, there's nothing important about me that you do not already know."

CHAPTER 2

The Kazakh

Chinese Turkestan
1883

Leighton enjoyed an oasis. But unlike the oases of the Arabian deserts, this particular oasis had no date palms. Though it did have farmlands and orchards that suddenly leaped into the view of the weary traveler, the verdant acres lively and defiant against the endlessly arid Takla Makan Desert, never far to the south.

There were also no natural springs. The crops and the fruit trees were irrigated by melted snow that had traveled miles from the nearest mountain, along an ancient and complex system of underground tunnels that had been constructed entirely by hand.

There were, however, Bactrian camels, a train of them just outside the courtyard of the open-air restaurant, feasting on grass and oats. Inside the courtyard, beneath the shade of grapevines growing on overhead trellises—he wondered what the French would think of the *terroir*—the clientele consisted mostly of traders and travelers, lured by the sizzling fragrance of spiced mutton grilling over an open fire and the yeasty aroma of freshly baked bread.

Once, great caravans had teemed on these routes, carrying

precious bolts of Chinese silk across the vast steppes of central Asia to the coast of the Caspian Sea, to Antioch, and finally to Rome, to feed the empire's ever ravenous desire for luxury fabrics.

The rise of great ocean-faring vessels had rendered the land courses obsolete hundreds of years ago. The caravans that still plied the route were small, sometimes no more than a few camels, trading between towns. And most of the legendary cities of yore were either lost or reduced to mere shadows of their former glory.

Yet a sense of continuity still lingered in the air. Marco Polo had drunk the same sweet, cool wine as that in Leighton's cup, made from oasis-grown white grapes. A thousand years before that, Buddhist missionaries from India had braved the same perilous paths, carrying the teachings of the Tathagata into the western provinces of China.

Leighton, too, had traveled to China once—alone, with almost nothing in his pocket, and little more than an irrational hope in his heart.

Now he was again in China, at least technically. But Chinese Turkestan, currently controlled by the Ch'ing Dynasty, was of a different character altogether, a place of endless desert, vast blue skies, and snowcapped mountain ranges.

A new customer walked into the courtyard, a young Kazakh dressed in a knee-length robe and a fur-lined, long-flapped hat. They were in a predominantly Uyghur part of Tarim Basin, but one encountered Kazakhs, Kyrgyz, Han Chinese, and even Mongols on the road. The diners looked up for only a moment before returning to their food and conversation. Leighton popped another chickpea into his mouth.

"Bring me soup and bread," the young Kazakh ordered as he sat down. "Mind you skim the fat off the soup. And the bread had better be still warm."

Leighton cast another glance at the Kazakh. Why did he think he had seen that face before?

The Kazakh now had a dagger in hand, scraping at the dirt underneath his nails. The weapon was six inches of deadly, gleaming blade, and he wielded it with no more care than if it were a toothpick. A man seated close to the entrance of the courtyard, who had been looking at the Kazakh with the interest of a pickpocket, turned back to his stew of sheep's brain.

The Kazakh's food arrived. He sheathed his dagger and attacked the round disk of bread, pausing only to wash it down with soup. Halfway through his meal, he flicked Leighton a hard look.

All at once it came to Leighton. Not when or where he had seen the Kazakh, but that last time he saw the face, it had belonged to a *girl*.

The memory was hazy, almost dreamlike, the kind of recollection that felt more imagined than real. Add to it the Kazakh's unfriendly bearing, grimy appearance, and affinity for sharp objects—Leighton was inclined to dismiss the notion out of hand.

And yet, now that the idea had arisen, he couldn't help but notice that the Kazakh was a tad too old to have such a perfectly smooth face. And wasn't his wrist, when it peeked out from his sleeve, a bit delicate in size for a man?

Not to mention his thick robe and close-collared shirt. At the edge of the desert, temperatures plunged directly after sunset. But now it was high noon on a spring day; the sun seared, the air hot and heavy even in the shade. Most of the other travelers had loosened their outer garments, but the Kazakh kept his closed and belted, even though he must be perspiring underneath.

She stopped eating—Leighton realized that he had changed the pronoun he used to think about the Kazakh. Instead she watched him, her gaze frosty. Her dagger, which had never left the table, was now once again unsheathed, the naked blade pointed directly at him.

He was not in Chinese Turkestan to make trouble. The goal

of the British was to pass entirely unnoticed on their intelligence-gathering mission. In fact, he was already leaving, on his way to meet his colleagues in Yarkand. There they would debate whether to brave the Karakoram Pass directly into Kashmir, or tackle the relatively easier Baroghil Pass, still two miles above sea level, for a more circuitous route back to the raj.

The wise choice would be to stop gawking at the girl, finish his meal, and ride out. Until he was on Indian soil, he was not entirely safe—the Ch'ing authority, who had recovered control over the territory only recently, was not kind to spies. And anything that could delay his return added to the risk of being found out.

Yet he could not shake the feeling that his seemingly unreliable memory of having seen her before was not something to be ignored. That it had not been a case of two random strangers passing each other, but an encounter of significance.

The nature of which significance just happened to elude him entirely.

He drank from his wine, then stood up, jug in hand, and seated himself opposite her—the unwise choice it was, then.

The people of these parts were by and large friendly and hospitable. It was not uncommon for strangers to sit down together and chat. "You look hot, friend," he said in Turkic. "Have some of this wine."

Up close, her eyes were the color of a desolate sea, charcoal grey tinged with blue. Her lips, greasy from lunch, were the dark red of aged claret.

Without a word, she picked up the wine jug he had pushed across the table at her, held it above her head, and poured a fine stream straight down her throat.

The grace and precision of her action, the way her throat moved as she swallowed—his awareness of her was suddenly the sort to elevate his heart rate.

"Good wine," she said, sliding the jug back to him. "Many thanks."

When he glanced down at the wine, he saw that the dagger had also found its way across the table, its tip no more than two inches from his chest. He turned it around, and with a flick at the pommel, sent it skidding directly back into its scabbard.

"Good blade," he said.

Her eyes narrowed. She slapped the table from underneath. The sheathed dagger leaped up a foot off the table, still perfectly horizontal. She knocked the dagger with her soup spoon. It flew directly at him.

He barely deflected it with the wine jug. The dagger fell to the table with a loud clatter.

One thing was clear: The show of force removed any doubt of her gender. Only a young woman traveling by herself would be so wary of being approached by a man offering wine and friendship.

"Is this how the Kazakhs repay hospitality?" he asked.

She glanced around at the startled diners. Quickly, eating and talking recommenced on the part of the latter. She turned back to him. "What do you want, stranger?"

"Am I a stranger to you?"

"I've never laid eyes on you before. Of course you are a stranger to me," she said scornfully. But she did return the dagger to her belt.

"But I have seen you. I don't remember when or where, except that I have seen you."

"So what?" Her small teeth sank into a piece of carrot from the soup. "I have seen a thousand strangers on these roads. Passed them without a backward glance."

She was full of thorns, and just short of loutish. But strangely enough, he felt more at ease with her than with a roomful of eminently proper English misses.

"Where are you headed?" he asked.

He wasn't usually so loquacious. Though he absorbed languages with the ease of white cloth in a vat of dyes, he rarely spoke unless spoken to, in any of those languages.

"West," she answered tersely. "You?"

She was studying his face. There were places in the world where his green eyes would be a dead giveaway of his racial origin. But fortunately, in the heart of Asia, there existed natives with eyes of sky and forest, and every color in between. And he was now sufficiently tanned to pass for one of them.

"West, too." Then he surprised himself by telling something close to the truth. "Kashmir is my eventual destination."

"Lucky you."

"Have you been to Kashmir?" And was that where he might have met her?

She shook her head. "No, but I've heard it's a nice place."

There was an odd wistfulness to her voice, the way an invalid stuck at home might speak of the world outside. She lifted the wine and drank as she did before, her fragile-looking wrist remarkably steady as she suspended the heavy jug above her mouth.

He swallowed. There was nothing retiring, modest, or pliant about her. Yet for reasons he couldn't fathom, he found her blatantly, ragingly feminine, like a pearl at the tip of a knife.

She set down the jug. Their gazes met—and held. She had been wary and hostile, but now she was tense in a way that seemed not entirely related to her earlier distrust of him.

Pushing away what was left of her soup, she asked, "Where are *you* from?"

She knew, the thought came to him. She knew that he had seen through her disguise.

"Persia." He gave his standard answer—Parsi was one of his strongest languages.

"You are far from home."

There was an accent to her Turkic, and not a Kazakh one— the only thing Kazakh about her, as far as he could see, was her clothes. Perhaps Turkic wasn't her mother tongue. But so many different variations of the language were spoken over such a large territory by so many different people, it was quite possible that she hailed from an area or a tribe unfamiliar to him.

"Some of us are not meant to grow old where we are born," he said. "You, my friend, are you also far from home?"

A shadow passed over her face, something almost like pain, as if home was so distant as to be beyond reach. Then she shrugged. "Home is wherever I am."

Oddly enough, he felt an answering pang of longing. Not so much for the mortar and bricks of home, but for the idea of it, that safe, happy place he had once known. "Where will you be making your home next?"

She thought for a moment. "Kashgar."

He would reach Yarkand much more conveniently by turning south a hundred miles or so before Kashgar and following the course of the Yarkand River upstream. But he found himself reluctant to contemplate that faster path. He did not want them to part so soon, still strangers.

"Perhaps we can share the road for a few days, if you are traveling alone."

After having traversed the territory all the way to the Altai Mountains and back, another hundred miles or two hardly mattered.

If, that was, she agreed to it.

Surely she must understand the average criminal would gravitate toward an easier quarry. And she was a poor target if one were out for gold: Her blue tunic was frayed at the cuffs and the hem, the embroidery along the lapels long ago soiled into squiggles of greasy black.

She popped the last piece of bread into her mouth. A desire to kiss her, bread crumbs and all, shot through him like a bullet.

"Well, the road does get lonely," she said.

She did not move—or at least he could swear she did not

move. Yet all at once she twirled a palm-size grape leaf by its stem. It was early yet in the year; the vine that spread on the trellis overhead was not weighed down by ripe clusters of fruit. He would have to stand with an arm stretched to pluck a leaf. Yet she had done it while remaining perfectly still in her seat.

As a warning, it was far more sobering than a rattling of the dagger. She was stating, quite plainly, that she could cut his throat before he even knew what happened.

He smiled, thoroughly impressed. "So you will permit me to accompany you?"

She, too, smiled, now that she had established she needed barely lift a finger to take his life—a smile as sharp as her blade. "Yes, do come along."

*Y*ing-ying would like to think that she spoke as a smug cat, looking forward to toying with a foolish mouse. But the truth was, short of actually incapacitating the Persian, she had run out of deterrents to lob at him.

Other than Master Gordon, in her life she had dealt with only three men who mattered: Da-ren, who kept a reproachful distance from her; Shao-ye, Da-ren's son, who lusted after her; and Lin, who would kill her the moment he located her.

The Persian was a completely new experience, a man who found her deadliness interesting, rather than dismaying.

She had taken note of him as soon as she had walked into the vine-shaded courtyard: He occupied the seat she'd have chosen—in a corner, nothing but walls behind him, good view of the other diners and of the road beyond. And instead of a *dopa*, the embroidered, domelike cap that was more popular among the Muslims of Chinese Turkestan, he had on a turban, a rather dramatic one at that, black with accents of gold, in contrast against his flowing white robe.

But she'd have remarked his green, steady eyes even if he

had been dressed in rags. Though his gaze seemed to stray no further than his jug of wine, she knew instinctively that he was fully aware of everything that went on about him. And as she sensed the danger in him, the stillness that belied his strength, he grew more watchful of her, observing her minutely without seeming to do so.

She must have grown accustomed to all manners of non-Chinese in her years beyond the westernmost pass of the Great Wall. She found nothing to fault in his deep-set green eyes, his high cheekbones, or even the full beard that obscured most of the lower half of his face—and she had always thought excessive facial hair barbaric.

He had beautiful balance as he walked, tall and lithe. And when he sat down opposite her, all wide shoulders and cool assurance, she felt as if she had awakened from a very long hibernation, perhaps for the first time in her life.

The rustle of the grapevine on the trellis, the cool, green-flecked light that filtered through the canopy of new leaves, the scent of lamb skewers sizzling over hot coals—she had stopped at many, many such dusty roadside eateries in her travels, but now the place pulsed with color and sensation.

Too much color, too much sensation, like an all-too-vivid dream that wouldn't let her wake up.

As she wiped her soup bowl with the last morsel of her bread, he commented mildly, "My friend has a manly appetite."

She sneered at him. "Your friend has manly everything."

He laughed, and not in mockery, but with a mirth that was full of genuine delight.

She rose to her feet, perplexed and ever more suspicious, and resolved to be rid of him within the half hour. "Come. The road beckons."

He left enough coins on the table to pay for both their meals and stood up unhurriedly. "Ah yes, the heroic gallop of friendship. I can scarcely wait."

* * *

*S*he rode a handsome, fleet bay stallion. Leighton followed three lengths behind, watched her beautiful posture and fluid motion, and speculated how someone who didn't seem to have two pennies to rub together managed to acquire such exquisite horseflesh.

How quickly things changed. This morning he had been a man with, essentially, no concerns—he was young, he was free, and he did not doubt his ability to reach India quickly and safely. And now he had taken up with the deadliest girl north of the Himalayas.

Midafternoon she led them through a defile that opened into a green valley with a shallow but wide stream running through the center—they were in the foothills of Tian Shan, the Heavenly Mountains, and it was the season of snow melt.

Another few miles along the stream and she reined in her horse. "We had better stop while there is still daylight. You want to hunt us something, friend?"

An ironic inflection on that last word. He dismounted. "Any preferences?"

"That you do it without using a firearm. We don't want bandits in the mountains to hear you."

He didn't ask how she knew he had firearms—he carried a revolver on his person and a rifle that had been taken apart in his saddlebag. "You have a spear you can lend me?"

"No."

Fortunately he still had a slingshot. Close to sunset he returned with a brace of wild hares. She already had a fire going and was drinking tea out of a metal cup. The beverage was clear in color and light in fragrance, nothing like the salted milk tea the locals consumed.

"What kind of tea is that?"

"An infusion of snow chrysanthemum from the Kunlun Mountains. They grow at a height of ten thousand feet."

The Kunlun Mountains were four hundred miles to the south, on the other side of the Takla Makan Desert. "My friend has refined tastes."

"Some of us are born for luxury." She tilted her chin toward the hares. "You will prepare and serve those?"

"Of course."

He skinned and gutted the hares, and rubbed them down with the salt and ground black pepper that he carried in his saddlebag. Then he constructed a makeshift turning spit and put the hares to roast.

"Would you like some?" He offered her a bag of dried apricots as they sat around the fire.

"Thank you," she said. "But, no."

On reflection he supposed it was possible for him to hide some sort of narcotics in the apricots, which would probably be the only way a man could bypass her lethal skills.

He ate several of the apricots, which were wonderfully sweet. She watched him, her thoughts hidden.

The sun had nearly disappeared below the horizon. Temperatures were dropping fast. He leaned forward and turned the spit. The hares glistened; a few drops of fat fell into the fire and sizzled. When he sat back she was still watching him.

Hope leaped, in spite of his tendency to suppress such things as hope.

"What is a Persian doing in these parts," she asked, "far from home?"

"I had goods to sell." Again his standard answer.

She took another sip of her tea. "Where are those goods—and where is your caravan?"

Made of nothing but peril and skepticism, this girl. "My goods I have sold—and not all goods need a caravan to transport."

She smiled slightly. "You know, if I were a merchant at the end of a successful trip, I would not invite a stranger as a travel companion. I would fear for my coins."

In the flickering, warm-copper light, her features were pure, flawless. With a start he realized that she was almost unbearably lovely, now that it was too dark to be distracted by the grime on her face. "But you are not a stranger to me—I cannot remember where I have seen you, that's all."

With a metallic hiss, she pulled a sword out of the bedroll to her side. "And you would risk your gold to satisfy such a silly curiosity?"

The sword was not a curved scimitar, but straight and slender. Flames danced upon the steel, beautiful and deadly at once.

Another warning. But he only smiled. "With a friend like you by my side, who would dare touch my gold?"

"Exactly. Leaving me to rob you blind."

"For a master thief, you don't seem to have prospered." He lifted his waterskin and took a long swig.

"If thieves knew how to handle money, they wouldn't be thieves," she said quite reasonably. "I, for one, am much too fond of the brothels of Kashgar."

He nearly choked on the water he was drinking. Spitting it out, he looked her up and down, this time openly. No, he was not mistaken. If she were a man, then he was a chimpanzee in London's zoological garden.

"Aren't you too young for such places?" She was what? Eighteen? Nineteen?

She smiled toothily, all knowing, predatory gorgeousness. "No one ever asks for your age. Only your money. The girls there would fuck my horse if he trotted in with enough gold."

He gaped at her, speechless.

"Perhaps you can treat me, friend." She leaned back slightly and arched her eyebrow. "I'd like to take two girls to bed at once."

He recovered his voice. "Would you now?"

"Every night, it's all I can think about before going to sleep," she answered smoothly. "So what say you? I escort you and your gold safely to Kashgar and you buy me the night of my dreams."

His life hadn't been so interesting in long, long years. "I will," he said, "as long as I get to watch."

She didn't bat an eyelash as she sheathed her sword. "Agreed. I'll bet you can learn a thing or two. The girls, they go wild for me."

When the hares were done, they ate with knives and fingers. And throughout their meal, he was conscious of her gaze. She looked at him often, and did not bother to look away when he caught her at it, as if their positions were reversed and *he* was the most unlikely person *she* had ever encountered in her life.

He could not recall the last time he'd felt so completely alive.

*Y*ing-ying could not recall the last time she was so unsettled, she who led a hunted life, no less.

Sometimes it surprised her to remember that she had not spent most of her days riding from one end of Chinese Turkestan to the other. That until a few years ago, she had not only never stepped out of the great imperial city of Peking, but almost never stepped out of her own front door.

Behind that front door, however, life had been anything but ordinary: years of grueling, secret training under the tutelage of her amah, undertaken not because Ying-ying had burned with a particular desire to master the martial arts, but because she would otherwise always be at the mercy of others, a girl with no say in the direction of her existence.

Being deadly, however, was no assurance that one would be free from misfortune. Amah's death at the hands of an enemy had come as a devastating blow to Ying-ying—that night she had truly become an orphan, bereft of everyone who had ever cared for her.

By strange coincidence, the next day, a decree had come

down from the Forbidden Palace, appointing Da-ren, Ying-ying's stepfather—her late mother had been his concubine—to the governorship of Ili.

It was a punishment, an exile to the farthest corner of the empire, where Da-ren would no longer be able to agitate for reform and modernization at the imperial court. His family was granted leave to remain behind in Peking, but he chose to bring Ying-ying.

Trouble in the form of Lin, disciple of Amah's enemy whom Ying-ying had killed in self-defense, found her within weeks of their arrival in Kulja, the capital of the territory. She'd managed to escape Lin's wrath, but it became clear that she could not remain in one place.

So she roamed. The hardship of the road was beyond anything she had known: the bandits, the monotony, the unrelenting heat, and the terrible cold—these last two often within the same day. Yet every time she returned briefly to the governor's residence in Kulja, by the next day she was already preparing to set out again.

She was no more truly free than a kite, but still, it was the most freedom she had ever known. Except . . . when the young girl who was not even allowed to venture into the streets of Peking had dreamed of the outside world, she had not thought it would be so lonely.

Was that why she kept delaying the hour she rid herself of the Persian, because no one else ever wished to accompany the prickly traveler that she was?

At the end of their meal, he rose to do the washing up. She stared at the hem of his robe, golden in the firelight, strangely fascinated by its billow and swirl, which accentuated the fluidity of his every movement.

When he was done, he sat down on the opposite side of the fire and fed it another handful of broken branches. "What do you do in the evenings, my friend?"

She performed her breathing exercises and practiced with

her blades and her hidden weapons—Lin could find her at any moment and she desperately needed to be as accomplished as he to have a chance to surviving their encounter. "I study the fires I make."

"You never stay at inns?"

Most inns she came across were not luxurious establishments. And even if she fancied sharing a room with a half dozen men, she wouldn't, for the simple fact that in the wilderness she could see Lin coming from miles away, but in more civilized surroundings she might not have any warning until it was too late.

"They have fleas."

Again that smile, again that delight: He found her company, which she would rate as questionable at best, a first-rate pleasure. She could not understand his reasons, but she could not deny that his smile was warm and gorgeous.

"And of course my friend is fastidious," he said, his tone plainly teasing. "I can tell from your attire."

She was half annoyed and half amused that she, who truly was rather fastidious—or at least used to be—should be going around clad in such rags.

"What do you know of good fabric? This is made from the wool of the frost sheep, which graze on the highest slopes of the Heavenly Mountains."

"And only wool from the first shearing of virgin ewes, of course. Am I correct?"

Now he was openly making fun of her. She thought about brandishing her knife in a show of force, but she actually did not mind being called out good-naturedly when she was just making things up.

"My sword is forged from the adamantine remains of a meteor that fell to earth," she said.

"And Allah the great and merciful plucked stars from the night sky for your eyes, I do not doubt—your very manly eyes, that is."

She had to make an effort not to smile.

He leaned forward slightly. "Would you like to hear a story?"

She'd never had such an offer in her life. "As long as it is not about my manly, starry eyes."

"No, but it does have thieves."

She stretched out her hands to the fire. "Go ahead."

And so he told her the strange and wonderful "Ali Baba and the Forty Thieves." He had a raconteur's voice, rich and seductive. When he described the cave, she could see the glow thrown off by the treasures and hear the trickle of the coins as they fell off too-high heaps in golden rivulets.

She gazed at him as he spun his tale. It had been a very long time since anyone took the trouble to entertain her, or even cared whether she enjoyed herself. But the Persian cared: It was as if he sensed not only her hunger for the outside world, not only her desire for a thrilling narrative that culminated in a satisfying outcome, but also her deep-seated need to know that such a happy ending could be made possible by the efforts of a woman. For though Ali Baba and the thieves were named in the title of the tale, it was the slave girl Morgiana who saved the day again and again, and who was, in the end, rewarded for her cleverness and her resolve.

And that hint of understanding on the Persian's part was an enchantment far more powerful than that of any mere story, no matter how fantastical.

Even after he lay down in his bedroll, she kept studying him. Amah had warned her, when she turned fourteen, to beware of mindless attachment to a man. She had not given the advice much credence then: Just because Amah had lost her head over some wastrel didn't mean Ying-ying would.

Now she was beginning to understand what Amah had meant: It was not something one could ignore. When she made herself look elsewhere, a few seconds later her eyes were again fastened to him, as if the very sight of him offered sustenance. Worse, she wanted to touch his turban, and the fabric of his robe—perhaps even his beard, a quick graze with the back of her hand, for an idea of its texture.

Amah would counsel her to leave now, slip away in the night. Ying-ying ought to. But she only wrapped her arms about her knees, listened to the tranquil rhythm of his breaths, and gazed upon him until the fire sputtered and turned to ashes.

CHAPTER 3

The Window

England
1891

Most of the time, Leighton Atwood could hike for fifteen miles and not feel a twinge of discomfort, his limbs as fresh and nimble as those of an adolescent. This state of health and well-being would go on for weeks, sometimes months. And then, without warning, without rhyme or reason, the agony would return, like a hook piercing through his flesh.

In much the same way, the girl from Chinese Turkestan would fade from mind, long enough for him to almost believe that she no longer mattered to him. To almost cease turning sharply in the street when a dark-haired woman of similar figure and gait passed by. But the memories always came back: her face in the firelight, her laughter, the dirty overcoat she had worn as part of her disguise, the embroidery on the lapels hopelessly soiled.

He preferred the physical torment. Pain as a matter of seared nerves cleared the mind beautifully. He took no laudanum and forced himself to never curtail his activities during those attacks, to walk, ride, and even run, launching himself headlong at the pain.

Against the pain of *her*, however, there was little he could do. He would jerk awake at night, unable to breathe for the weight on his heart. There were others he missed as ferociously, but they were dead, whereas she was presumably still alive, still somewhere in this world.

He had not recognized the woman who came with Mrs. Reynolds and Mrs. Chase. She was different—that much he had sensed instantly. But he had not connected the subdued, almost fragile-looking woman in the old-fashioned brown traveling dress to the girl who had stolen his heart with her swagger and vitality.

Until he looked into her eyes, the color of the Atlantic in winter, and understood the joke fate had chosen to play.

The chaos inside him had been such that he forgot the pain in his leg, which, until that moment, had demanded nearly all his attention, so that he would not lose his balance to the next spike of agony.

He could only hope he appeared normal at luncheon: It was all he could do to not stare at her. It was her, of that much there could be no doubt. But to experience her speaking the Queen's English almost without accent and in general conducting herself with ladylike modesty—his disorientation, fierce to begin with, turned dizzying.

Who was this woman, all her sharp edges sheared off and scrubbed smooth?

He was grateful for the conclusion of luncheon—he wasn't sure how much more of it he could have taken. They had risen from the table and were saying their good-byes when Annabel turned to her and asked, "Won't you join us for dinner, Miss Blade?"

Of everything disconcerting about her reappearance in his life, that she had a name probably ranked near the top: For eight years he had thought of her only in pronouns.

Miss Blade.

Real or not, it was a fitting name, bright, sharp, and potentially deadly.

"It will be a very small affair," Annabel continued. "Just the present company, plus two of my cousins and a few of our friends."

He had an urge to warn Annabel. But of what, exactly? *She is a creature of venom and fangs—approach at your peril*?

"A marvelous idea." Marland took up the cause, Marland who had no idea the kind of woman he was speaking to. "I would love to hear more about your life in China, Miss Blade."

Her life in China. Leighton's own memory of the north of China was built on a foundation of immense cold—he had arrived in the middle of winter and departed before the beginning of spring. Everything seemed to have been white or red: Snow blanketed fields, roads, and the curved roofs of temples and manors; against this pristine backdrop proliferated red doors, red lanterns, and innumerable squares and rectangles of red paper, inked with wishes for happiness and prosperity.

He could not place her in that world, a place that hid its women behind walled courtyards and covered litters. Could not imagine her without a fast horse and a gleaming sword.

It would be like locking a wolf in a broom cupboard.

"Yes, do come, Miss Blade." Mrs. Reynolds added her voice to the chorus. "You should make it a priority to broaden your circle of acquaintances."

Even Mrs. Chase, indebted to Miss Blade for saving her life, was obliged to mumble syllables of agreement.

Leighton said nothing.

Miss Blade smiled. "What a lovely invitation," she murmured. "But I don't wish to intrude on an intimate family gathering."

He could not get used to her demureness: The most decorous of spinster aunts would barely rival her in propriety—this, from the same woman who had once said, *The girls there would fuck my horse if he trotted in with enough gold.*

That might have been the moment he fell in love with her.

"But it will be fun for everyone," said Annabel. "Just think of how much more diverting it would be to spend your evening among friends."

That sentiment was heartily echoed by Marland. But Miss Blade very correctly declined again. "It is most wonderfully kind of you, but I shall feel quite overwhelmed to be out and about so soon after my arrival. Better for me to proceed at a more manageable pace."

There was no arguing with such reasonable prudence.

"In that case, let us wish you a very pleasant day," said Mrs. Reynolds. "I hope we will have the pleasure of calling on you very soon."

"I look forward to it," said Miss Blade. Her gaze skimmed lightly over Leighton, a caress like fire. "I look forward to meeting everyone again—at the earliest opportunity."

Mrs. Reynolds's private carriage had smelled of beeswax and freshly cut tulip stems. The interior of the hansom cab Catherine had hailed, on the other hand, reeked strongly of tobacco, spirits, and a large dose of turpentine that had been used to clean the upholstery.

The driver spoke with an accent she found difficult to understand—had he come from the provinces? But at least he did not say much, except to warn her to be careful as she climbed in.

Rain still fell, stolid and gloomy. The pedestrians shielded themselves with large black umbrellas. The drivers of hansom cabs and private carriages hunched beneath their black raincoats. London was like a living photograph, leached of color, leaving behind only shades of charcoal and grey.

Before his death the same night as Amah's, Master Gordon, Catherine's English tutor and her only true friend, had always liked to brew Darjeeling tea during Peking's few wet days.

Together, they would listen to the sound of rain falling on his roof.

Once she had written out for him a Sung Dynasty song that her mother had loved. After his death, she had found the poem among his possessions, along with an English translation he had been working on.

> As a youth, I listened to the rain from the bowers of
>   pleasure houses,
> Red silk drapes translucent in the glow of candlelight.
> In my prime, I listened to the rain as a traveler,
> The sky low, the river broad, the calls of the wild geese
>   harsh and cold.
> Now, grey at the temples, I listen to the rain beneath the
>   eaves of an abandoned cloister.
> Has mine been a futile life?
> I have no answers, only the sound of raindrops upon
>   worn stone steps,
> And long hours yet to pass before the light of dawn.

Catherine was not much younger than Master Gordon had been when she first met him. While this English rain had been to him the romantic embodiment of his youth, the music that accompanied carefree pleasure and easy lovemaking, it was for her very possibly the rain of the lone, weary traveler, one who was beginning to fear the wilderness of old age.

A cold, gnarly pain gripped her side as she descended the hansom cab on St. Martin's-le-Grand. The injury from the night of Lin's death she had been able to contain; what she truly needed, however, was a long retreat, nothing but the building and repairing of chi, to expel all the poison.

But she had too much to do now.

The rain-slicked street was boxed in by imposing buildings that belonged to the General Post Office. Catherine asked at the poste restante office for any dispatches that had come for her during her travels—from Shanghai, before she left China, she had telegraphed a request for the office to hold her mail.

There was a single telegram dated three weeks prior, from Da-ren's secretary, alerting her to the fact that news of the jade tablets' appearance in London had reached the Dowager Empress's ear and that she had dispatched an agent of her own to find them for her.

Had Lin been that agent? If so, he was no longer in the Dowager Empress's service, but feeding fish at the bottom of the Atlantic. And with luck, Catherine would complete her task and depart England, the jade tablets in tow, before the Dowager Empress could send a replacement.

Next she visited the Bank of England, to check on the funds she had wired from Shanghai. She withdrew a fraction of the money and headed to her next destination: the office of a private investigator.

After she had saved Mrs. Chase, Catherine had found a staunch champion in Mrs. Reynolds. Not that Mrs. Reynolds hadn't been kind and helpful before, but now she stressed repeatedly that Catherine must—must—allow her to do everything that a wealthy, well-connected widow could do for a young lady.

When Mrs. Reynolds made such offers, Catherine believed her. She had therefore told Mrs. Reynolds that she would like to pay her respects at her former tutor's final resting place. Would Mrs. Reynolds know how she could track down the late gentleman if all she had was a name?

As soon as they'd disembarked in Southampton, Mrs. Reynolds had sent off a telegram to her man of affairs. And by the end of luncheon, Catherine had the name and address of a private investigator who could be relied upon to make discreet inquiries.

Seated in Mr. Lochby's clean but utilitarian office behind Bow Street, a cup of hot, overbrewed tea before her, Catherine laid out her case.

"I am almost certain that Mr. Gordon arrived in China sometime around 1875. He passed away early in 1879. His remains were entrusted to the British Legation in Peking. And I'm afraid that is all I can tell you. I do not know his place or date of birth. Or the names of his family members."

"Was he a gentleman?"

Sometimes Catherine still interpreted "gentleman" as "gentle man," which Master Gordon certainly was. But Mr. Lochby was asking after Master Gordon's pedigree, whether he came from that specific class of English landed gentry, a man of means and leisure.

"Yes," she said.

"You have some idea of his age?"

"He must have been around thirty-five or so when he died."

Mr. Lochby's pen scratched as he wrote in a notebook. "It is my belief we probably do not have many native sons shipped back from the Far East in caskets. I should be able to cable the legation in Peking for more information. And I will send inquiries to harbormasters at our major ports of entry: Dover, Southampton, Liverpool, and so on. And in the meanwhile, I will also look into scholastic records—there are certain schools the gentry prefer for the education of their sons."

"That would be very good. Thank you, Mr. Lochby."

They discussed his fees and Catherine paid him a portion up front. As she rose to leave, she turned around at the door and said, as if in afterthought, "If possible, I would like to learn the contents of Mr. Gordon's will."

Mr. Lochby was surprised. "Are you expecting a bequest, Miss Blade?"

"No, not at all. I do, however, believe that a man's will is the most succinct statement on whom he truly loved."

Master Gordon had possessed, at one point, both of the jade tablets that had left China—his father had acquired them from an antique expert in Nanking. One of the tablets Master Gordon had kept for himself; the other he had given, as a token of his affection, to the man he loved. That man died long ago, but he had a son, who would have inherited the other jade tablet.

Master Gordon's will could point Catherine in the direction of this son, which would prove helpful in her search. But what she wanted above all was for the will to lead her to someone who had adored Master Gordon as she had, and who, like her, felt the impact of his untimely death to this day.

If nothing else, this alone would make the long journey to England worthwhile.

The rest of Catherine's afternoon was spent in her hotel room, sitting cross-legged on a rug before the fireplace, her breaths carefully controlled to aid the movement of her chi, laying siege to the knot of cold venom that Lin had left behind.

At seven, she rose and ate two sweet buns that she had purchased from a bakery—after months of steamer travel, during which she had dined on a steady diet of Western foods, she had grown somewhat accustomed to the omnipresence of butter. Then she dressed and left the hotel on foot, since it had stopped raining and she was not going far.

Brook Street, Regent Street, Oxford Street, Great Russell Street. And there it was, the British Museum, all granite façade and huge fluted columns, as imposing as Master Gordon had said it would be, even at night.

Electrical illumination had been installed in the museum the previous year, Mrs. Reynolds had told her, and now the museum opened from eight to ten in the evening, every day of the week except Sunday. Tonight, according to the information given to the public, the ethnographic gallery, including the Asiatic Saloon, could be viewed.

She passed under the grand, coffered ceiling of the entry hall, restraining herself from running up the stairs to the upper level. *I believe someday I will donate this to the British Museum*, Master Gordon had once murmured, gazing down at the jade tablet, as if it were a window through which he could see the years of his youth and the greenery of an English countryside.

Then she hadn't known what a museum was: The very idea of giving one's collection of beautiful things to a public institution had seemed breathtakingly radical. Now, well inside one of the greatest museums in the world, she still barely had any idea what a normal museum-going experience should be.

She was very nearly sick with excitement. The interview with Mr. Lochby, the calls she intended to pay to London's antique dealers, those were necessary steps. But deep down she had always known that it would be at the British Museum that she'd find the jade tablets—or at least the one that Master Gordon had kept.

Her heart pounded dizzily; her fingertips shook. Her eyes perceived only slightly blurred shapes, ringed with the glow of the incandescent electric light from the ceiling.

It would be—a bittersweet understanding pierced through her—almost like seeing Master Gordon again.

At the doorway to the Asiatic gallery, she made herself stop and take slow, deep breaths. She could almost see it, the creamy radiance of the jade tablet, the ecstatic drift of the dancing goddess. *Watch over me, you who were my truest friend*, she prayed to Master Gordon's spirit. *Let me find you.*

The first thing she saw was the head of a Buddha—an excellent sign. The room seemed to be filled with religious artifacts, Buddhist, Hindu, and other faiths that she couldn't readily identify.

But no jade tablet among them. She moved a little farther, to cases of teapots, inlaid stoneware, and colored pottery bricks. And then past them to huge vases, small plates, bronze figures, wood carvings, and even musical instruments.

The beating of her heart had slowed, but now each one felt like a hammer strike. She turned around. There in a table case, small, pale, rectangular, with vertical lines of Chinese characters—

She rushed over. But a lurch in her stomach told her it was not the jade tablet she was looking for, but a different one, the mineral a very light green, the scene that of a well-tended garden rather than one of spiritual bliss. And the words were not those from the *Heart Sutra*, but a poem by Chien-lung Emperor, who had reigned a hundred years ago.

She felt nauseated again—this time from dread. Table cases, wall cases, displays affixed to pillars, she went through them one by one, methodically, meticulously. And when she had exhausted all the items in the Asiatic Saloon, she went down the entire length of the Ethnographical Rooms, but though the gallery started with some Chinese weaponry, the main focus quickly shifted to far-flung islands from Java to Hawaii.

She came back up the other side of the gallery and went through the Asiatic Saloon one more time, her footsteps heavy with disappointment.

But it was a disappointment that did not last long. Already, as she walked out of the museum, she realized how ridiculous it was to think that on the same day she found out that her lover was alive, she would also locate the first of the two jade tablets.

This was but a small setback—not even that, really; merely a correction of overly optimistic estimates. It was still a good day. An excellent day. The best day she'd had in a very long time, coming so soon on the heels of at last avenging her daughter: She had not killed the man she loved and she would never again live under that soul-crushing guilt.

* * *

*Wh*at Annabel had characterized as an intimate evening at home was now a gathering of more than thirty guests. Several of the guests sang lustily to Mrs. Chase's accompaniment at the piano, and quite a few of the rest, Annabel included, were enjoying an impromptu dance, after having pushed the furniture to the walls.

Annabel, of course, cut a dashing figure on the dance floor. Her golden hair had been done up in a Grecian style, which complimented the subtly Grecian draping of her white evening gown. Though she was engaged, the young man who was her partner still gazed at her adoringly, more than half undone by the beauty of her person and the vivacity of her presence.

Leighton had met her not long after his return to England, on a night much like this, at a gathering of young people clamoring for fun and games.

At some point during the evening, she had approached him. *Sir, you are a man of handsome mien and independent means. And I have volunteered to inquire, on behalf of all the young ladies present, whether you are earnestly seeking a spouse or merely browsing the available selections.*

He had been charmed. *I have been told I should be married.*

Her eyes twinkled. *Ah, so you are one of those gentlemen making the rounds out of a sense of obligation.*

More or less.

I see. If you will excuse me, I must return to my friends and report my findings.

As she turned to leave, he had asked, *And do those findings matter to anyone besides yourself, Miss Chase?*

Her response had been a cheeky wink.

The present-day Annabel glanced in his direction and, as if reading his mind, gave him another comely wink.

It would be an excellent story to tell his future children

about how their parents had met. A proper, drawing room–friendly anecdote. No gore, no lies, no poisoned wound that would never heal.

Only sunshine and sweetness.

The dance ended. Immediately another man came up, clamoring for Annabel's next dance: Edwin Madison, her second cousin and Leighton's former colleague in India. If Mrs. Reynolds meant to introduce Miss Blade around, then inevitably she and Madison would meet.

The girl he could not forget had spoken excellent Turkic. Her facility in that language, along with her blue-grey eyes, had made him assume that she was who she had appeared to be, a stray from a nomadic tribe.

Miss Blade spoke nearly perfect English. But this time, he could not possibly accept the façade she so capably presented, that of an Englishwoman visiting the homeland for the very first time, not when he was already certain that she was an agent of the Ch'ing government. Did he, then, have an obligation to pull aside Madison, a fellow agent of the crown, for a word of caution?

But what could he say without giving himself away? And if he had met her for the first time today, would he have believed there to be any danger to this slightly dowdy–looking woman, whose every smile seemed to finish on a note of melancholy?

Oddly enough, it was not her melancholy that unfurled the old pain in his heart, but her dowdiness. There had always been a trace of sadness to her, even during their days along the ancient caravan route; but there had been fire, too, a fierce resolve to not let herself be defined by everything she had lost. And because of that, though she had dressed little better than a beggar, she had been utterly dashing. Riveting.

Now the light had gone out of her, a flame reduced to a coil of smoke, a shadow of its former self.

"One can always count on you to be the center of calm,

Captain, when there is a frenzy of merrymaking going on," said Mrs. Reynolds, coming up to stand next to him.

She was a good hostess—the reason he stood apart was so that she would approach and make sure that he was enjoying himself.

"One could say the same of you, ma'am," answered Leighton.

"But I'm twenty years your senior, Captain. When I was your age I took an active part in the merrymaking."

He smiled, allowed a few seconds to pass, then said, "Mrs. Chase seems to have recovered well from her ordeal."

Mrs. Reynolds glanced at her sister, who was having herself a riotous good time. "Well, thank goodness."

"And you, ma'am?"

"I am also in fine form."

She slid her fingers along the closed fan in her other hand. Leighton willed her to speak of the one he truly wanted to hear about. Mrs. Reynolds exhaled, a rather heavy sigh, and gazed up at the overcast sky outside the window.

"Something the matter, ma'am?"

"A little worried for Miss Blade, that's all."

For all that he had been expecting it, her name fell upon his hearing with the force of boulders. "Oh?" he made himself say lightly.

"I wish she had agreed to stay with us. Somehow I feel that dealing with that awful man has weakened her and that I am remiss in not having her under my roof and taking care of her."

Was she injured? Was that why she had looked so fragile?

He remembered the near reverence with which he had looked after her, when she had been crumpled and helpless. It was the first and only time he had ever had the care of someone stronger than himself, and he had been driven with the need to see her restored to her former glory.

But then it had taken nearly a dozen bandits—with rifles—to

drive her to the edge of defeat. Who could have single-handedly taken her on?

Unless it was the man she had been running from for half of her life . . .

"A Chinese man, Mrs. Chase had said, was it not?"

Mrs. Reynolds hesitated. "I am not entirely certain—I saw him only briefly. And he spoke French."

Leighton knew of a man, reputed to be half French, half Vietnamese—a man who could scale any wall, penetrate into any fortress, and crack the skull of any who stood in his way. In fact, only a week ago Leighton had returned from the Côte d'Azur, in an unsuccessful attempt to locate the lair of the Centipede, so called because the man always left behind a brush-and-ink drawing of a centipede.

"You and Mrs. Chase met him on Gibraltar?"

"Only my sister did. Miss Blade and I went ashore together; my sister did so with two other ladies from our steamer. When we returned, she said she had met a French gentleman named Monsieur Dubois who had spent some time in Gibraltar, and was now headed to England. Only after the chaotic events of the night did she claim that he was instead Chinese."

Leighton would have liked to ask more questions, but he judged he could proceed no further without betraying too great an interest, especially given the probability that Mrs. Reynolds, like he, suspected some sort of physical intimacy between Mrs. Chase and her assailant before their eventual falling-out. "Well, now you need to think no more about him."

"A very comforting notion, that." Mrs. Reynolds sighed again, opened the window, and leaned out slightly. "Ah, a bit of fresh air."

Her house backed onto a large, shared private garden. The moon had just broken through the clouds, its nimbus copper-colored, its light dancing faintly upon shadowy branches. A fountain trickled. And somewhere in the darkness, someone's mouser—or perhaps a stray cat—meowed softly.

The sound pricked his attention: Certain times of the year aside, felines that roamed the night were not usually noisy creatures.

A hand landed on his elbow. "Won't you take me for a round in the garden, my dearest Captain?" teased his fiancée. "I told Edwin I needed a minute to breathe before I can dance more."

He turned to her winsome, flushed face. "Of course, my dear. It would be a pleasure."

"Don't forget your wrap," warned Mrs. Reynolds. "The wind can be quite chill."

"Yes, Auntie darling," answered Annabel, already pulling Leighton along.

He made sure she had the wrap Mrs. Reynolds prescribed before they stepped outside. Mrs. Reynolds remained at the window, not exactly standing guard, but, well, standing guard.

The aunt approved of him as a man, but he had the impression that she was not entirely convinced that he was the right match for Annabel. He did not disagree with her: The right match for Annabel would be someone like Marland, someone simpler, more high-spirited, and more inherently happy.

But that someone would not be as grateful as he was to have Annabel's hand—a man who had not survived a storm at sea could not truly appreciate the solace of a well-sheltered harbor.

The night air was as cool as Mrs. Reynolds had warned. Near his left femur, pain leaped and spiked. Not too much longer now—the flare-ups were unpredictable in their onset, but they lasted exactly seven days, no less, no more.

"A delightful night, don't you think?" said Annabel with a sweep of her hand.

He liked seeing the world through her eyes. The night, to him, was rather ordinary, overlaid with London's crowded odors and a damp that promised a deeply unlovely fog in the near future. But she preferred to consider the commonest patch of grass and the most unremarkable clump of trees worthy of a Constable canvas—in which case this night could very well have graced the ceiling of a great cathedral.

"Yes, most delightful," he answered. "I enjoyed how much fun you were having."

She sighed, a contented sound. "And that's why I adore you. You actually mean it when you say something like that."

A sensation of being watched came over him—or rather, it had been there for a while, but now it had become too strong to ignore.

He had spent several of his formative years fleeing from the men his uncle had hired to track him down. A large part of the reason he had evaded them for as long as he had was that he had never hesitated to run, whenever he felt the pressure of an unfriendly gaze.

This attention was not unfriendly, per se, merely close and minute, making him feel as if he had been put under a microscope.

"Is something the matter?" Annabel asked.

He realized that he had stopped moving. He resumed his progress. "Just thought I'd heard something."

She chortled. "Do you think we have company?"

"Stray cats and other such trivial creatures," he said. "Nothing I plan to pay the least mind to."

"Good. Because in five years you will snore when I talk, so now you must be extra solicitous," Annabel teased. "So that in the future, when I realize you have fallen asleep again while listening to me, I can at least think back to moments like this and sigh over how romantic you once were."

How could any man not treasure her? "If all I have to do is remain awake to be considered romantic, then I can promise you a great deal of romance in our marriage."

She giggled and pulled him onto a bench. "So let's set a date. We've been engaged since Christmas. If we want to be married before the end of the Season, it's time to put events into motion. I helped with my cousins' weddings and let me tell you, Napoleon had fewer decisions to make when he marched into Egypt. And I want plenty of time for preparations, so I won't turn into one of those brides who bursts into tears in the middle of a discussion about whether to serve soup for the wedding breakfast."

Sensible as well as sparkling—how much more perfect could a woman be?

I, for one, am much too fond of the brothels of Kashgar.

The feeling of being watched intensified further. He touched a hand to Annabel's cheek. "In that case, set any date you'd like."

She wrapped her arms around him. "You are so good to me, Leighton."

He lifted her chin and kissed her, a long, deep kiss. She panted a little when he let go.

"Well, Captain, I'd say you have just signaled that you'd like for us to be married sooner rather than later."

"You have read my mind," he said, to both Annabel and the unseen presence in the shadows. "Let us be married at your earliest convenience."

*S*he ought not to be out at this hour of the night, Catherine thought. Amah, if she were still alive, would have disapproved of this kind of recklessness. But then again, Amah, while she yet lived, had been the most reckless woman Catherine ever knew.

Her fingertips glided over the books on the shelves. Western books, with their pasteboard covers and leather binding, had such a different feel to them, bulky and unyielding. And such a pronounced scent, nothing of the almost tealike fragrance of their Chinese counterparts.

She moved to the fireplace. On the mantel were photographs, in rectangular and oval frames. She struck a match. A picture of

Marland Atwood. Next to it, the portrait of a couple, neither of whom she recognized—his parents, perhaps?

And then, a profile of the luminous Miss Chase. She gazed somewhere just off camera, a look of both hope and serenity.

Let us be married at your earliest convenience, Leighton Atwood had said, after that impeccably staged kiss, angled just so for Catherine to take in every detail, despite the murkiness of the night.

She endured a sharp stab of pain in her heart. Life had been less complicated when she'd thought him dead and herself bound for hell. But no, he was alive and set to marry someone else, someone younger, gentler, sweeter. Someone perfect for this English stranger he had turned out to be.

Was there any trace of her lover left, beneath the tailored coat and the cool detachment?

The meadow was almost purple with wildflowers, the sky a piercingly brilliant blue. In the distance, the jagged peaks of the Heavenly Mountains soared, ramparts of God's own castle.

Near the edge of the meadow, her silky black hair long and loose, the girl collected wildflowers with her dagger, slicing through the stems of those stalks she found worthy. The sight made him smile: Those who lived by the sword played by the sword.

She sheathed her dagger, tied the flowers she had collected with another stalk, set the bouquet into his slingshot, and pulled on the strip of vulcanized rubber—all the while still standing with her back to him.

The bouquet sailed through the air with such perfect aim that from where he stood he had but to stretch out his hand for it to fall into his palm.

Only then did she turn around, a small smile around her lips.

"You are showing off."

Her smile deepened. *"You like it."*

He lifted the bouquet to his face. It smelled of sunshine and nectar. "I like an arrogant, intractable woman."

Leighton opened his eyes. He could just make out, from the moonlight streaming into the room, the face of the mantel clock. Ten minutes after three.

He had not been sleeping long—he had still been awake at two. His leg hurt, but for the moment, the pain was tolerable, almost subdued. Something else, then, had pulled him out of his dream.

He closed his eyes and listened. Nothing. But he grew increasingly certain that she was in the room with him.

How long had he tottered at the edge of death? How had he made his way out of Chinese Turkestan to a British outpost? He had only the flimsiest recollection of scorching days, raw cold nights, and constant, marrow-rotting pain.

She had been like those mythical females of woods and dells, nymphs who took their deadly vengeance on men who elected not to remain with them. Except she had been a product of desert and mountains, as beautiful as the sudden spring in the foothills, as harsh and dangerous as the black sandstorms.

He flung aside the bedcover, got up, and lit a cigarette for himself, breathing in a lungful of acrid smoke. Suddenly he was back at the edge of the meadow, sharing his dwindling supply of tobacco with her.

Why don't you frown upon my smoking? she had asked.

The day I quit smoking myself, he had replied, *is the day I start lecturing you on* your *filthy habit.*

And she had laughed as if it were the funniest thing she had ever heard.

He walked to the fireplace and tapped the ashes into the grate. Did he turn on the light and look? Did he return to bed and pretend as if nothing were the matter?

She was directly behind him. No sounds, no movements, but the heat she radiated was palpable, almost coercive.

"You should not be here," he said.

They lived in uncertain times. Those who protected the crown were tense and jumpy. She would not wish to be caught.

No response from her, except . . . did she move even closer to him?

The air was thick with her intentions. She wanted to touch him, with her hands, her lips, and all the rest of her, a desire as primal as the origins of the world.

She wanted to hold him within her.

His own pulse accelerated. His awareness of her grew excruciating. And the answering desire that arose within him shocked him with its vehemence and recklessness.

He drew on the cigarette again; his other hand closed into a fist. "I am going to walk out of this room. You have two minutes to make yourself scarce."

When he returned, one window of his room was wide open, the curtain whipping in the draft.

Someone with her skills could have easily closed the window behind herself, if she wanted to.

Instead, she had chosen to acknowledge her presence. Her invasion of his privacy.

And in doing so, reaffirmed the desire on her part that had set him on fire, like a city already ransacked.

CHAPTER 4

Fools

Chinese Turkestan
1883

The Persian was up at the crack of dawn. He first saw to the horses, grooming them and taking them to the stream for water. Then he went down to the stream by himself. When he returned, he packed up his things and walked around, gathering fuel for a new fire.

Ying-ying was not the kind to remain on her back while a stranger moved about. But this stranger's movement was quiet and soothing, almost like a lullaby. She allowed herself to sleep on to the rhythm of his morning routines.

When she woke up again, it was quite bright. The Persian was tending to the fire, kneeling with his back to her. He was not wearing his turban, revealing a head of thick black hair that curled at the ends. This fascinated Ying-ying more than she would have thought possible: She wondered whether touching his hair would feel like plunging one's hand into a sheep's wool.

That hair was also slightly damp. Foreigners. Her amah would have been livid if Ying-ying had washed her hair first thing in the morning in the ice-cold water of a snow-melt stream—that kind of chill, according to the principles of Chinese medicine, was terribly injurious to the health.

The Persian, however, did not seem to suffer any deficiencies, healthwise. And despite the loose fit of his clothes, she could tell, by the way the fabric stretched across the width of his shoulders and upper arms, that he was well built and well muscled.

"Good morning," he said, without turning around.

"Good morning."

"Do you take tea in the morning?"

"If there is hot water." She was usually too lazy to do such things for herself.

He turned around at last. "There will be, in a few minutes."

She smiled a little. "Perhaps I ought to make friends more often."

His gaze swept her person before returning to her face; she did the same to him. Alas, he had not become less handsome—or confident—overnight. Had he been anyone else, looking down at her in her bedroll, she would be on her feet in a fraction of a second, a weapon in hand. But he was not anyone else, so she stretched, her hands clasped together, her arms extended beyond her head.

His expression did not change, but something did. She had the feeling that he had to restrain himself, and rather violently.

"Help me get up?" she murmured, wanting, perversely, to test that restraint.

Slowly he approached, his eyes never leaving hers. He sank to one knee—a surpassingly intimate act, as if he had sat down at the edge of her bed. Her breaths came in shallower.

He took hold of her bedding and flung it aside. Underneath she was fully dressed, of course, but still she tensed. His eyes seemed to turn darker as he took her in. Her stomach felt strangely light, the rest of her strangely heavy.

He wanted her, she had no doubt. He wanted to see her, touch her, and press himself into her.

But what did *she* want?

Old habits die hard—for too long she had defended her virtue, sometimes at terrible costs. Of their own volition, her fingers closed around the hilt of her sword.

He noticed. She sensed no anger or frustration on his part—not even surprise. He only took a deep breath, and then another.

When he spoke, his voice was almost playful. "Do you never wash your face?"

She needed a moment to find her voice. "It isn't manly to be too clean."

The Persian took her hand and pulled her to her feet. "And we would never question *your* manliness, would we?"

*L*eighton was used to letting women talk. Whether by temperament or by the requirement to be amiable, women talked, their speech the unguent that greased the gears of polite society.

The day before, there had been no question of conversation while they traveled, as the girl always rode ahead of him. Now she spent as much time riding alongside him as she did out in front, yet still, for hours not a single word would be uttered. And when they did say something to each other, almost invariably it concerned such impersonal matters as feed for the horses and the amount of fluid that remained in their waterskins.

He was at a loss, faced with a woman who spoke as little as he did. Even worse, he *wanted* her to talk. Everything about her fascinated him. She could speak of herself for a fortnight without stop, and he would listen raptly.

But she felt no such need to unburden herself. From time to time, he would try a question. *Will you return to the bosom of your family to celebrate Eid? Where did you acquire this fine horse of yours? Are you meeting anyone in Kashgar?*

Her answers were always short, sometimes to the point of brusqueness. *I'll think about it when it's almost Eid. It was a gift. No.*

He was beginning to despair of ever learning anything about her when they stopped that afternoon. When she wanted to travel fast, she used the caravan route; to rest and water the horses, she preferred to find meadows and valleys where there was fresh water—and groves of poplar for her privacy.

When she returned from this particular grove of poplar he already had a fire going and water nearly at a boil. She made herself a cup of her snow chrysanthemum infusion. He spared a pinch of his own tea leaves—there was hardly any left—and set it to steep, while he knelt down facing the direction of Mecca and pretend-prayed like a good pretend-Muslim.

"Is that tea from Darjeeling?" she asked as soon as he finished, her expression oddly intense.

"Yes," he said, surprised, as much for her quick identification of the tea as from being spoken to at all. He extended toward her his dwindling supply of sultana raisins. "You know of it?"

She declined his offer—she did not accept any food or drink from him the preparation of which she had not witnessed—but she did answer his question. "I once had a friend who drank this tea. Black, without milk or sugar."

He, too, once had such a friend, the friend for whom he had made the long trek to China. "A very dear friend?"

After a moment, she said, almost as if to herself, "Yes, a very dear friend. Although when he was alive, I had thought of him more as a teacher, because he was much older than me. It was only after he passed away . . ."

Her face had gone blank, but it was there, a grief that had not yet lost its anguish.

He remembered his own disbelief when he'd been informed

of Herb's death. *No, it cannot be*, he had said numbly. *I saw him only yesterday. He told me he was coming back today. With firecrackers for Chinese New Year. And when I get well we are to go to a teahouse theater—and eat candied haws in the street.*

That night he had wept, for Herb, for Father, for the ten thousand miles that he had journeyed in vain. With the passage of the years he had come to see that he had been fortunate to have met Herb again at all, even if it was only for half an hour. But her pain, just beneath the surface, called to the sorrow he would always carry.

"Did you often take tea together?" he heard himself ask, his voice quiet.

"Yes, quite frequently in those days."

"And what did you talk about?"

It was never the tea, but the conversation.

Her eyes took on a faraway look. "We talked about the outside world. The places he would like to see again. The places I would like to see for the first time."

He remembered the wistfulness in her voice, when they spoke of Kashmir. "Was he the one who told you that Kashmir was a nice place?"

"Yes. He had visited Kashmir in his youth—and a great many other places in India. The white marble palace that a king built for his beloved, the holy river in which tens of thousands of people seek blessings, and hill stations like Darjeeling, where the British go to escape the heat of the plains of India."

Leighton felt a little light-headed. Herb had toured India many years ago. And before his exile, during those years when he visited Starling Manor regularly, sometimes he, too, had spoken to Leighton of those places he had loved best.

How marvelous would it be—

He stopped his wishful thinking. No, the world was full of people who had traveled through India; she was talking of someone else altogether.

"I have been to Darjeeling," he told her. "From the hills of Darjeeling, if you look north, you'll see a wall of glacier-covered peaks—so massive that the tallest of them was once thought to be the highest summit in all the world. There is nothing like standing outside at the end of the day, a cup of tea in hand, and watching the mountains. The snowcaps are golden, and sometimes the slopes turn the color of the setting sun itself."

She looked down into her cup—did he see a sheen of tears in her eyes?

"What a sight to have seen," she said, her voice soft.

"Come and see it for yourself," he said impulsively.

She laughed a little. "Darjeeling must be as far as the sky itself."

"About a thousand miles as the crow flies. But once we cross into India and reach lower elevation, it will be forty miles an hour by rail most of the rest of the way. I should be very surprised if it takes us more than two weeks before you are walking between rows of tea bushes."

A light of wonder came into her eyes, as if he had told her that the very end of the universe was within a day's journey. But that light extinguished as quickly as it had come to be.

She shook her head. "I can't."

"Why not?"

She shrugged. "I'm too poor."

"You can sell your horse."

She shook her head again. "Far better to have a horse here than to be a beggar in Darjeeling."

He doubted that was truly her reason, but her tone was quite closed: The matter was not one for debate. "Where are you going after Kashgar then?"

And how long could he reasonably—or even unreasonably—follow her around?

"Somewhere that won't bankrupt me so thoroughly."

"A shame," he said, leaning back on his elbows. "There are still places in India where the teachings of the *Kama Sutra* are practiced. And two girls well versed in the *Kama Sutra*, my friend, will give you every taste of Paradise in a single night."

"Add insult to injury, why don't y—" Her expression changed. "Don't move an inch. And don't speak." He held perfectly still and silent. Something hissed softly in the grass.

She felt on the ground about her person and made a seemingly careless flick of her fingers. He did not see anything leaving her hand, yet he heard their impact, two tiny thuds. The hissing stopped.

Signaling him to remain motionless, she rose to her feet and came to inspect the grass just beside him.

"You are safe now," she said.

He turned and saw an adder, lying dead six inches from his hand. The snake's bite was usually not fatal, but it was definitely poisonous.

He looked up at her. "Allah willing, my friend, you will always be by my side to save me from certain death."

She snorted and sauntered away. "No use wasting your prayers. We already know I won't be."

*T*he Persian took care of Ying-ying as no one had in a very long time.

Every time they stopped, he saw to the horses. In the evening he hunted, cooked, and did the washing up afterward. The next morning he packed everything to get them back on the road.

All without asking for anything in return.

She did not understand it, this giving. It made her suspicious and it made her . . . Well, not outright unhappy. But it made her think dangerous thoughts, thoughts that more often than not involved herself standing on the balcony of a house in Darjeeling, a cup of steaming tea in hand, looking northward at sunset, with him draping a warm cloak over her shoulders.

And after the sunset, they would . . .

Ceaseless as the waves of the sea, those thoughts were. But they always broke upon the rocky shores of reality.

Some of her earliest memories were those of herself as a toddler, perched on a chair, peering out into the courtyard as Da-ren strode across toward her mother, who waited beneath the gallery outside her door, her eyes decorously lowered. Such authority he had exuded, such gravitas, this man who guaranteed their safety and happiness—Ying-ying had wanted nothing more than that he should be her father.

But he was a stern man, not given to displays of affection. So instead of his love, she began to long for his esteem.

But would that still be possible, if she were to bring back a foreigner with no one to vouch for his parentage? An insignificant merchant who plied his wares along the caravan road?

And as terrifying and potentially humiliating as *that* scenario was, it was the very best she could conjure, one in which the Persian, full of honorable intentions, bravely faced Da-ren's wrath while she quaked in her boots.

When the Persian was probably just waiting for her to give in and sleep with him.

With time she could find out. But she had no time: This detour toward Kashgar had put her behind schedule. Her route was her own to manage, but she must always report back on the appointed day. Da-ren did not like her to be late, and any thought of Da-ren's displeasure made her lungs feel completely airless.

Was it any wonder that every mile west set her further on edge?

"Would you like some chocolate?" asked the Persian.

His offer vexed her. Everything about him vexed her. If he tried something untoward, then she could leave him a few choice bruises and gallop off, back to the life she knew. But he only ever pampered her, and lured her farther and farther away from where she needed to go.

"Chocolate is bitter," she said, half angrily. "And sticks to the roof of the mouth."

"You must not have had the newer chocolates—the Swiss have wrought marvels. Try it," he coaxed her. "If you don't like it, you can spit it out."

She snatched the small rectangle of confection from his hand, only remembering, as she was already putting the chocolate into her mouth, that she had not witnessed its making.

But she did not spit out the chocolate for that reason. Nor did she spit it out for any other reason. For this chocolate was smooth, decadent, with the perfect depth and darkness to complement a milky sweetness.

She ate it too fast—and almost could not look at him as she licked the back of her teeth, desperate to extract every last bit of flavor that still remained inside her mouth.

He promptly offered her a bigger piece. "Some more?"

She wanted to eat this piece slowly, to savor the utter deliciousness of it, but she didn't—she wolfed it down as she had the other morsel. What was the point? It would be over soon anyway. And even if his entire saddlebag turned out to be filled with the same chocolate, it would still not be enough.

Kashgar was no more than a few hours away. And then he would be but a memory, like the all-too-brief pleasure of milk chocolate, a sweetness after which everything else would only ever taste bitter and vinegary.

"Do you have an address?" he asked quietly. "I can send you chocolate, if I have your address."

The only address she had was the governor's residence in Kulja, which of course she could not give him.

"And we can write each other," he added.

She stared at him. She spoke Turkic just fine, but she was almost completely illiterate in that language. "I can't write."

"Neither can I—not in Turkic, in any case," he said. "But I'm sure I can find someone to read your letters for me—and write my replies."

Implying she could do the same. But she simply could not have his letters arrive at the governor's residence. How would she explain them to Da-ren? "Letters are stupid. It would take me less time to walk to India."

He smiled. "You could do that also."

Could she? The idea struck hard. Of course she could not go with the Persian anywhere now, but someday, perhaps someday not too far into the future, after she had proved herself and rendered Da-ren a great service, she could leave to marry. And then, if she knew where to find the Persian . . .

"What is your address?"

Did he hesitate? "It won't be very useful for me to give you my address now, as soon I might move."

He didn't want her to have his address. A horrible understanding dawned. "You have a wife."

"What? No!"

His surprise seemed genuine. But a girl never knew with men, did she, to what lengths they would go? "More than one wife?"

"*No.*" He rose to his feet, as if to further emphasize that syllable of denial. "I am not married."

"How old are you?"

"Twenty-one."

Much closer to her age than she had thought. With his competence and maturity—not to mention his luxuriant beard—she had believed him to be at least twenty-five. But twenty-one was still more than old enough to be married—or at least betrothed. In China, in good families, the matter of a child's matrimony was often settled before the latter reached adolescence. That no such agreement had ever been spoken of for her was as much a black mark against her as it was a relief.

"Why has your father not arranged a marriage for you?" she demanded.

"My father is no more. He died years ago."

"Have you no mother?"

"I do, but she will let me choose for myself."

She drew back. "What kind of mother is that?"

"A slightly negligent one—I'll grant you that. But the point is, there is no wife, fiancée, or sweetheart waiting for me in India. Or Persia. Or anywhere in the world."

And they were back where they started. "Then why keep your address a secret?"

*L*eighton could not tell her his address because when he was not on the road, he lived at the British garrison in Rawalpindi.

Not that he suspected her of any ties to the Ch'ing authority, but he had not only his own safety to consider, but those of others on the expedition. And though the main concern of the local officials was to keep the Russians out, they would not hesitate to treat the presence of spies as evidence of the British Raj's desire to expand its territory at the Ch'ing Dynasty's expense.

"It is as I said, only because I will be moving to a new place." She rose to her feet.

"I still have a bit more chocolate left. Do you—"

"No." She untied her horse and leaped upon the saddle with jaw-dropping athleticism, not even bothering with the stirrup.

He stood still for a moment, staring after her as she galloped away. Was this it? Was this the last he would see of her?

The very thought jolted him into action; the next minute he was in pursuit. But then he realized she was not trying to be rid of him—she wasn't riding at a full sprint and she was headed back to the caravan route, rather than a more obscure path that would make it easier for her to shake him loose.

He followed her from a furlong behind and let a half hour pass before he caught up to her. She cast him an unreadable look and said nothing.

And Kashgar drew nearer with every second.

Finally he could stand the silence no more. "From Kashgar I go to Yarkand. You?"

She glanced toward the mountains. "It's spring. I shall go sightseeing."

"I will miss you."

"I will forget you by next week."

He bit the inside of his cheek at her merciless reply. But why should she have mercy on him? He was a man following her about, proposing that she should leave everything behind for the unknown, and then refusing to even divulge where he lived.

"I will not forget you—ever."

"No, of course you won't," she said, her tone biting. "Next time you are in Darjeeling, I will be all that you can think of."

No need for Darjeeling—she had been all that he could think of from the moment they met. But he did not know what to say to convince her of it. Whatever words he chose would still be only words, of no more value than grains of sand in the Takla Makan.

Silence again.

He groped around for something to say. "Your friend, the one who drank Darjeeling tea, was he the one who taught you how to use a sword?"

She snorted. "My amah taught me."

"Your what?"

"You are obviously a foreigner. Here everyone's nannies teach such things."

He could not tell whether she was mocking him. "Tell me more about her then."

"She is dead."

"What was she like when she was alive?"

"She was a fool." She laughed harshly at his expression. "Do you think a woman who can kill with her little finger can't be a fool? Well, she was. She was addicted to gambling. To keep gambling she turned to thievery. When I was eleven a bounty hunter chased her all the way home. She killed him in the courtyard and we had to drag his body for miles to dispose of it."

He blinked, trying to digest this revelation.

She bit her lower lip and then snarled at him. "Still want to send me chocolate?"

"Yes."

"Why?"

"Why shouldn't I, just because your amah was foolish?"

"Because I am just like her."

Her tone was all defiance, and yet he heard quite something else, the fear of a girl who was all alone in the world. "That's fine," he said quietly. "There is no law that says fools cannot have chocolate."

She looked away. "Good thing, for you are a fool, too."

He gazed at her still-dirty face, her exaggeratedly thread-bare hat, and the much patched sleeve of her coat. "Yes, I know."

A much bigger fool than she could ever suspect.

From a distance, Kashgar was almost indistinguishable from the desert. The city wall was a dun color identical to that of the sand. The houses inside, built of brick, mud, and straw, appeared just as dull and weathered.

And yet here and there Leighton would catch a glimpse of bright blue minarets, or the underside of an arcaded passage-way that had been painted the colors of a kaleidoscope. Children stood on balconies decorated with pointed arches and looked down curiously. At least twice they rode by residences from which issued the soft, clear music of a bubbling fountain.

She led on, past the livestock market, past the stalls sell-ing dried and sundry goods, past the streets populated with old men drinking tea and playing chess.

When they reached a quieter section of the town, he asked, "How did your amah die?"

He was beginning to believe the woman had not perished of natural causes.

"She was killed," the girl answered brusquely, confirming his suspicions.

"Are you ever worried for your own safety?"

She pulled her lips. "No, I carry a sword and three daggers for my amusement."

"If you need help—"

"Should my nemesis arrive, you will be no use to me whatsoever."

"Nemesis?"

"What would you call someone who killed both your master and your only friend? Anyway, we are here."

She turned under an arched gate into a courtyard. Long balconies, decorated by white lacelike fretwork, enclosed the courtyard from three sides. She dismounted and walked into the dim interior beyond a doorway. When he followed her in, she was already reclined on gold and purple cushions, her booted feet spread apart in a casual and entirely convincing male pose.

Loudly she called for wine and sweets. And when two giggling girls came with the trays, she pulled one down onto the cushions next to her, set an arm around the girl's shoulder, and kissed her on the neck.

So she did know the brothel quite well—at least well enough to find it without asking anyone. He waved away the girl who approached him, his eyes only on his girl.

She watched him as she caressed the serving wench's throat and shoulder, a strange glitter in her eyes. He could scarcely breathe. From arousal, yes, but at the same time, a suffocating pain in his chest: They had so little time left, and she preferred to spend it playing games.

She rose, pulling the serving girl up with her, and sending her off with a whispered word in the ear and a slap on the bottom. The serving girl left, all giggles. She came toward him. "You said you still have more chocolate?"

He had one last bar left. He had meant to save it for the ascent of the mountain pass into India, but now he handed it to her.

"And your tea," she demanded. "Must set the proper mood for lovemaking, don't you know."

He handed over what little remained of his supply of tea as well, wrapped in pages from a Parsi-language newspaper published in India.

She filliped the package. "I haven't forgotten our deal— you can come and watch, just give me a few minutes to get the girls ready."

"Of course, make sure you get my money's worth," he said.

"I'd better get inside. Don't want the ladies to become impatient."

"Should we meet here again, this day next year?"

"This day next year by whose calendar?"

He grimaced inwardly. He had forgotten that for the Islamic calendar, which relied on lunar observation to determine the beginning of the months, a different locality might have a different set of dates.

"Let's just say three hundred fifty-four days from today."

By then he should have accrued enough home leave to make the trip to Kashgar.

"And what? Will you bring more gold for me to steal?"

With that, she slapped him on the chest and left, disappearing through a curtained doorway.

Almost immediately he went out to the courtyard, but her horse was already gone. He ran out of the courtyard, but there was no sign of the horse on the street outside. He stood in place, his hand on the support column of an arch. It was completely unsurprising, her departure. She had always given every indication that she would go her own way, but for some reason, he had not wanted to see the inevitable.

Now the inevitable was a void in his chest.

His head lifted. He felt inside his robe. The velvet pouch of gems that he always carried on his person, in order to pass for a diamond dealer—it was gone. He remembered her slap across his chest. He remembered her warning that she would rob him blind.

You are a fool, too, she had told him.

Yes, I know.

He didn't know. He didn't know at all.

"Sir?"

He turned. It was the serving girl she had taken to "bed."

"Your friend asked that this be returned to you, sir."

This was the package of tea, as evidenced by the Parsi newspaper from four months ago.

"Thank you," he managed to say. "How much do I owe for your . . . hospitality?"

"Your friend has already paid very handsomely for the wine and the sweets."

Of course she would have, the beautiful bastard.

But something felt different about the tea package. He made sure he was alone before he peeked inside. The velvet pouch. And it did not feel lighter in his hand, but slightly heavier than he remembered.

Nestled among the uncut gems he had brought, a round bead of green jade, from the tassel of her sword. And next to it, several dried flowers—snow chrysanthemum from the Kunlun Mountains, grown at an altitude of ten thousand feet above sea level.

She had not robbed him after all.

Except of his heart.

CHAPTER 5

The Lady

London
1891

Mr. Lochby, the private investigator, had excellent news. He had easily found information on Master Gordon, who, he informed Catherine, had indeed been a gentleman, a member of an old landowning family of Devonshire—the cadet branch, but all the same, very, very respectable stock.

Young Herbert Gordon had been educated at Harrow and Cambridge—Trinity College, to be exact. After that, he had lived the life of a man about town. He displayed an interest in the Far East, since his father had spent some time there, but it was the interest of a dilettante, nothing terribly serious. Most of his time was spent doing what pleased himself.

And then, in October of 1873, he left England abruptly, never to return except upon his death.

Some of this Catherine knew, some she had guessed, but still, there was so much more she did not know. As a child, she had defined the adults in her life by their roles and never sought to learn about them as individuals until it was too late: She had no knowledge of her mother's upbringing in a scholarly household, just as little of her amah's girlhood under the eaves of the legendary Abode of the Shadowless Goddesses, and only slightly more of Master Gordon's youth, for all her eagerness to hear of everything there was to know about the outside world.

Before she left England, she would rectify her ignorance about Master Gordon. But for now, despite her hunger for every last detail of his life, she must remember her purpose: She needed to find out what happened to the jade tablet that had been in his possession.

"This is investigative work of very fine caliber, Mr. Lochby," she said.

Mr. Lochby preened a little, stroking his mustache. "My pleasure to provide the services I have promised."

"Would you mind telling me if you were able to locate any of his surviving family members?"

"Unfortunately, no. He did have a sister elder to him, but she passed away two years ago."

This was not what Catherine wanted to hear. "Did his will name any particularly close friends?"

"Mr. Gordon never made a will."

"What?" Her exclamation hung in the air, a half octave too loud.

"I inquired at the Principal Probate Registry and was told that there is none on record," said Mr. Lochby.

"I see." She did her best to keep the dismay out of her voice. In an almost casual tone, she asked, "Out of curiosity, to whom does a man's possession go when he leaves no will?"

"I am no solicitor, but I would say his closest of kin, which in this case would be his sister."

"Who is also dead."

"True, but I do have the address of Mr. Cromwell, the Gordons' solicitor, if you should care to speak to him about Mr. Gordon's and Miss Gordon's estates."

Catherine's heart leaped, all her earlier distress gone. The solicitor would have far more information to offer her. But more important, he must have known Master Gordon in the old days—the first such person she would come across in all her years.

"Yes, thank you," she said, again trying to keep her voice even. "I would very much like to speak to the solicitor."

She left Mr. Lochby's office with Mr. Cromwell's address in hand. The latter's office was not very far away. She would have walked to conserve her limited funds, but rain came down quite insistently, and she had learned from bitter experience that even one as nimble as she could not keep the hem of her dress completely safe from all the splashes caused by horses, carriage wheels, and other pedestrians.

She had not seen a clear sky since she'd disembarked in Southampton. Rain, always rain, pausing only to let a round of fog roll in and out, before coming down again, a state of permanent sogginess. Such weather was common enough in the south of China—reams of poetry celebrated the beauty of spring rain—but for a city as northerly as the uppermost reaches of Manchuria, it felt all wrong.

And now, because of the rain, her moldy-smelling hansom cab was stuck in a traffic logjam. She stared out of the water-blurred window, imagining this Mr. Cromwell, hoping he would have something to tell her about Master Gordon beyond what the latter's signature looked like.

Her heart seized: A stylish couple came down the sidewalk, the woman in a violet mantle and the man in a black cloak with upturned collars. But they turned out to be strangers Catherine had never seen before, not Leighton Atwood and his fiancée.

Catherine had been good. She had not gone back to his house or tried in any other way to insinuate herself into his presence. Instead she had been busy looking for a serviceable flat at a respectable address that catered to single women—and then busy fitting out the flat so that it would be presentable when Mrs. Reynolds came to call.

But what she really wanted was for *him* to see her place.

For years she'd assumed that he'd left her because all his promises had been lies. Now she wondered whether his decision hadn't been in part prompted by his belief that it would be impossible for a nomad girl to fit into the life of an English man of property. But there were entire swaths of her life that he could not have remotely guessed at, the long years confined behind high walls, the sea of etiquette through which she swam daily, the elaborate pretense she was capable of putting on, to appear the most docile and ladylike of creatures.

She would have had not a bit of trouble negotiating the relatively uncomplicated English rules of politesse.

And she wanted him to understand this and regret his choice.

She sighed. Why did she persist in assuming that their unexpected reunion was a matter of earth-shattering significance to him, simply because it was the case for her? He had left her years ago. Without a backward glance. Her reappearance was an inconvenience, probably a minor irritant—nothing else.

Rain fell and fell. The hansom cab barely moved. With another sigh, Catherine got out, paid the cabbie, and sloshed in the direction of the sidewalk.

*M*r. Cromwell was a small man with almost entirely white hair and a warm twinkle to his eyes— Catherine liked him instantly. Once she explained who she was and her purpose for visiting him, he tasked his secretary to hang her coat near the fire, and welcomed her into his dark-paneled, thickly carpeted office.

"Miserable weather, is it not?" he asked cheerfully.

"Indeed it is. I am beginning to believe that it never stops raining in England."

It was Master Gordon who had first told her that whereas Chinese chitchat often led with mealtimes, English small talk tended to revolve around precipitation.

"Ah, but you must have greater faith, Miss Blade," the solicitor admonished her gently. "The sky *will* eventually clear. And our summers are all the more glorious for how much we must yearn for them."

Catherine smiled a little. "I see you are a philosopher as well, sir."

This quite pleased Mr. Cromwell. "Oh, I imagine any old lawyer must have done a fair bit of pondering upon the nature of life and humanity. But do let us proceed now to the purpose of your visit. You said you would like to know more about Mr. Herbert Gordon."

"He was a beloved friend and I was looking forward to reading his will. Not because I expected there to be anything for me but because I hoped the will would tell me the names of those he held dear, people I could call on to reminisce about him."

Mr. Cromwell nodded sympathetically. "And you found that he left no will."

"Is that not a bit rare?"

"Not as rare as you'd think, given how easy it is to make and execute wills in this country. For a relatively young man like Mr. Gordon, with no dependents, no complicated holdings, and no expectations that he would come into a great fortune, not having a will might be more common."

"So whatever belongings of his would simply have gone to his sister, his closest of kin."

"Not very much of what belonged to him came back from China: a trunk of books and letters and a trunk of clothing."

"And his remains, of course."

"His ashes have been scattered, according to the late Miss Gordon."

"He was *cremated*?" She had seen his body delivered to the British Legation, but she herself had left Peking the following day, for the long journey to Chinese Turkestan. "But cremations are not performed in China."

"Except by Buddhist monks," said Mr. Cromwell. "The legation staff took his remains to a Buddhist temple, from what I understand."

This was most unexpected. But she was only surprised, not dismayed. There was something dramatic and final about cremations—the soul had already departed, no need for the body to remain behind. "You wouldn't happen to know where his ashes were scattered, would you, Mr. Cromwell?"

"I'm afraid I do not. Miss Jane Gordon mentioned it in passing and I did not inquire in detail."

And there went Catherine's nascent hope of perhaps taking a handful of that soil to keep as a memento.

She had to think for a moment before she could remember where they were before the conversation veered off to cremations: Master Gordon's belongings, which she had packed in a daze the morning after he died, trying desperately to hold herself together.

"You mentioned a trunk of books and letters and a trunk of clothes, sir. But surely those could not be the entirety of his worldly possessions."

"He did have a house in London. But about two years after he left England, I received instructions from him to transfer the house and its contents into the possession of one Mrs. Robert Delany."

At last, the name of someone Master Gordon had treasured and esteemed above all others. Catherine forced herself to remain still, to not leap up from her chair in sheer excitement. "Would you happen to know how Master Gordon knew this Mrs. Delany and where I can find her?"

Mr. Cromwell shook his head. "I'm afraid all I can tell you is that she is an Englishwoman who married an American and lives in San Francisco."

San Francisco was an ocean and a continent away. But with steamers and trains, an ocean and a continent could be crossed in a matter of weeks. In no time at all, she could be sitting in Mrs. Delany's sitting room, listening to the latter tell her all about Master Gordon.

Except Master Gordon had left England in 1873, which meant the gift of his house and its contents had been made in 1875. But Catherine had seen the jade tablet in his possession as late as 1877, so it had not gone to Mrs. Delany with everything else.

At least not then.

And Catherine, as much as she wanted to, could not simply jump on the next steamer out of Southampton, not until she could reasonably claim to have exhausted any and all leads in England.

But she could write Mrs. Delany. Or, if she allowed herself to be a little reckless with her budget, she could even cable Mrs. Delany, in hope of a faster response.

"Do you have Mrs. Delany's address, Mr. Cromwell?"

Mr. Cromwell wrote Mrs. Delany's address on a crisp sheet of stationery and handed it to Catherine. "I did not know Mr. Gordon very well outside of my capacity as his solicitor—and I regret it. May I tell you something about him?"

"Of course," said Catherine, who was just about to inquire whether Mr. Cromwell had any anecdotes to relate. "Please."

"Twenty years ago, I lost my daughter Julia to illness."

"Oh, I'm so sorry!"

"As am I to this day, but life goes on," said Mr. Cromwell quietly, with neither awkwardness nor feigned nonchalance. "We were all devastated. But Julia's twin sister, Portia, then eight years old, was absolutely inconsolable.

"One day, a package came for her in the post, a package

that contained two books, a puzzle, a pair of opera glasses, a model train set, two ostrich plumes, stamps and coins from all over world, and several miniature paintings meant for a doll's house. A note in the package, addressed to Portia, said that the sender had heard that she was having a difficult time without her sister and hoped that the contents of the package would offer some distraction. It also said that there would be one package a month for the next two years.

"And so twenty-four packages came, each filled with a variety of interesting and often unexpected items. Sometimes there would be seashells and geodes, sometimes a whole book of pressed flowers, and once there was even a necklace made of shark's teeth, which fascinated Portia to no end.

"The packages helped Portia immensely—they helped all of us immensely." Mr. Cromwell's voice caught. He exhaled slowly. "But it was not until after Mr. Gordon had passed away that we learned he had been the one to send all the packages, he who had never met either one of my daughters but had felt moved to do something when he learned of Portia's grief."

Catherine's eyes prickled with tears. "That sounds like him. He was the kindest man I have ever met."

"You are fortunate to have met him," said Mr. Cromwell with tremendous sincerity. "Portia would have dearly loved to."

Catherine gazed upon Mr. Cromwell. There was still a hint of sadness in his eyes, but the twinkle was back—despite the loss of a beloved child, Mr. Cromwell remained a man who found much to enjoy in life.

Could she hope for a fraction of his joie de vivre someday?

He accompanied her out of his office to the reception room. They shook hands warmly.

"Look forward to your summer, Miss Blade," said Mr. Cromwell. "And trust that it will come."

* * *

Mrs. Reynolds approved of the elaborate music box Leighton had chosen for Annabel. "Yes, Captain, I do believe she would quite enjoy it."

"Thank you, Mrs. Reynolds. In that case, I will take it back to the shop and have the spring mechanism replaced." He rose. "Let me not take up any more of your time."

Mrs. Reynolds hesitated—as he had hoped. "Captain, would you mind if I asked for a favor?"

"Please, go ahead."

"I have arranged to call on Miss Blade this afternoon. It is the staff's half day, so I am without a coachman, which I didn't think would matter much as I could always take a hansom cab or walk. But this fog . . ."

This fog was spectacular even for London, thick enough to scoop with one's hands, with the bouquet of an overripe Stilton that had fallen into a sludge pond.

Leighton inclined his head. "I will be glad to put my carriage at your disposal, ma'am."

Twenty minutes later, they were walking up a considerable number of flights of stairs. The fog was such that from the street it had been impossible to assess the height of the building. But it would seem that the block of flats was at least six stories tall, and Miss Blade had taken a flat at the very top.

Mrs. Reynolds huffed as she staggered up the last flight, her fingers digging into Leighton's arm. "Ah, there it is, at last. I daresay Miss Blade would have no trouble keeping her figure svelte if she but went out and came back once or twice a day."

Before they had walked halfway down the corridor, Miss Blade's door opened. The expression of the quiet, shadowlike woman who stood waiting altered only a little as she took him in: She would have already known, from the sound of their footsteps, that a man had come with Mrs. Reynolds; the only question in her mind would have been whether Mrs. Reynolds had brought Marland or himself.

"Captain Atwood was kind enough to ferry me over on this rather horrible day, Miss Blade," explained Mrs. Reynolds. "And I could not possibly allow him to remain in the carriage while I enjoyed myself up here."

Leighton had known for approximately twenty-four hours that Mrs. Reynolds would call on her while Annabel and Mrs. Chase attended Edwin Madison's indoor birthday picnic. He had not meant to do anything with that knowledge until the fog rolled in. Now here he was, about to walk into the dwelling, however temporary, of the one who, to him at least, always belonged under a wide-open sky.

"No, no, of course not," said Miss Blade graciously. "I am delighted to see you both. Do please come in."

The redolence of incense wafted toward him. He had never cared for incense, with its heavy, cloying smell. But the incense she used produced a much lighter fragrance, one that reminded him, more than anything else, of the scent of Chinese ink.

She herself was dressed very simply in an afternoon gown of light grey. He would not have thought of it, but the color suited her well and lent her an air of unmistakable refinement.

She led them into the flat's vestibule.

There were items of appropriate furnishing in the vestibule, but all he saw was a curtain made of strings of ceramic beads that took the place of a door that separated the vestibule from the parlor.

We had a curtain made of beads, she had once told him, in those long-ago days.

He swept aside the curtain for the ladies to pass, the beads sliding along his palm. They were cloisonné enamel, blue and white. As he let go, the strings of beads swung back and forth, striking one another with soft, melodic pings.

"Oh, how atmospheric," said Mrs. Reynolds admiringly.

Atmospheric indeed, and also quite effective at making sure that no one could sneak into the parlor unheard.

The parlor was sparsely furnished, but rich in artwork. On one wall, a large black ink painting of a mountain landscape, the ridges sharp as swords, one lone tree in the foreground, bare and gnarly. On the opposite wall, the exact same landscape, but depicted in color, the summits a rich, deep green, the tree laden with riotous pink blossoms. Grouped scrolls of Chinese calligraphy hung beside and above the paintings. Pale smoke drifted from a brilliantly green jasper incense holder on the mantelpiece.

"I hope you don't mind the incense," said Miss Blade as she offered them seats. "The smell of the fog was rather overwhelming earlier."

"The incense is most certainly a vast improvement over the *eau de brume*," answered Mrs. Reynolds. "Ghastly weather of late, is it not?"

Miss Blade lit the spirit lamp on the tea table and hoisted a small kettle above the flame. "I certainly hope so. I should hate to think that this is normal weather."

"It *is* normal weather," Leighton heard himself say. "That is what is so ghastly about it."

She shot him a quick glance, as if astounded that he had spoken to her without being forced to by the weight of etiquette. He was no less shocked himself.

"I'm afraid Captain Atwood has hit the nail on the head." Mrs. Reynolds chuckled. "But do tell me, Miss Blade, that you have not been kept inside all this time."

"I saw a good bit of London during my search for a flat. I have taken a walk on the Embankment and seen Parliament from a distance. And since you recommended it so highly, ma'am, I have paid a visit to the British Museum."

Leighton experienced a frisson at the thought of a self-professed master thief visiting a depository of valuable objects.

"How did you find the museum?" asked Mrs. Reynolds, gratified. "I have always enjoyed my visits there."

"The vastness of the collections is most impressive."

The kettle sang. She warmed the pot and made tea, her motion graceful and unhurried—that of a woman who had never ridden a horse astride or drawn blood with a sharp sword.

Darjeeling tea, the scent was unmistakable.

And then, from another tin, she scooped a spoonful of dried chrysanthemum flowers into a teacup and poured hot water on top.

An Englishman was assured of coming across a cup of Darjeeling every once in a while. But the delicate fragrance of chrysanthemum tea he had not known since her.

For a moment the void inside threatened to engulf him.

"What is that?" asked Mrs. Reynolds.

"It is a tisane of chrysanthemum blossoms."

"How interesting. Where do you get these blossoms?"

He braced himself to hear the words *Kunlun Mountains* and *a height of ten thousand feet.*

"These are from Huangshan, or the Yellow Mountain, as sometimes it is called—a place of otherworldly beauty, much celebrated in the art and literature of China," said Miss Blade, removing the spirit lamp and the kettle from the table to bring out a plate of Madeira cake slices.

She poured for Mrs. Reynolds and Leighton. He was transfixed by her ease with these small rituals of life. It was not the afternoon gown that gave her that air of refinement—this woman *was* refined, accustomed to sophisticated surroundings and the intricacies of polite society.

What did you do to her, that untamed and untamable girl? And what exactly is your purpose here in England?

"Was there anything in particular you wished to see at the British Museum, Miss Blade?" he asked.

Her face was bent over her own teacup; she looked at him

out of the corner of her eye. She had heard his suspicion then, which he had not tried too hard to hide.

"I did my best to avoid accidentally coming upon the mummies. But as for what I *wished* to see . . . I had rather thought there would be a larger selection of oriental art." She turned toward Mrs. Reynolds. "You see, ma'am, in China there is no equivalent of the British Museum. There are no public museums at all, as far as I know. The only works of art one can experience must either be in one's own possession or that of a friend's. So I was quite looking forward to the treasures of the British Museum—and therefore a little disappointed that the display was rather paltry."

"Oh, but you mustn't think that the collection on display is everything the museum holds. Far from it!" Mrs. Reynolds cried. "I have a cousin who sits on the Board of Trustees for the museum. And he tells me that plans are under way to bring more oriental artworks out of storage to fill the space that has been opened up by the building of the White Wing. I recommend you wait some time and visit the museum again, Miss Blade. I am sure you will meet with a far wealthier exhibit than the one you saw."

Miss Blade leaned forward slightly—Leighton felt her excitement as surely as if she had stood up and somersaulted. "I had no idea," she said.

"Oh yes." Mrs. Reynolds nodded. "Even now there are collections you can see at other locations around London. And you can always ask to see the accession catalogues, which would give you a better idea of the true extent of the museum's holdings."

"Fascinating," Miss Blade murmured.

"I have a guide to the museum's exhibits at home, and it mentions where some of the additional holdings are archived. I will find it when I get home and have it sent to you as soon as the fog clears."

"Thank you. That would be much appreciated."

So she *was* looking for something, an object of Asiatic origin that she expected to see in the British Museum.

As if she heard his thoughts, her eyes came to rest on him, eyes the color of the North Sea, of cold water and approaching storm. "And you, Captain, how do you do?"

He took a sip of his tea, his hand surprisingly steady, considering the rest of him was all agitation and frayed nerves. "Very well, thank you."

"My soon-to-be nephew-in-law is a man of few words," said Mrs. Reynolds, in a tone that was meant to be indulgent, but came off more resigned than anything else.

"Is he?" Miss Blade murmured, no doubt remembering all his attempts to induce *her*, the strong, silent one, to speak. "I'm sure Miss Chase would disagree—even the quietest gentlemen become chatty when they are with their sweethearts."

Mrs. Reynolds turned her teacup around on its saucer: It was one of Annabel's running jokes that it was easier to milk a stone than to pry words out of him.

"I enjoy listening to Miss Chase," he said. "I am convinced that every time she speaks, a rainbow appears somewhere in the world."

"What an extraordinarily lovely sentiment," said the woman who specialized in turning his life upside down. "Miss Chase is a very fortunate young lady."

"No," he said, "I consider myself the far more fortunate one."

She traced the tip of her index finger along the handle of her teacup. Her hand, slender and elegant, gave every impression of delicateness. But he remembered the calluses on her palms, the calluses of one who always had a set of reins in her hands. And he remembered the sensation of those calluses under his lips—and upon his skin.

"I am sure you and Miss Chase will be very happy together for years to come," she said.

Would they?

He tried to detect an undertone of mockery, but could not.

She believed it, that he would settle into an easy wedded bliss, untroubled by such things as her reappearance in his life.

When he hadn't breathed since the moment he'd recognized her.

"Speaking of my niece," said Mrs. Reynolds, rising, "Captain Atwood and I had better leave soon to retrieve her—and my sister—from Mr. Madison's house, before this fog gets any worse."

Miss Blade walked them to the door. "Thank you for calling on this dismal day, Mrs. Reynolds. And it is excellent to see you, too, Captain—as always."

*C*atherine thought it a little odd, the way Leighton Atwood placed himself in the vestibule, as he and Mrs. Reynolds retrieved their overcoats. When they had departed, she immediately noticed that he had left his walking stick behind—he had been blocking the older woman's view of the umbrella stand so that she wouldn't realize this omission.

Catherine opened the door and listened. They descended one, two, three stories before they halted and exchanged a few murmured words. And now one set of footsteps reascended at an easy, healthy pace.

It was because of this gait that until she saw his face, she had believed Mrs. Reynolds to have brought Marland Atwood.

She left the door ajar and carried the walking stick with her into the parlor. The stick was straight, slender, and surprisingly dense, forged entirely of blue steel. As a weapon, it was sturdy and well balanced, with just enough flexibility to make things interesting—for a short burst of use, that was. As a cane . . . she would need a severe disability to turn to something so heavy.

He was now on the sixth floor, approaching her door. Following a moment of silence, he entered—and closed the door behind himself. The curtain of beads parted and swayed, a sprinkling of mineral raindrops.

Ever since they'd parted ways eight years ago, she had wished for this moment, her lover walking back into her life again. Through hundreds of doors and in thousands of guises he would return, crossing the line that separated life and death. And now here he was, somber and beautiful, the only person other than Master Gordon to have believed that something wonderful would become of her.

Perhaps Mr. Cromwell was right. Perhaps the summer of her life had not yet passed her by. Perhaps—

"Did you know Mrs. Chase's assailant, the man you sent overboard?" he asked, his manners entirely official.

She wanted to laugh—to keep from crying. So much for dreams coming true. The walking stick left her hand, passed an inch before his face, and landed with a hard rattle inside the wrought iron umbrella holder, fifteen feet and a strange angle away. "Why do you want to know?"

To his credit, he didn't bat an eyelash—not that he ever had: Her deadliness he simply took for granted. "Not many men can injure you in single combat."

"So?"

Only after the word left her lips did she realize that she had never told anyone, least of all him, that she had been injured.

"There was only one man you feared."

That man had killed her daughter. *Their* daughter. But Leighton Atwood knew nothing of what had happened afterward. He had gone back to India, attended garden parties, and saved boys from escaped tigers to universal acclaim, while she had buried their child alone.

"I did not know Mrs. Chase's assailant. And I fear no man, now or ever," she said coldly. "You should go, Captain. You don't wish to keep Mrs. Reynolds waiting, do you?"

CHAPTER 6

The Ambush

Chinese Turkestan
1883

The girl moaned hot, obscene words like a cat meowing before a dish of fried fish. The Tajik warlord growled in approval and pumped into her with renewed frenzy. She opened her legs wider and began to emit short screams of delight.

Her smooth skin glistened in the dancing orange light of a crackling fire. His large body straddled hers like a bear vanquishing its prey. Their frantic shadows jiggled on the arabesque tapestry that covered the wall. Silk pillows were falling off the low bed, one soft plop after another.

Ying-ying, on the roof, barely heard or saw anything. She was in distant Darjeeling again, walking between rows of tea bushes, the Persian next to her.

Was there enough room for a couple to walk abreast between two rows of tea bushes? Probably not. She might have to put him beyond the next row, just slightly out of reach. And what would she be wearing? Definitely something other than this grimy old coat. Perhaps something Indian, dazzlingly bright and shot through with gold threads—or maybe even something English, very prim and proper, with a lace parasol to match.

He, who had seen her only in her ratty coat—and liked it—would be full of admiration for her lovely new clothes. And would ply her with Swiss chocolate. They would—

She was brought out of her reverie by a rafter-shaking roar. But it was only the Tajik warlord, at last done. He collapsed onto his Chinese concubine, who stroked his neck and shoulders and praised his prowess in a mixture of Chinese and Turkic.

Da-ren, despite his anger at his exile, devoted himself to his post. He saw his role as far more than keeping peace and collecting taxes. No, it was up to him to make sure that Chinese Turkestan never slipped from the control of the Imperial Court again.

The land itself was harsh. Agriculture was practiced only on a minor scale. Nor did the earth yield enough precious metals to recuperate the cost of holding it. Yet from the Tang Dynasty onward, those who ruled the Central Plain had tried to impose control over this vast tract of territory.

Bound on the north, west, and south by impassable mountains ranges, with the great Takla Makan Desert blocking any direct passage across, Chinese Turkestan, under the dominion of the Imperial Court, assured security on China's western border. But the natives were restive. The Russians openly coveted it. And who was to say the English, who already held the Subcontinent, would not be similarly greedy?

Da-ren had decided in the earliest days of his tenure that pacification of the natives was key to his goals. Among the tactics he employed to achieve that end was the gifting of beautiful Chinese girls to influential local chiefs.

An old tactic, probably one of the oldest there ever was. China produced an endless supply of lovely, clever girls whose parents had no use for them. They were grateful to be purchased by Da-ren, instead of by a brothel, and eager for a chance to become a warlord's favorite concubine.

But Da-ren did not trust them. Some might be content simply to be fed. And some might be content simply to be a favorite, forgetting that they were there to pillow-talk closer links to China.

When Lin had proved a danger even at eight thousand *li* from Peking, Da-ren had wanted to send Ying-ying back to the interior of China and hide her under heavy guard. But such a fate would have been almost worse than death, so Ying-ying proposed instead that she be the one to go from one warlord household to the next, spying on the girls in their nocturnal duties, rewarding successes, and putting fear in those who slacked in their efforts.

At first, Da-ren had adamantly refused. It was too dangerous. How would he answer her mother in the afterworld if something happened to her? But Ying-ying persisted. To be surrounded by a contingent of guards was tantamount to announcing her exact location to Lin; far better to pass herself off as yet another weary—and male—traveler, in a land that was still a crossroad between China and the world to the west. Besides, could Da-ren really entrust a man to deal with dozens and dozens of pretty and shrewd women?

In the end, Ying-ying had prevailed. For three years, until she was satisfied that her Turkic was good enough, she'd dressed as a Mongolian boy. And now, taking advantage of her fluent Turkic and her malleable features, a Kazakh youth.

"I'm so glad Da-ren gave me to you," the girl with the Tajik warlord whispered. "I never knew such pleasure was possible."

The man flipped on his back and grinned broadly.

The girl dabbed off his sweat and drew the covers over him, all the while speaking in that lovely, hypnotic murmur that she had been taught. She told him how she could not live without the bliss he brought her nightly, that he must not put himself in danger. When the natives rebelled, men died, and all they'd get was a new foreign master. Let the others assuage their doubts of their manliness that way. He didn't need to. Didn't he hear her moans of joy?

The man nodded sleepily. Ying-ying wondered whether the

Persian could be steered like that, with a pair of soft thighs and a great deal of flattery. She liked to think that he would see through such staged affections, but she could not be entirely certain. Men were as stupid about women as women were stupid about men.

Tomorrow Ying-ying would have some coins for the girl. After that, the road to Kulja, on which she hoped to travel fast and make up for some lost time. But first, at sunrise, she would mark off one more day on the little calendar she had made for herself.

Three hundred fifty-four days, the Persian had said, the length of an Islamic year. She meant to be there at the brothel in Kashgar. And if he came, if he was true to his word, then she would go to India with him, see the holy river, the white marble tomb, and, of course, Darjeeling, in the foothills of the Himalayas.

And perhaps then, her life would truly begin.

She rose to her feet, bounded to the next roof, and then the next, sinking to a crouch between each leap to make sure she hadn't been seen. But from the last roof to the fortified earthen wall that surrounded the warlord's compound, the distance was too great for a single leap.

With some reluctance, she dropped into a narrow alley between two buildings, grimacing at muscles made stiff by lying motionless several hours in the still-cold night. There came a whimper. She tensed, expecting to see men on patrol. But no one came. Her task was only to make sure the Chinese concubines did as Da-ren bid. Night thieves, illicit trysts, and other goings-on in a warlord's household were no concern of hers.

But if the warlord had dealings with Russians . . .

She clambered up the roof again.

*L*eighton heard the soft landing. If someone had leaped off the roof, that someone had remarkably quiet feet. He moved a step backward. Edwin Madison, feverish, whimpered before Leighton could clamp a hand over his mouth.

Leighton had arrived in Yarkand eight days ago, to be met with ill news. Madison and Singh, their Punjabi stepper, had been caught on the periphery of an argument involving a Tajik chieftain's nephew. And when a horde of the latter's men descended on the scene, they had been taken to the chieftain's custody stronghold.

The other Punjabi on the mission, Roshan, had attempted a rescue and almost got himself killed for his trouble. Under different circumstances they would have taken their time and bargained for the release of the prisoners—a long, drawn-out process that the warlords and their underlings enjoyed, to see how much profit could be squeezed out. But now there was no time for such leisurely proceedings: In a week or so, Madison's hair would start showing its not-so-black roots, and the Tajik chieftain, said to be on friendly terms with his Ch'ing overlord, might turn Madison over to the governor of Ili.

Half of the remaining members of the expedition had set out with Leighton. The Tajik chieftain's stronghold was north of the Takla Makan Desert and farther east on the caravan route than where Leighton had met the girl—his chest had felt quite hollow as he'd galloped past the open-air eatery.

It was spring. Was she sightseeing?

He had needed to touch the jade bead from her sword to reassure himself that she did not give such gifts lightly. That he would see her again in little less than a year.

At least the rescue attempt seemed to be going off smoothly. The moon was nearly full, but they had stumbled upon the chieftain's birthday celebration. A little stealth and handkerchiefs soaked in chloroform had done the rest.

And they weren't that far from where he and Roshan had climbed in and hidden the rope ladder. Ten more minutes, and he would have them safely out and on the road again.

But if they had been seen . . .

He led the men into the next alley—one step closer to the exit. There was no one. Had he been imagining things?

But his hearing rarely led him astray The hard-packed earth underfoot gave little clue. He looked up—height was an ambusher's best advantage. He saw nothing at first. But he heard a quick indrawn breath, so faint it barely registered. Then he saw the figure stretched flat on the roof, fingers gripping the eaves.

He'd recognized that tatty hat anywhere. *Her!*

Well, he supposed a master thief had to steal at some point. He must have smiled, for she winked in return. Suppressing another smile, he tore his gaze away before anyone else could catch on to what was going on.

That was when he heard the running footsteps, a percussive wall of them. The guards must have discovered the prisoners missing. Thankfully they weren't shouting—probably out of fear of disturbing their chieftain on his birthday night. But they were coming fast and from several directions.

A loud crash. She ran across the roof, as agile as a cat, and lobbed another tile, creating a distraction to lead the pursuing guards away from them.

"What should we do?" Roshan asked in Urdu, as the noises escalated.

"We keep going," Leighton answered.

With her on his side, he had no fear.

They moved as fast as they could, hauling a half-delirious Madison and a limping Singh. But they must have been sighted; despite the ongoing crash of the tiles, one particular contingent of guards kept coming after them.

The last thing he saw, as he climbed over the fortified earthen wall, Madison on his back, was the sight of her landing lightly before a group of pursuers, her sword gleaming in the moonlight.

$\mathcal{I}$t was almost dawn before Leighton and his group met up with the other two men he had brought with him. He ordered everyone to head back to Yarkand.

They were puzzled. What of him? Was he not coming?

In a day or two, he said. If there were to be pursuers, he wanted to remain behind and point them the wrong way. His colleagues believed him—he was known for his trustworthiness. For his part, he experienced not a twinge of guilt, his head too full of her for any qualms.

Going back was not a wise thing to do; the chieftain's men were combing the town. Leighton went from mosque to mosque, and almost wore his knees out praying, since even the warlord's minions couldn't disturb worshippers of God. Late in the morning, after the search appeared to have been called off, he made a tour of all the nearby eateries.

No sign of her.

Just as he was about to pull his hair out, inspiration struck. She had said she was fond of the brothels of Kashgar. What if she had been speaking the truth? What if that was where she went to sleep? The inns along the caravan road often piled travelers into one or two big rooms, but at a brothel, one could be assured of a bit of privacy, at least.

He asked his way to the only house of ill repute in town and was amply rewarded for his efforts. Yes, the young man meeting his description had indeed left word, in case a man with green eyes inquired after him: He was headed for Kulja.

Leighton barely remembered to hand the woman a coin before leaping on his horse and galloping away.

It had not been easy getting back into the Tajik warlord's compound in the morning to speak to his Chinese concubine. But eventually Ying-ying had managed, and learned that two traders from Punjab, who had been arrested by the warlord's men, had disappeared overnight.

So that was what the Persian had been doing. She had been delighted to see him, but later, his presence, so far away from where he'd said he was going and inside a stronghold, no less, had made her feel uneasy. Now it was all explained: He was just helping his friends.

After that, she had left town for her own safety, headed toward Kulja. But she did not hasten at all—she didn't want to make the Persian work too hard to find her. Well past noon, having made only half the progress she should have, she stopped to eat her lunch in the shade of a poplar. The air was warm, the scent of wildflowers everywhere, and as she slowly chewed on a piece of stale bread, she could not stop imagining him hurtling in her direction, riding so fast that his turban flew off.

Maybe it was meant to be, or their paths wouldn't keep crossing. Maybe a foreigner with a dead father and a "slightly negligent" mother was just the kind of man she ought to marry—Amah certainly had no confidence in her ability to please a Chinese mother-in-law. And maybe—

A clicking sound caught at the fringe of her awareness. The dark barrel of a rifle emerged from behind a boulder on the slope opposite her. She ran toward Fireborn, hooked one heel in the stirrup on the flank away from the rifle, and grabbed the bridle. Shielded this way, she kicked the stallion into motion.

The first shot missed. Bandits. She had come across them twice before, along the caravan route much farther east, the old-fashioned type who worked with long knives and broadswords. Once she had simply outrun them, Fireborn being a descendant of the breed from the Altai Mountains that the Chinese had called Heavenly Horses and waged war for. Another time she had fought the few who could keep up with her, cracking her riding whip on their skulls with stark satisfaction.

What did one do with bandits with rifles? She gripped tighter. The nomads made it look so easy, hanging on to one side of the horse so that the steed appeared riderless. She was a good rider, but not an acrobatic one.

Another shot ran out. This time it came from her exposed side. She wanted to slap herself. This was what came of mooning over a man: She had been so absentminded that she had stopped and lunched in the bottom of a valley, though one wide and shallow. This area wasn't as infested with bandits as some other parts of Chinese Turkestan. But still she had no excuse for being so careless.

She slid under Fireborn's belly, fingers digging under the saddle straps, legs about the steed's flanks. If she slipped off, she'd be trampled by Fireborn's hind hooves.

The ground quivered. Riders were approaching her at oblique angles from both sides, the leading riders hoisting rifles.

"We want only the horse. Hand over the horse and you can go."

She knew of no bandits who wanted only one thing. A man was lucky to escape with his trousers. And she was not even so lucky as to be a man. She urged Fireborn on.

But Fireborn was slowing down. She dropped her head. From between the horse's front legs she saw a row of mounted men blocking her way, the blades of their machetes glinting in the sun.

The machetes gave her hope. If they all had rifles, she was doomed. But if only a few did . . .

Fireborn stopped and turned nervously. She set her feet down and ducked out from underneath him, her hand on his mane to keep him calm. Nine men surrounded her, four machetes, two broadswords, a mace, and two rifles.

"My mother rides a horse better than you," one of the rifled men said with a laugh.

It was likely true. "I don't know about her with horses," she said. "She rode me exceedingly well."

Anything to keep them from realizing that she was a woman.

Several men chortled and whistled. "What will you tell your father, Yakub?"

Yakub growled and bared his teeth at Ying-ying. "I think I'll shoot a bullet into your teeth and see if you are still so mouthy."

She spit, as big a gob as she could manage with her dry mouth. "Allah willing, you will not disgrace yourself so. When I travel east of here, the men who want my horse are at least man enough to fight for it. What's wrong with you? Can't lift a machete?"

Yakub leaped off his horse, surprisingly agile for a big man. He snatched a broadsword from another bandit. "You son of a pig. You are stepping on your own prick, don't you know?"

"And you will teach me better, no doubt. You and your friends, together."

Yakub brandished the broadsword. "I don't need anyone's help to feed your balls to the vultures."

A one-on-one fight. Just what she was angling for. "Won't be a fair fight. I'm young and strong, but you"—she leaned back against Fireborn, feigning insouciance—"my friend, the years have not been kind to you."

"Shut up and draw your sword!" Yakub bellowed.

She grabbed her sword from the saddle, scabbard and all. "And when I have you defeated, what then?"

"You and your horse are free to leave." He charged. "But you dream."

She dodged the heavy broadsword and rammed the hilt of her sword into his side. He grunted, stumbling to his right. She followed with a kick to the center of his back, the tip of the scabbard poking hard into the acupuncture points on his lower body.

"What's the matter?" she said. "Get up and fight."

Half of the epithets he sputtered out she could not fully understand, no doubt having to do with her mother and various domesticated animals.

"Guess the fight's over then, if you won't get up," she said when he paused to take a breath. "I'd better get going."

The other men couldn't object; they still had their mouths hanging open. Quickly, sword still in hand, she lifted her left foot into the stirrup. At that moment her hat fell off, her hairpins not quite enough of a match for riding upside down. But it was no great disaster. She wore her hair in a Chinese man's long braid, wound about her head. Still a man, to all appearances.

The bandits' faces, however, changed. "The Chinese killed my father," said one.

"They killed my brother," said another, older bandit.

"Killed all of my great-grandfather's family," said yet another, grinding his teeth.

But that massacre had to have been more than a hundred years ago, when the Manchu garrison from Ili retook Kashgar. As for the father and the brother, they probably took part in the native uprising some twenty years ago, during which thousands of Chinese residents of Chinese Turkestan were also slaughtered.

But what could she say? *I didn't do it, so don't blame me*?

One by one the bandits raised their machetes. Her hands suddenly trembled with fear. She was going to die a pile of minced meat.

"Aaaaahhhhh!" she screamed, her fright fueling the skull-cracking shriek. She stepped atop Fireborn, bounded high, and dove at one of the men who still held a rifle. The force of her impact knocked him off his horse. As he fell, she yanked the rifle clean from him.

She turned and pointed it at the man to whom Yakub had given *his* rifle, her finger on the trigger. "Drop it. Or I'll blow your nose off your face."

His rifle was still cradled against his left arm. He let it thump to the ground.

"You coward!" shouted the man whose father had been killed by the Chinese. "I can live without a nose."

He charged her on his horse. She swung around and pulled the trigger.

Nothing happened. For a moment she stood stunned, staring at the oncoming horse and the machete raised high in the air. Then she dropped the useless rifle, ran toward the bandit's horse on the side away from the machete, caught the bridle, swung her feet up, and kicked the man off. She'd have liked to get atop the saddle and ride away. But already someone else was coming at her from behind—the mace, whooshing down, death in motion.

She rolled under the horse, barely avoiding the unnerved animal's hooves. Her sword, which she had dropped in order to fire the rifle, lay only a spear's length away, but another bandit already stood on it, his machete at the ready.

She pulled out a handful of golden needles from her sleeve and let him have it. As he yelled and danced in pain, she knocked him down and grabbed her sword, unsheathing it with a heartening screech of metal.

Machetes and broadswords came at her. She parried one with her blade, one with the scabbard, and ducked the third one. The mace swung down. She knocked it aside with the scabbard. Someone slashed a machete low, at her ankles. She stepped on it and hacked at the attached wrist, forcing the man back.

Not all the men attacked at once. In the back of her mind, she was aware of the four or five men who circled, ominously, outside the immediate ring of bandits who were doing their best to slice her in two. How long could she last, one against so many? All the training, all the subtleties of martial arts would do her little good when her arm became too sore to wield her weapon.

She was tiring, her feet more sluggish, her wrists less steady. But so were the three men around her. Maybe they were more accustomed to bursts of savagery, rather than sustained fighting. She smashed her scabbard against one man's head. He went down and did not immediately get up.

There might be a bit of hope for her yet. No replacement fighter had come forward. Perhaps some of them really were cowards, brutal before the weak, pusillanimous when true courage was needed. If she hurried and brought down the remaining two—

"Step back, you two!" someone howled. "Step back."

The two men pulled back. She spun around. A rifle, no more than ten paces away, was aimed directly at her head. She froze. A voice in her head screamed for her to move, something, anything, but she only stood, heart pounding, limbs paralyzed.

"Put down your sword!" the bandit demanded. He was the one who had lost some distant ancestors.

He didn't shoot. Why didn't he shoot?

"Drop the sword or I'll shoot!"

He didn't want her dead. He only wanted her helpless at her own butchering. Sweat was dripping down the back of her neck, cold and clammy. Slowly she opened her left hand and let drop her scabbard.

"The sword."

She lifted her sword, bringing it across the front of her body. Could she do it? Could she be that quick? Her left hand darted up the sleeve of her right arm, yanked out the knife sheathed in her vambrace, and hurled it at him.

The bandit ducked, then aimed at her again.

She threw herself down and rolled away. A shot exploded, echoing in the valley. It missed her by a hair.

Machetes came at her, forcing her to stand up and fight. Between ducking and parrying, she looked back at the bandit with the rifle. He had the rifle between his thighs, busy doing something to it.

With a few wild swings, she forced back those attacking her and rushed past them. If she could stop the rifle from being reloaded, then perhaps she might be safe from it.

But she wasn't fast enough. He set the rifle against his shoulder and fired. She swerved—and screamed as her upper right arm burned, a streak of agony.

Another shot rang out. Something scalded just above her ear, ripping off a long strip of scalp. Too stunned to scream this time, she slapped a palm to the side of her head. Her hand came away bright red, slick with blood.

The machetes came again. The broadswords, too. She parried, dimly surprised that she was still capable of motion and reaction. But the air had become thicker, viscous. Her arm felt as if it were parting water. She had barely pushed back one machete when another one was at her throat.

A bandit kicked her in the back. She stumbled. A blade slanted down, a harsh glare in the sun. She met it with her own blade. Her arm hurt as if she had cleaved into a mountainside.

The air behind her sizzled. She sprang forward. But not far enough. An angry welt of pain clawed into her lower back. A lacerating pain in her thigh. She fell to her knees. Before she could get up, someone kicked her in the head.

As she collapsed, another shot blasted.

Blackness came over her.

CHAPTER 7

The Report

England
1891

$\mathcal{T}$he fog was a pea-souper.

The first time Catherine had heard the term from Master Gordon, it had befuddled her. Soup, to her, meant a base of clear broth—therefore, transparency. He'd had to explain that certain European soups contained ingredients that had been pureed, resulting in something that was almost a slurry.

This slurry of a fog, the color and density of phosphorous smoke, but cold and damp, with a smell at once industrial and faintly rotted, had dismayed her when it had first spread. But now she was glad of its all-obscuring powers: It enabled her to stand outside a house and fiddle with the lock of its front door without fearing detection.

Well, she couldn't be completely careless: There was a night guard on duty—she'd heard his movement from outside the service door that led to the basement. But as long as she was reasonably quiet, the guard's tea drinking and newspaper rattling, plus the muffled grinding of carriages that rolled by unseen, would be enough to mask any sounds she made with her lock picks.

She stopped: Footsteps approached, those of someone ungainly and possibly drunk. The vague outline of a man, smelling heavily of gin, tottered toward her. She flattened herself against the door and waited until he and his personal fog of liquor had disappeared again into the murkiness of the pea-souper.

She had not sat around for Mrs. Reynolds to find her copy of the guide to the British Museum's exhibits. As soon as she was sure Leighton Atwood had truly left, she had gone to the museum to buy her own copy. The fog had been an unpleasant medium for moving through, but not an impossible one, and, to her at least, preferable to a Peking dust storm.

The guide, purchased at a cost of sixpence, produced the address of a house on Victoria Street that held a significant store of oriental artifacts. Now if she could only persuade this stubborn lock to cooperate.

She gritted her teeth. It wasn't the lock, it was her: She was too agitated for the delicate and precise work of lock picking. For eight years she'd been filled with remorse, certain in the belief that she had killed the man she loved. But now, with her initial and overwhelming relief behind her, anger surged again in her heart.

He had taken everything, everything she'd had to give, and left her to face all the consequences alone.

When the lock yielded at last, she listened at the door for a full minute before slipping inside. It had been dark outside, but there had still been a stray particle or two of light from the street lamps. Inside the house, with the shutters drawn, the blackness was almost absolute.

She gave her eyes some time to adjust as she listened for the night guard. The latter seemed content to remain in the basement. She moved about slowly and quietly, mapping out the room in her head. Thankfully, the furnishings were sparse: a desk with a chair behind it, an additional trio of chairs by the windows, and a plant stand in a corner.

An antechamber of some sort, then. Two doors led out

from the antechamber, both locked. One seemed to have no particular features; the other bore a plaque. Her fingers, tracing over the letters of the plaque, told her that it was the office of a keeper of the British Museum by the name of G. Baker.

It seemed reasonable to assume that the accession catalogues would be found inside the keeper's office. This lock gave much faster, and when she had closed herself inside the office, she finally dared to light the tiny lantern she had brought.

Mr. Baker's shelves were indeed full of records. She pulled out one marked *Victoria Street Accession Catalogue 1877*. That year marked the last time she had seen the jade tablet in Master Gordon's possession and the earliest it could have made its way to the museum.

Each entry in the catalogue recorded the date an object was received at the Victoria Street storage site, the catalogue number of the object, its description, the name of the donor, the person responsible for its reception, its current location, and, if applicable, the date it left Victoria Street for either some other off-site location or the British Museum itself.

Tonight itself she could find out the jade tablet's exact whereabouts. Tonight itself she could look upon it and be transported back to the sweetest hours of her childhood.

The 1877 volume did not yield what she sought. She moved on to that for 1878. In the middle of a seemingly endless run of records on Japanese sword guards, she heard the night guard's footsteps. She extinguished the lantern and slid behind the table. But he did not come into the antechamber or the keeper's office, presumably since they didn't have anything worth stealing.

When he retreated back to the basement, she went on with her task. 1879. 1880. And there it was, an entry in 1881, the transfer to Victoria Street of an item that had been accessioned into the British Museum in 1880. *Dancing Devi*, read the description, *white jade bas-relief carving, circa 900 A.D. Buddhist motifs with quotes in Chinese from the* Heart Sutra.

The donor was none other than one Mrs. Robert Delany of San Francisco.

Catherine didn't know how she managed to go through all the remaining entries in all the remaining catalogues. But she did, methodically—she would feel terrifically stupid if both the jade tablets she sought were here and she missed that fact by being too impatient.

Alas, the other jade tablet did not seem to have been donated to the British Museum. Nor were there any other items attributed to the generosity of Mrs. Robert Delany. Catherine set all the catalogues back in their original places, extinguished her lantern, and left Mr. Baker's office.

The lock of the other door leading out of the antechamber did not prove difficult to pick. She entered the dark corridor beyond and immediately located the door at the far end that led down to the basement, by the light coming from beneath. The other doors had small plaques beside them on the wall, and it was easy enough for her fingers to run over the letters and inform her that only rooms A–F were on this floor.

Up a flight of stairs and she immediately encountered room H. Unfortunately its lock proved stubborn. She was still on the last, elusive pin when the night guard began making his next round. She grimaced, trying to concentrate, trying not to let his footsteps distract her from her task.

The pin tumbled into place only as the guard started up the stairs. She hurried inside and locked the door behind herself. The room was full of dark, hulking outlines of laden shelves. She could discern no ceiling beam for her to get up on, and the door was too close to the wall to stand behind. But the shelves did start ten inches from the floor—to protect the artifacts on the lowest shelves from water damage, perhaps?

The guard, humming to himself, had his key in the door. She slid under a shelf and made herself as small as possible. The key turned; the door opened. The guard, still humming tunelessly, shone the light of his lantern into the space between the shelves.

He approached the shelf Catherine was hiding under. She grimaced. It would be easy enough for her to temporarily overpower him. But at some point he would still come to and still have things to report to the police.

The man's feet were now directly before her. She forced herself to breath slowly and with no sounds whatsoever. Now his knees were on the ground. She flexed her fingers. As soon as his head leaned down to look . . .

But he rose and left. Catherine clamped a hand over her heart, straining her ears to make sure that his footsteps receded all the way downstairs before slipping out and lighting her lantern.

A note had been left on the shelf she had been hiding under—the reason the bored guard had come close for a look: *Contents of Shelf J, Rung 5 to be delivered to Bloomsbury on Thursday.*

The jade tablet was on Shelf J, Rung 5. It was Tuesday; she was just in time.

She was almost afraid to open the box that contained item 1880.18.06.05. But when she did, when she had pulled aside the protective tissue paper, nestled inside was the exact object she sought. At its center was a goddess, her eyes half closed in joy, her pliant back arched, and the ribbons on her flowing robe dancing all about her, as if lifted by a gentle breath. To her left and right were the famous words of the *Heart Sutra*. *Form is no other than emptiness; emptiness is no other than form. Form is exactly emptiness; emptiness exactly form.*

Tears welled in Catherine's eyes.

At long, long last.

*L*eighton was half convinced that he still reeked of gin, though he'd bathed twice and changed into new clothes. But clerk at the Victoria Street house, the one that held a large portion of the British Museum's oriental collection, did not seem to find anything amiss with him. "May I help you, sir?"

"I would like to see an item in your keeping," said Leighton, handing over his calling card and a slip of paper with the jade tablet's accession number.

The clerk rose. "One moment, if you would, sir."

He disappeared into the museum keeper's office, and a minute later, Mr. Baker, a slight, balding man, emerged. He took a look at Leighton and handed the slip of paper back to the clerk. "Have Mr. Broadbent retrieve the item, Mr. Harris."

The clerk named Harris nodded and left.

"May I inquire as to your specific interest in this piece, sir?" asked Mr. Baker.

"It belonged to a friend of mine. I promised him I would keep an eye on it."

"Yes, of course."

Was Leighton imagining things or could he still detect the faintest trace of Miss Blade's incense in the air? The scent of incense that clung to her was how he had known, despite the fog that obscured everything, that it had been her standing outside the house last night.

The location housed thousands and thousands of interesting and beautiful objects. He had no evidence that it was the jade tablet she wanted. But they had spoken of it in Chinese Turkestan, and she had known that it was rumored to be a clue to the whereabouts of a legendary treasure.

Leighton and Mr. Baker had barely made a dent in their discussion on the weather when Harris returned with a box. Mr. Baker checked the accession number against the one marked on the box, set the box down on the clerk's table, opened it, and gestured for Leighton to take a look.

With gloved hands, Leighton lifted the jade tablet out of its container. The carving of the goddess was familiar enough; the weight and texture of the white jade was also correct.

For a moment he could not tell whether the prickly sensation in his rib cage was relief or disappointment. But of course it was a crushing disappointment, because he wanted to see the hand of fate at work. He wanted to know that even if she had not met Mrs. Reynolds and Mrs. Chase in Bombay, what she sought on this trip would still have eventually led her to him.

As he turned the jade tablet in his hand, however, the markings on the edges came into view, and they were nothing of what he remembered.

The tablet was a substitute; she had taken the original.

The hand of fate was at work after all.

*R*ain fell steadily on Leighton's umbrella. He barely noticed, his mind far away.

A cave. Firelight flickering on the walls. A beautiful girl standing with her back to him, admiring the details of an ancient Buddha mural.

The night they had spoken of the jade tablets.

The night he had promised her that he would look after her, for as long as they both lived—the only promise he had ever broken in his life.

Was that why he still wanted to look after her?

There had been no other reason for him to bring up the topic of Mrs. Chase's assailant: He'd wanted to know whether the man she had sent overboard had been her old nemesis and whether he ought to worry about her injury. But her reaction— he could still feel the impossible speed of his walking stick, hurtling past an inch from his face, still hear the angry clamor as the stick landed in the umbrella stand.

Her fury had stayed with him as he stood guard outside the house on Victoria Street last night. It simmered in him even now, fueling an almost unbearable frustration.

He stopped in the middle of the sidewalk, prompting a mild exclamation from the man behind him.

Mrs. Chase's assailant had a name. And according to Mrs.

Reynolds, Monsieur Dubois had business in England. Leighton was inclined to believe that—Mrs. Chase was not an ugly woman, but not exactly one a man would get on a steamer for, if he wasn't already headed in the same direction.

Which meant he probably had luggage with him, luggage that was sitting in Southampton unclaimed, because its owner had fallen into the Atlantic.

Leighton raised his hand and hailed the nearest hansom cab.

*T*he *Maria Augusta*'s passenger manifest indeed showed a man by the name of Dubois. With that information, Leighton, pretending to act on behalf of Dubois's estate, managed to retrieve the latter's luggage from a warehouse in Southampton with little hassle.

From there he proceeded to Starling Manor, his estate in Sussex. To the lavender house, specifically, which hadn't been used in years. With all the windows open, a clear, bright afternoon light flooded in—Sussex was a much sunnier place than the rest of England. Leighton put on a fencing mask and a pair of falconer's gloves and set to work on the portmanteau's lock.

The Centipede's reputation as a master of poison and hidden weapons preceded him. If Monsieur Dubois was indeed the Centipede, then Leighton had no reason to suppose he would be careless with his possessions. The thick gloves made it more difficult to maneuver, but Leighton would rather lose a few hours than a few fingers.

Twenty minutes later, he was beginning to feel that his precautions had been ridiculously excessive, when the locking mechanism disengaged and two tiny, barbed balls shot out from the keyhole and embedded themselves in his gloves. He dropped the balls into a glass of water; the water immediately turned black.

Leighton exhaled. The fencing mask and the falconer's

gloves now felt insufficient as protective measures. But this was why he had chosen the lavender house in the first place.

He closed all the windows except one and went outside. After making sure that his person was shielded by the wall, he inserted a pole that had been fitted with a hook at the end through the remaining open window and pried apart the portmanteau. The sound the portmanteau made as it opened was that of a minor battlefield, the air hissing with flying objects that struck windows and walls.

When he peeked into the lavender house to inspect the damage, a dozen small, black-tipped arrows littered the floor. In all directions. So even if he had been standing behind the trunk, or to the side, he would still have been hit.

One would expect such a highly secured portmanteau to contain state secrets. But one side of the portmanteau was given over entirely to the Centipede's wardrobe. Half of the other side was also taken up by clothes and haberdashery. And then items that firmly marked the Centipede as human, rather than a well-dressed ghost: packages of tea, candied plums, and slender, hard-cured sausages.

The last and most interesting item was also one that required the most careful handling: a box. But it was unlocked and no projectile or noxious fume met Leighton. The inside of the box was thickly padded, the items the padding protected shrouded in additional layers of batting and cloth. Under all the wrapping he discovered half a dozen small porcelain jars, each filled with a paste of a different color and odor.

The jars reminded him of the ones the girl from Chinese Turkestan had used for her ointments—the woman who lived in a parlor flat in Kensington he thought of as Miss Blade, but he could not attach that name to his lover from another life.

He put the jars back into the box and turned to the satchel. It was nowhere as dangerous as the trunk, since it was meant to be carried by Monsieur Dubois on his own person, rather than entrusted to strangers. Unfortunately it contained only some toiletries, a scarf, a map of London, and a few calling cards.

Leighton was unsatisfied. He wanted answers. Did Miss Blade know Monsieur Dubois? Was he her old nemesis? And why had she been so furious when he had inquired into the matter?

And that was when he saw the envelope peeking out from underneath the packages of candied plums. When he opened the envelope, he held a stack of precisely trimmed papers, each bearing a brush-and-ink painting of a centipede.

Well, here was one answer, at least.

There were several safes at Starling Manor, one in the study, another in Leighton's bedroom, and a third in the mistress's dressing room.

The safe in the mistress's dressing room seemed empty, until one removed the false bottom to reveal yet another locked compartment. Inside the compartment was a steel case. And inside the steel case was everything Leighton had of the girl from Chinese Turkestan.

The black tassel with a bead of jade that she had cut from the handle of her sword. The few heads of dried chrysanthemum blossoms, quietly crumbling into powder in a tightly sealed glass jar. The small, white porcelain pot that she had given him upon their parting, which still contained a bit of the once rose-colored salve, now dried into several brown, brittle clumps.

Under the porcelain pot was a letter, from the man in charge of the best chemical analysis laboratory in all of England. As soon as Leighton had safely returned to Rawalpindi, he had sent in a sample of the salve for testing. But the report that should have been posted at the beginning of 1884 had come to him only this past December, when an ownership change at the laboratory had brought about a thorough examination of all the accumulated paperwork.

He could recite the relevant paragraph word for word. *The laboratory has not been able to determine the chemical structure of all the substances found in the salve. But after consulting with several eminent botanists and biologists at Cambridge University, I am confident in the conclusion that the salve as a whole is indeed highly toxic. Fatally so in sufficient quantities.*

Leighton had strongly suspected it, of course, or he wouldn't have arranged for the analysis in the first place. But during the intervening years, he had managed to convince himself that it didn't matter whether she had poisoned him: He was still alive and that was enough.

Yet when the long-lost report had at last arrived, ten days before Christmas, his first at Starling Manor in many, many years, he had been fragmented by the blow.

It had been, objectively speaking, a perfect day, snow falling softly outside the windows, a fire roaring in the grate, the garlands of fir and spruce draped over the mantel smelling green and resinous, a lovely fragrance that recalled some of his earliest memories of Christmas.

And then the bitter, scientific summary of her murderous intentions.

Two days later he had forced himself to attend a house party in the next county. Annabel had also been invited. She had proposed to him at the end of the Season, the previous August, and he had turned her down as gently as he could— she deserved better than a man who still dreamed of another.

But when she brought up the subject again during the house party, an hour after the agony in his limb had returned, he had answered in the affirmative. That bridge had been burned long ago; it was past time for him to stop standing on the bank, wishing that the girl from Chinese Turkestan would somehow punt, row, or swim her way across.

At the very corner of the steel case from the safe's secret compartment was the pouch of gems in the rough that he had carried with him on each trip to Chinese Turkestan. The gems that she had briefly stolen. The ones that she had refused, in the end, because she had wanted nothing more to do with him. Because she had already decided that he must die.

But when she had stood behind him in his bedroom . . . When he had walked back into her parlor twenty-four hours ago, before his questions had rankled her . . .

Sometimes things that did not possess shape or substance nevertheless had weight and impact—thoughts of a thousand sleepless nights, prayers uttered in the darkest hours, regrets that never lessened, despite the passage of time.

Her task had brought her ten thousand miles to England. But who was to say that what had led her to *him* had not been the exact same flickering hope that he knew all too well?

He pushed away that useless thought, put everything back, and locked the safe.

Would that everything could be stowed away so neatly and safely, never coming to light except with his permission.

*L*eighton returned to London late, left Victoria station on foot, and walked until he was exactly where he should not be.

Beneath Miss Blade's window.

He stood in the dark, beyond the light of the street lamps, bitter tendrils of cigarette smoke curling about him.

Her reappearance had been a seismic event, the aftershocks of which he felt daily. But it was not because she symbolized everything about a certain moment of his past. No, her presence jarred because he had thought the question of his future settled, only to realize that he had been lying to himself.

That, in his heart, he had never left the foothills of the Heavenly Mountains.

CHAPTER 8

The Promise

Chinese Turkestan
1883

His heart pounding madly, Leighton reined to a full stop and aimed.

He didn't know if he could keep his fear under control—the slightest tremor in the wrist, the least excess of tension in his shoulders, and the shot would go wide. He exhaled and let his mind go blank.

The two bandits closest to her fell. He reloaded and took out two more. One bandit aimed a rifle at him. Leighton fired his revolver and the bandit went down. The last two bandits still on their feet looked at each other and sprinted for their horses.

He galloped down the slope, leaped off his horse, and ran to her. She was bloody, limp, and completely unconscious. She was also unreasonably lucky. The two gunshot wounds were grazes; there were no bullets in her. With shaking hands, he tore strips of cloth from her trousers and stemmed the bleeding of her arm and her head.

Something cold and metallic seared into his left thigh. He looked down; the knife was an inch and a half into his flesh. He pulled it out and hurled it back at the bandit who had thrown it. The bandit fell sideways, the knife sticking into his chest.

Somehow he shoved her up on her horse. She lay on her stomach, her head and feet hanging down the horse's flanks.

He forced himself up on the saddle and took up the reins.

She was alive. It was all that mattered.

*Y*ing-ying was crawling through the desert at high noon, sand scalding every inch of her body. Then the sun disappeared and she could not stop shivering; so cold, she would never be warm again. Abruptly the heat returned, scorching her from the inside out, drying her until she shriveled.

She cried for Amah. *Help me. Water.*

Someone did help her. Water trickled down her throat until she turned aside, too exhausted to swallow. When she burned, a cool, damp cloth wiped her down, bringing her relief. And when she shuddered, blankets came around her; warm hands rubbed her icy feet.

Sometimes the person hurt her, too, pouring a cool liquid on her that made her groan from the fiery pain. A low, reassuring voice came then, telling her that it was all right, her wounds must be kept clean.

At last the temperature stopped swinging between extremes. Warm and cozy, with the scent of wood smoke in her nostrils, she slept, long, solid, dreamless hours.

She awoke to the chirping of birds and the falling of water in the distance. A ceiling of rock greeted her sight. She was in a cave, but not the nasty kind, cramped and full of animal smells. Rather, the cave was quite decent as caves went, dry, large, and almost airy.

A soft blanket covered her. Beneath her, another blanket. And beneath that was neither cold rock nor packed earth. Someone had made something close to a mattress for her out of grass, some blades with faded flowers still attached.

Her head throbbed a little. Her person was limp. But other than that, she felt almost fine, almost in form. And hungry enough to eat the grass mattress. She pushed herself up to a sitting position—and gasped.

Underneath the blanket she was naked. She choked. Had she been—

Footsteps. She looked around frantically. Her vambraces lay against the far wall. She held the blanket about her and ran for the vambraces. One lone knife remained. She pulled it out and pressed herself against the surprisingly smooth cave wall.

A man ducked inside. The Persian, a rifle slung over his shoulder. Her jaw dropped.

He glanced at the knife in her hand. "Well," he said, smiling, "I guess this is how you'll always greet me, isn't it?"

The girl smiled back, her eyes crinkling a little at the corners.

A huge relief rolled over Leighton. Even though her fever had broken a while ago and he knew she was going to be all right, it still wasn't the same as seeing her awake, alert, on her own feet, and ready to cut down any intruder.

"Are you hungry?" he asked.

"I—" Abruptly her smile disappeared. "Where are my clothes?"

The soles of his feet prickled with the sensation of danger. "I needed material to bandage you. And since your clothes were ruined anyway, they were what I used."

Her eyes narrowed, her suspicions as hard-edged as her knife.

"There are strips of them drying nearby in the sun if you don't believe me." He had made sure to wash the bandages under the nearby waterfall and then scald them with boiling water.

She remained ominously silent.

He was beginning to feel distraught. "I didn't take any liberties."

He had even tried his best to not look at her.

She switched her hold on the knife several times, the blade alternating point at and away from him, as she considered his answer. "Why *didn't* you take any liberties?"

The concept was alien to him—and repugnant. "With a girl who is hurt and unconscious? I am not an animal."

She regarded him for another long moment, then dropped the knife back into its slot on her vambrace. "Let me dress and you can feed me."

He exhaled, ducked out, and leaned limply against the rock face. The idea of her in a violent fury did not bother him, but the possibility of losing her trust did—he would rather she broke every bone in his body.

When she called him back, she had put on a change of his clothes, a black tunic that came almost to her ankles and a pair of loose black trousers that she wore with the cuffs folded. Dressed like this, there was something raffish about her—he could see her as a pirate captain, commanding a ship the sight of which struck fear into the hearts of salty old sea dogs.

An outcrop rose from the floor of the cave and had been made flat on the top. He set out the food he'd bartered for her on this tablelike surface: fried bread, cheese, and shelled pieces of walnuts. For a chair he laid their two saddles, one on top of the other.

She watched him silently, her gaze still wary. It occurred to him that she could be girding herself for what he might demand in return for having taken care of her. The thought did not please him—she should know by now that he wasn't that kind of man— but it was her right to err on the side of caution. "You eat. I'll go hunt something. You'll need more substantial food to recover."

"No," she said immediately.

His heart thumped. It might have been the best "no" he had ever heard.

Looking away, she sat down and picked up a piece of fried bread. "Tell me what happened. I thought those bandits would be the end of me."

He walked to the fire that had nearly died down and added more firewood. "I shot some of them and the rest fled."

It had to be an unsatisfactory answer for her, but he was unwilling to relive the terror of those moments. The fear that had pulsed in his veins had been as cold and heavy as mercury.

She raised her brow. "You saved the day. If ever there is a time to elaborate—and maybe embroider the story a little—it is now. I promise I will listen raptly, no matter how long-winded you are about it."

At the hint of teasing in her voice, he relaxed a little. "It was all of two minutes. How much can I elaborate?"

She shook her head—and did not seem to be bothered by the wound there. It was healing well, but she must also be hardier than most people. "You have never tried to impress a girl, have you?"

He put water to boil over the fire. "Are you the kind of girl impressed by a long, boastful tale?"

She lifted a strand of her long, loose hair and tucked it behind her ear, just under the bandaging still wrapped around her head. "No."

He had not looked at or touched her unclothed person except when necessary. But he had allowed himself to run his fingers through her hair during the long hours he had watched over her, hair that was smoother and softer than the finest silk in the world. "Then I'll stick to the facts. I shot some of them and the rest fled."

Her gaze swept over him as he folded the blankets on the grass mattress. "That doesn't explain why you are walking with a limp."

He'd thought he wasn't. "A knife wound—nothing to worry about."

"Why didn't you tell me right away?" she chided him—and the concern in her words made his heart somersault. "I have a good balm for knife wounds."

"I'd rather you save it for yourself. You lead a far more dangerous life than I do."

Had he been delayed, she would have been killed, pure and simple—the thought had haunted him ever since.

She, on the other hand, seemed to have already shrugged off the mortal peril, her demeanor breezy, with a hint of cheekiness. "Anyone could run into bandits. You, on the other hand, were in a warlord's compound, breaking out prisoners."

She looked at him askance, an expression more of mischief than of misgiving, but doubt was there, beneath the surface. He tried to lie as little as possible. "Remember I told you I was going to Yarkand? I was there to meet some friends with whom I had made the trip north from India. But when I reached Yarkand, I learned that two of those friends had fallen into trouble. We couldn't just leave them behind."

"So you rode across the width of the Takla Makan to break into the warlord's compound?" She shook her head again. "You should have bargained for their release instead. A warlord needs money more than he needs another corpse."

He would have, had Madison not been fair-haired. "See? If only you had been there to advise me, I wouldn't have needed to risk my neck."

She tilted her chin up slightly, as if in a challenge. "You would allow yourself to be advised by a woman?"

"I take advice from those who know better. And in this instance, you obviously do."

Her eyes brightened with pleasure. And it was with a smile that she began to attack her meal in earnest. He would have liked to just watch her, but that would probably make her uncomfortable. So he turned his head away and set himself to chores around the cave.

Wishing, of course, that he could sit down next to her and place his arm around her shoulders.

*A*ll the while Ying-ying ate, her mouth too full to speak, the Persian kept busy. He brought in armfuls of already dried grass to plump up the mattress, remade the bed afterward, and, when the water he'd placed over the fire had boiled, steeped her a cup of chrysanthemum tea.

"Were you a woman, you would have make your mother-in-law very happy," she told him, as she blew on the surface of the infusion.

"And you would have made your mother-in-law very docile, whether you are a man or a woman," he answered from where he knelt before his saddlebags.

She smiled and inhaled the steam rising from her cup, warm and fragrant. Alas, his very interesting turban sat very securely on his head and she could not see his even more interesting hair. "How long have you known that I'm a girl?"

He cast her an arch look that implied it was a question she needed not ask. "From the beginning. And how long have you known that I carry gems on my person?"

"Not until I held them in my hand." She had seen him checking its contents, however, and had deduced it must contain something valuable. "No wonder you don't need a caravan."

He rose to his feet. "And no wonder you haven't prospered, if you are in the habit of returning a fool his diamonds."

She shrugged. "It was too easy, stealing from you. There was no glory to it."

For the first time since she called him back into the cave, he was standing still—tall, loose-limbed, and so handsome her eyes risked becoming permanently glued to him if she didn't move her gaze elsewhere.

"Well, I was thoroughly impressed. I had no idea I'd been pickpocketed—and usually thieves don't get the best of me."

She had heard so few words of praise in her entire life. Her efforts at music and calligraphy never met Mother's exacting standards. Amah at best nodded and said, *Practice some more*. And Da-ren, well, a piercing look from him made her feel inadequate for days. Only Master Gordon had complimented her—but some of his compliments had concerned her command of the Chinese language, which was a bit like congratulating a fish on knowing how to live in water.

But the Persian seemed like a man who could tell a good thief from an incompetent one and she quite puffed up at his assessment of her skills. "We had a curtain made of beads. My amah took it apart and sewed a string of beads on some old clothes. And I had to reach into the clothes and take out the coins without making any noises."

"And your parents permitted this kind of training?"

There was no judgment in his voice, only interest—fascination, even. She felt like preening. "My father died before I was born. My mother never knew—she died soon after my training started. Her health was never good, you see. I didn't know what would happen to me after she passed away—that was part of the reason I undertook the training, so I could at least defend myself."

"So your mother didn't have the same kind of training?"

She chortled at the very thought. "No. My mother was a different kind of woman altogether."

"What was she like?" The Persian came a few steps toward her, as if pulled forward by the force of his curiosity.

"Beautiful. And talented—she played instruments, painted, and wrote poems. Not to mention she was incredibly elegant, both in motion and in stillness—you could look upon her all day long and there would not be a moment when she was less than perfect."

"But she could not have defended herself?"

Her words had been full of admiration, but he must have heard the note of pity in her voice.

"No." Ying-ying sighed. "She could not have defended herself."

"Then it's much better to be you. You are also talented." He spoke from beside her, the hem of his robe almost brushing her upper arm.

Her heart skipped a beat. "The talents of a miscreant."

He sat down crossed-legged on the other side of the stone table. "The talents of a fighter. I admire that."

She kept looking at the way the fabric of the robe draped across his wide shoulders, but she was not so distracted that she didn't puff up some more at this newest compliment. "Why? Most men don't. Not in a woman, anyway."

"I suppose—" He hesitated. "I suppose it's because I wish my own mother had been more of a fighter."

This caught her attention. She looked up into his eyes, eyes as green as an Ili valley at the height of summer. "Your slightly negligent mother who has failed to find you a wife?"

He smiled a little. "Yes, that one."

"What did she do? Or not do?"

He hesitated again. "When my father died, my uncle, whom we all despised, told her that if she did not give me to him, he would take both me and my younger brother from her. I convinced her to go away with my brother where my uncle could not reach them—and she did."

It was an unexpected glimpse into his life—somehow she'd had the impression that he had sprung into life with a turban on his head and a horse under his seat. But even more unexpected was the glimpse into his soul: He was not angry at his mother. "You have forgiven her."

"There was nothing to forgive—it was an impossible situation. Even if I sometimes wish she had fought for me, the important thing was that we protected my brother."

"But you had to live with this uncle?"

"For a while, but then I ran away to find a friend."

Always happy to skip over unpleasant details, her Persian. "Did you find this friend?"

"Briefly. I managed to see him once before he passed away."

She heard regret, but also gladness. His composure had been the first thing she'd noticed about him. But only now did she realize that it was not a carapace to hide a core of turmoil—as was her case—but a reflection of his equanimity within.

The winged brows, the deep-set eyes, the beautifully angled ridge of his nose—she studied him as if he were a text that she needed to translate. "You are an optimist."

He seemed surprised by her statement. He tilted his head to one side and answered only after a long moment. "Yes, I suppose I am."

Now it was her turn to hesitate over what she was about to reveal, this secret sense of foreboding that had long festered at the edge of her awareness. "Ever since I was a little girl, everyone around me has always feared for my future— everyone except my friend who loved tea from Darjeeling."

Mother, Amah, and Da-ren, they all sensed something in her—a wildness, an intractability—that would prove to be her undoing. It had been there in Mother's anxiety, in Amah's watchfulness, and in Da-ren's case, something akin to resignation beneath his sternness. Her hopes and dreams, such as they were, must always pass through this inner prism of dread and emerge on the other side muted. Lesser.

"I don't believe it," said her Persian. "I see wonderful things for you, many, many wonderful things."

The music of the spheres could not have sounded lovelier. And the warmth and certainty of his expression—for the first time she knew what it looked like when someone had complete faith in her.

She had to turn her head away to hide the tears in her eyes.

* * *

*T*he mouth of the cave opened to a rock fissure that was barely wide enough for one person to walk through without turning sideways. The fissure angled several times before giving onto a green slope. From the slope, Ying-ying had a panoramic view of a wide meadow turned purple-pink by the flowers of spring. In the distance rose the sky-piercing peaks of the Heavenly Mountains.

When Da-ren had told her that she would come with him to Chinese Turkestan, she had thought it would be nothing but a vast wasteland beyond Jiayu Pass, the westernmost terminus of the Great Wall. And even after she discovered that there was far more to the territory than desert and desolation, some part of her still thought of it as a prison, a prison two thousand *li* across, but a prison all the same.

But now, with the sky the blue of mountain lakes and everything drenched under a clear, warm sun . . . she was filled with a fierce gladness that she had lived to see this land once again. A fierce gladness to be alive, no matter what loomed ahead.

And along with that came the realization that this time, she would not let go of her Persian.

But to need anyone was to risk losing them. Mother, Amah, Master Gordon—she was still picking up the wreckage left in the wake of their departures. Did she really dare to open herself to that kind of devastation again?

The Persian had carried the saddles out and placed one of them on the grass as a seat for her, so she'd have some fresh air while he groomed the horses. The gold cords in his black turban flashed in the sunlight. His movements were efficient but without haste. And such an innate calm radiated from him, a mesmerizing tranquility.

She tried to imagine going back to her old life, the one

without him—and the void in her heart was instant and fathomless.

He set the other saddle on the back of his horse and she grew alarmed. "Where are you going?"

Her tone must have been strident, for he glanced at her, surprised. "We need more food. Or there will be nothing to eat for supper."

Right, of course—she'd eaten everything except the cheese. But her fear was not entirely assuaged. "What about your friends? Have they already departed for India or are they waiting for you?"

And how long could he keep them waiting?

Did he frown? "Don't worry about them," he said. "They are grown men."

"But won't they worry about you?"

"They know I can take care of myself."

She chewed on the inside of her cheek. What she really wanted was to make sure he didn't go anywhere without her, but she hadn't the least idea how to broach such a subject. "When will you be back?"

He came toward her. As he approached, her anxiety faded—and even began to seem ridiculous: His calm was already beginning to envelope her.

"A couple of hours, perhaps a little more," he said, "depending on how long it takes me to find the nomads and whether I come across suitable game for hunting. Will you keep this for me, while I'm gone?"

He handed her the pouch of gems. She closed her fingers over it, knowing that she was holding a promise.

She grinned at him. "There will be only pebbles inside when I give it back."

He smiled back. "I would rather have pebbles from you than the Koh-I-Noor from anyone else."

She watched him ride away, her heart as bright and sun-drenched as the day.

* * *

*L*eighton bartered for food from the Kazakh and Xibe nomads who had their yurts nearby. And as he wasn't far from the stream that marked the way to Ili Valley, the administrative center of the region, he caught several fish, cleaned and filleted them, and wrapped them in wax paper to take back to the cave.

He arrived to see her sitting cross-legged on the makeshift bed, her eyes closed, one hand over each knee. He watched her for a minute, taking in the straightness of her posture and the evenness of her breaths—he loved seeing her strong and hale and she was well on her way to full health.

Leaving her to her meditation, he scoured the surrounding area for edible plants. When he came back to the cave again, she was just about to step out, the bucket he had bought from the nomads in hand.

"Don't tire yourself," he admonished her. "I'll do it."

He fetched water from the nearby waterfall, heated it up for her, and left for a wash of his own. At dusk, upon his return, a mouthwatering scent greeted him. But instead of bending over the fire, cooking, she was studying the walls of the cave.

"Have you seen this?" she asked, cleaning the wall with a piece of wetted bandaging, uncovering the painted surface underneath.

With proper restoration, the images of Buddhas and bodhisattvas would have been almost unbearably brilliant, saffron and lapis lazuli against a background of ivory and black. But even after a millennia of neglect, the mural was still vivid and colorful, a fluid playfulness animating the eyes and faces of its enlightened subjects.

"It's the reason I know about this cave," he answered.

She wiped at the hem of a painted orange robe. "Oh? How?"

"When I was a child, I was told the story of a tremendous

treasure, hidden by Buddhist monks during a time when their monasteries were destroyed all throughout China."

She stilled. "I didn't know people outside China knew this story."

"You have heard of this story yourself?"

"Yes, many years ago. It's a legend."

"And legends travel. The story left a deep impression on me."

Not that he believed in a hoard of gold somewhere, but anytime *Buddhist* and *cave* were used in the same sentence, he was always deeply curious. In India he had visited the Karla Caves and the Ajanta Caves. When he passed through Afghanistan, he'd made a trip to the Buddhas of Bamiyan and the nearby caves. And when he had met her, it had been just after his visit to the Kizil Caves farther east on the caravan route.

"I came through this area earlier on my trip," he continued. "A nomad told me that there was a Buddha cave nearby, so I investigated. And this was what I found."

"But it's so far from anywhere."

"Probably it was the home of a single hermit monk."

She wiped some more at the walls. "And now we are cooking fish in his temple."

"That tends to be the fate of temples after a thousand years."

She turned around. "Do you know—" She gasped. "Your hair is still so wet! You will catch a chill!"

He had a knife wound and she a miscellany of injuries. But she was worried about wet hair? "It's almost summer."

"All the more reason not to be careless." With her foot, she pushed one of the saddles to just in front of the bed. "Sit down."

He obeyed, wincing slightly at the discomfort to his leg. She sat down behind him and, with a thin towel, rubbed his hair vigorously. Mercilessly.

"Ow."

"This is how my amah always dried my hair. Now take it like a man."

He smiled.

They were quite close; the ends of her hair brushed the back of his hand. He had to grip onto the edge of the saddle to keep from taking a strand of her hair between his fingers.

"What were you going to say when you noticed my wet hair?" he asked, to distract himself from her nearness.

"Oh, right. About that legendary treasure, it is said the Buddhist monks made three jade tablets that together would point to its whereabouts. After the First Opium War, the British took two of the three tablets out of China. But I've seen the third—or at least a copy of it."

"How?"

"You remember that my amah was a thief? She stole it."

He was astonished. "So you have it, this jade tablet?"

"No. But I know where to find it."

"Have you ever thought of stealing it back?" He almost hoped she would. It would be quite something to see if there was any truth to the legend.

Her voice turned stern. "Absolutely not. If my amah had never brought home that jade tablet, she might still be alive today—as might be my friend who loved tea from Darjeeling. So no, I don't ever wish for anything to do with the jade tablet. Not even if it were given to me, free and clear."

She tossed the towel onto the bed. He thought she was done, but she slid her fingers into his hair. Heat penetrated beneath his scalp, warm, strong currents that dispelled any lingering damp from his trip under the waterfall.

"How do you do that?" he marveled.

"Magic," she answered. "I guess I can always become a barber if all else fails. I don't mind putting a blade to a man's throat and I can give quite a head massage. Do you think I will have customers?"

"Not many, probably, but they will be the bravest men in the world."

She laughed softly. It was the first time he had ever heard

her laugh without derision or harshness—his heart constricted with the beauty of it.

After a few minutes, she removed her hands and said, "There. Now you won't suffer any ill effect."

He did not get up. He didn't know when he would have another chance to sit so close to her, almost in an embrace.

The fire threw their shadows on the wall. The shadow of her hand reached out and touched the shadow of his hair. Her master thief's fingers were so light and delicate that had he not seen it, he would not have felt it.

And then came the sensation of her hand on his nape, a barely-there touch, yet one that immediately set him on fire.

Before he could react, she rose. "I'm hungry. Let's eat."

*efore the Persian, Ying-ying had never touched a man, except in combat: With Da-ren, she only ever came close enough to kowtow; even with Master Gordon, in all their years of friendship, there had never been any kind of physical contact.

Nor had she ever *wanted* to touch a man.

But the Persian was like a magnet, pulling her toward him. Even after she'd mortified herself with her fingers on his nape—he had tensed as if she had put a knife to him instead—she still wanted more.

They ate silently, she tasting nothing of the simple stew she had made with the fish and the leaves he'd brought back.

"This is delicious," he said when he was done. "I didn't know you could cook."

"Why would you think I couldn't?"

He glanced at her. "You always made me do the cooking."

"Why should I lift a finger for a man, before he has taken the trouble to save my life?"

She had meant to tease, but with the state of her nerves, the question had come out all wrong: sharp and accusing.

He made no answer, only collected their utensils to wash outside. She grimaced. While she'd lived in Da-ren's household, she had been so sweet tongued, never without a compliment for anyone she came across. Her years of solitude had turned her into a boor.

Or perhaps more accurately, in the wilderness of Chinese Turkestan, she had tossed aside all the layers of courtesy under which she had hidden her true nature.

When he came back inside the cave, she said, "Forgive me. I can be prickly."

He had put some water to heat while they were still eating. Now he poured the hot water over a handful of herbs. The fresh, cool scent of mint rose with the steam. "It's all right. I already know that you have thorns."

Some of her agitation melted away at the quiet, reassuring tone of his voice—he was not angry at her, or otherwise displeased. But at the same time, an even greater ferment came to be. She wanted to know . . . she wanted an answer, even though she couldn't yet arrive at the exact question.

She gathered up her courage and went at it obliquely. "Why do you put up with me?"

He gave her a cup of the mint infusion and shrugged.

Perhaps that question wasn't so oblique after all. Perhaps it was as direct and aggressive as an unsheathed sword. She bit the inside of her lip. "Please give me an answer."

He stared down into his own cup. Just when she thought he would not reply at all, he said, "You left your destination with some ladies of the night. Was it for me?"

She had to think for a moment to remember that she had gone to the pleasure house nearest the warlord's compound, so that if he were clever enough, he would be able to catch up to her. "Yes."

"Why did you want me to find you?"

A question as problematic as hers to him had been. She drew a deep breath. "No one else looks after me."

That was true enough.

In the firelight, his eyes were a deep, piercing green. "You want someone to look after you?"

"Sometimes," she said, her heart thudding.

What if he asked next whether it was him she wanted to look after her? What would she say?

But he asked no such question. He only said, "I don't put up with your thorns. I like them."

Silence fell. She drank from the mint infusion—she had never tasted anything with such a strong flavor and yet at the same time, such a clean sensation. And she was . . . happy, almost.

He, on the other hand, did not appear happy. He gulped down his infusion and spread open his bedroll in a corner of the cave, far from the grass mattress on which she sat.

"So . . . " she heard herself ask, "those women who practice the teachings from that book of love, you have been to them?"

He stilled, down on one knee, his back to her. "I have only heard."

"Why have you not visited yourself?"

"I don't like that kind of transaction. And how can anyone be sure that a woman has not been swindled or even forced into that profession?"

"Then what do you do when you want to lie with a woman?"

She was being completely inappropriate. But then again, sharing a cave with a man to whom she was not wed was already in itself the height of unseemliness.

"Nothing," he said.

A unicorn of a man, her Persian. She leaned forward. "Nothing? Why not?"

*L*eighton's face heated. He could only be glad that his back was to her. Before him, on the wall, a bodhi-sattva regarded him with a gentle, steady compassion.

"What's your reason?" she pressed.

He couldn't explain, not in Turkic at least. And even in English he might have trouble articulating the true reason behind his celibacy, which was that he simply could not regard the sexual act with any kind of casualness.

His father had committed suicide after being caught with the man he loved. His mother had not been caught in the act, per se, but she had been caught by the result of her love: It was to protect Marland, her son with another man, that she'd given up Leighton, afraid that if she didn't, Sir Curtis, Leighton's uncle, would extract a pound of flesh from Marland. And even Sir Curtis, the seemingly invincible Sir Curtis, had been, in the end, destroyed by his own lust.

"I don't know," he said at last.

"But do you want to?"

Her tone was curious rather than seductive. But still, he had to swallow before he could answer. "Yes, I do."

And she was the singular focus of all his unfulfilled desires.

He waited with bated breath for more probing questions on her part, but she seemed to have run out of them. Silence descended. He smoothed his bedroll.

"Are you going to sleep without first changing my bandages?" she murmured.

His head came up. She had already changed her bandages at the time of her bath—he knew because she had washed the strips of cloth and placed them to dry on the makeshift rack he had constructed out of branches. "Are you sure they need to be changed again?"

Several seconds passed before she said, "Yes, I'm sure."

And that was an invitation even a fool could understand.

The Persian rose, turned around, and gazed down at Ying-ying. There was no greed or impatience in his eyes, only somberness.

Her fingers tightened on the blanket that covered the grass

mattress. *The Rubicon*, she thought. She could no longer recall Master Gordon's explanation of the events of ancient Rome that underlay that idiomatic usage, but she knew very well what it meant: a point of no return.

He regarded her not as a mere girl, but as if she were his Rubicon, a boundary that, once crossed, would alter history.

And then he was seated next to her, on the edge of the bed, the fabric of his robe brushing against her knee. The hem of the robe was trimmed in a blue embroidered band—that she already knew. But what she had thought of as an arabesque pattern of curves and shapes was actually a hunt scene, with men in chariots and on horseback.

He lifted a strand of her hair. Her already irregular heartbeat turned downright erratic—he didn't even pretend to check her bandages.

She looked at him, this beautiful foreigner who liked her thorns, and grazed the back of her hand across his beard.

He leaned in. She drew back a little, instinctively.

He did not follow further, but only rubbed his thumb across her cheek. She felt hypnotized, almost, by the contrast between the intensity of his gaze and the gentleness of his touch.

One of his hands curled around her nape. She understood what he meant to do: to hold her in place when he leaned in again. But he did not move closer. Instead, he smoothed her brow, a touch that both reassured her and made her restless.

She raised her hand again and felt the coolness of the gold hoop in his earlobe before taking that lobe itself between two of her fingers.

Now he applied a light but steady pressure behind her neck, lifting her slowly toward him. She heard herself exhale. His lips came close to hers. Closer. She held her breath.

His kiss, at the corner of her lips, was featherlight. But the heat that hurtled through her was beastly, as lawless and ferocious as a hill full of bandits. A startled whimper escaped her, she who could take a kick to the solar plexus without batting an eyelash.

He cupped her face, holding her firmly, and kissed her again, this time just below the center of her lips. She was scorched anew.

She touched the ends of his hair. Closer to his head the texture of his dark hair did not seem very different from hers. But whereas her hair fell as straight as rain, at his ears his hair began to curl into loose spirals and the way they coiled fascinated her.

In return, he kissed the shell of her ear; at the pleasure that spiked into her, she whimpered and buried her hands in his hair. He responded by parting her lips and kissing her *inside* her mouth. It shocked her. Though she had witnessed endless obscenities, the least of *his* moves seemed monumental, something no one had ever done before.

But it was delicious, what he did. When he would have pulled away she wrapped her hand around his nape and stopped him. He kissed her with greater force and urgency.

When she did let him go it was only so she could catch her breath.

What he did next made her lose her breath altogether: He opened her robe and pushed it off her shoulders. Without thinking, her hands came up to shield herself. But he caught her hands, leaving her exposed to his gaze.

For all that each of his movements had been slow and deliberate, she understood now that he would not stop, not until he had possessed her in full. A sudden panic caught up to her.

Her heart drummed in her ears as he kissed her again. One of his hands settled at the indentation of her waist; the other touched the undercurve of her breast.

She trembled and placed her hand on his chest. "If you make me yours, then you will be mine. Forever. And you can never leave me."

He gazed at her a long moment. "I am already yours. Forever."

The truth of his words resonated within her. And with it

came a fierce understanding. This was why fate had brought her to the wild heart of the continent, because it was only here that their paths would cross. It was only here that she would meet this remarkable man.

She kissed him, deeply and ardently, and tumbled him into bed with her.

"Your wounds—" he managed between kisses.

"Are mere scratches. And how dare you doubt my manly forbearance."

He smiled slightly and slid his palm over her nipple. "Forgive me. I can never be half the man you are."

She sucked in a breath at the sharp pleasure. He settled himself over her and she sucked in another breath at the rock-hard heft that now pressed into her thigh. The significance of what they were about to do overcame her once again.

She gripped his arms. "You won't leave me?"

Amah's lover had stayed with her for only six months.

The Persian took Ying-ying's face between his hands, his eyes at once intense and impossibly clear. "Never."

Her doubts evaporated before his absolute certainty. Suddenly she was impatient to claim him, to make him truly hers.

But he would not hurry. He caressed her as if the night were infinite and every square inch of her skin deserved its own hour of worship. And the places he touched—and kissed and licked. By the time he at last joined their bodies together, she was a mindless cauldron of lust. An entire storehouse of black powder that needed only the least spark to detonate.

How he ignited her.

Later, when they lay in each other's arms, their breaths finally quieting to something approaching normal, she said, "Tell me again."

He kissed her forehead, her eyelids, and her lips. "I will look after you, for as long as we both live. And there will never be anyone else but you."

CHAPTER 9

The Kite

England
1891

*T*wo minutes after Catherine left the antique shop, thunder boomed in the sky and rain poured as if Heaven meant to empty its entire reservoir.

She tried to hail a hansom cab, but the ones that drove by all had passengers—a miracle that she wasn't drenched to the knee with the sludge their wheels splattered. She had planned on visiting two more antique dealers this morning—perhaps the time had come to try the underground railway that she had heard so much about, primarily in friendly advice regarding things not to do while in London.

Or perhaps she ought to just go back to her flat, make herself a pot of chrysanthemum tea, and curl up with Master Gordon's jade tablet.

Every night since she had found it, she had sat with the jade tablet in hand, turning it over and over, examining every last detail. Even though she had seen it in Master Gordon's presence only a few times, knowing how important it had been to him, knowing that he had carried it with him across ten thousand miles . . .

He'd had many dreams for her, dreams of a life at once free and secure. Some of the happiest hours of her life had been spent sitting across a table from him as he wove a tapestry of possibilities, a whole wide world for a girl trapped behind high walls.

In truth, they had been fellow prisoners, staring together out of a single tiny window. But such was the beauty of friendship that when she had been with him, she never noticed the bars on that window.

A black brougham pulled to the curb some fifteen feet away. The door of the carriage opened just as she drew abreast to it. "I thought that was you, Miss Blade. Do please come in out of the rain."

Miss Chase.

And on the opposite seat, her fiancé.

The same shock overcame Catherine again: the same shock, the same searing happiness, then, the same throat-constricting realization that, dead or alive, he remained lost to her.

"It's most kind of you, Miss Chase." Catherine smiled with as much warmth as she could muster. "But I shan't drench your carriage. My flat is only around the corner."

Miss Chase turned to her fiancé. "Is it, Captain?"

The space of three heartbeats passed before he said, "No."

"Well, that won't do at all!" exclaimed Miss Chase, once again facing Catherine. "What would my aunt say if she knew that we left you out in a downpour? Now do please come in and let us take you home."

Leighton Atwood left his seat and descended. Something acrid lodged in Catherine's throat—he meant to leave. But no, he only intended to perform the gentlemanly task and assist her into the carriage.

He offered his arm and greeted her blandly. "How do you do, Miss Blade?"

She laid her gloved hand on the forearm of the man with whom she had meant to spend the rest of her life. There must be layers of clothes under his coat, cashmere, silk, linen. Nevertheless, her fingertips burned.

With a murmur of gratitude, she sat down next to Miss Chase. The interior of the carriage was polished wood and velvet, the seats dark red, the fixtures brass filigree—not Mrs. Reynolds's carriage, but his. He retook his seat and gave her address to the coachman.

"That's not around the corner at all," Miss Chase chided her. "You'd have been soaked if you were to walk all that distance, and it would have ruined your dress."

Catherine kept her eyes demurely downcast—a necessity, as he was directly opposite. Her gaze fell instead on his walking stick, the crutch of a man who never knew when he would become crippled by pain. "How fortunate for me that you happened to be passing this way."

"We were at a shop only two streets north—Captain Atwood bought me this most beautiful music box and had it restored." Miss Chase smiled at her fiancé. "You don't mind if I show off a bit, do you, Captain?"

"Of course not," he answered quietly.

Miss Chase opened the case on her lap. Inside was a music box of considerable size and complexity. Miss Chase wound it up, and half a dozen figurines atop the music box came to life, dancing, singing, playing trumpets, their eyes, mouths, and limbs moving in rhythm to the cheery tune.

"Adorable, isn't it?" Miss Chase laughed. "Captain Atwood gives the most delectable presents."

"Absolutely charming," Catherine managed.

When the music ended, Miss Chase put the music box away and indicated the package Catherine carried with her. "And did you also find something interesting, Miss Blade?"

"Not quite," said Catherine, unwrapping layers of cloth and oil cloth and then opening the box for Miss Chase to see. "I was rather hoping to purchase something that would go well with this, but I haven't had much luck so far."

"This" was a small, three-frame decorative screen that she always brought with her when she visited an antique shop. Each frame held a rectangle of mutton-fat jade of nearly identical density and creaminess to the *Heart Sutra* jade tablets, except the triptych depicted not a devotional theme, but scenes from a Chinese folktale.

She would show the screen to the antique dealers and ask whether they had anything that would function as companion pieces to the screen. In response, she had been presented with everything from a pair of stylized ebony African heads made in Vienna, to Delft chinoiserie plates, to a quartet of carved seals purporting to be imperial seals of the Ch'ing Court, when they were at best those of a midlevel provincial official.

Miss Chase laid a hand over her heart. "Oh, how beautiful. What does the scene depict?"

"A Chinese story named 'The Cowherd and the Weaver Girl.' The Cowherd and the Weaver Girl are lovers who cannot be together, so they spend their lives on opposite banks of the Silver River, which is what the Chinese call the Milky Way." Was that Leighton Atwood's gaze she felt on her? She slid the pad of her thumb across the mahogany latticework at the bottom of the panels. "But on the seventh day of the seventh moon of the year, a flock of magpies form a bridge across the river, and they are briefly reunited, before they must each return to their own bank for the long wait to begin again."

"My, but that is both so romantic and so sad." Miss Chase examined the screen more carefully. "I can't decide whether this bridge of magpies is in the process of forming or unforming."

"It is up to the beholder to decide whether the Cowherd and the Weaver Girl are about to reunite, or about to part again," said Catherine.

"They must be on the verge of a reunion," declared Miss Chase. "What do you think, Captain?"

He accepted the miniature screen and studied it. Fiercely, it seemed to Catherine.

"Well," prompted Miss Chase. "What is your verdict, Captain? Joyous reunion or more heartrending separation?"

Catherine didn't know why, but she held her breath.

Another two seconds passed before he spoke. "I cannot tell."

He handed the miniature screen to Catherine. Their eyes met. An almost blank look on his part, yet Catherine felt as if all the air in her lungs had been forced out.

Miss Chase laughed. "Leave it to a man to demand rock-solid evidence for something as silly as this."

Catherine busied herself putting the miniature screen away. Leighton Atwood should probably have said something, but he did not. Miss Chase tapped her fingers rather self-consciously on the seat—did she sense how out of place her laughter had sounded?

For some time no one said anything. Then Miss Chase turned to Catherine and announced brightly, "Captain Atwood and I have settled on a date. We will be married exactly four weeks from today."

A betrothal was a formal agreement to marry. Leighton Atwood and Miss Chase were betrothed. Therefore, it should not surprise Catherine at all that they had moved that much closer to the altar.

Yet she felt splintered by the shock.

I will look after you, for as long as we both live. And there will never be anyone else but you.

Her eyes strayed to him. Their gaze locked in a moment of wretched intensity. Yet as brief as it was, it did not pass unobserved. The tension between them was like a scent on the air, little noticeable in larger, more diffuse gatherings, but almost an assault to the senses in such close confines.

A shadow of disquiet crossed Miss Chase's sugar-and-spice features.

"Many congratulations," Catherine said, perhaps a beat too late. "What an exciting time this must be."

"Yes, quite—and busy, too!" Miss Chase said with great

cheer. "I have just been to my first fitting for the wedding gown yesterday. The invitations are due to come back from the printer's tomorrow. And according to my mother, we must produce a wedding breakfast menu no later than this afternoon."

The interlocking gears of a wedding, like those of a war machine, ground on inexorably.

It was another moment before Catherine realized a further reply was expected. Just as she was about speak, however, Leighton Atwood said, "Your generalship would put Napoleon's to shame, my dear."

A very nice compliment. Except to Catherine's ear, it sounded like an attempt to distract Miss Chase from the odd rhythm of Catherine's replies.

Miss Chase smiled at her future husband, a smile that was not entirely unclouded. Then she looked back at Catherine. "We are thinking of a big wedding, Miss Blade. Won't you honor us with your presence?"

A nearly inaudible crunch of fabric—Leighton Atwood had shifted in place. Had he been caught as much off guard as Catherine?

Miss Chase's gaze stayed on Catherine. Her cheeks had become more rigid, her shoulders taut. The girl might be young, but she was perceptive. And she did not hesitate to go on the offensive at the urging of her instinct.

The carriage stopped: They had arrived at Catherine's address.

She took a deep breath. "I will be delighted."

It would, if nothing else, cure her of false hopes. As the Chinese said, *All excellent remedies are bitter to swallow.*

The door opened. She thanked Miss Chase and Leighton Atwood again for their kindness. A footman, holding a large umbrella, escorted her to her front door.

The brougham rolled away and with every turn of the wheels, carried the pair inside closer to their wedded destiny.

* * *

For the first time since they'd become engaged, Leighton considered the possibility that perhaps he did not know his fiancée as well as he had believed.

The Annabel he thought he knew, the one who had charmed him with her frankness and transparency, would have asked if there was something the matter between himself and Miss Blade.

A thorny question for him, but one that would have been well within her rights to pose.

Instead she told him about her friend Miss Featherstone, who, unable to decide between her two suitors, had decided to entrust her fate to table-turning, that silly diversion whereby one spun around a table with letters on it until a letter had been picked, then another.

"And guess what the table's answer was? *The frog in the grass!*" Annabel cried triumphantly.

He obliged with a smile. "Not the answer she was looking for?"

"No, not when the suitors' names are Bloomsbury and Wellington. Now the poor girl doesn't know what to do, which goes to show that you should never leave important decisions to parlor games."

Her amiable chatter sounded scarcely any different from usual. It would be all too easy to suppose that she had noticed nothing, except he could not dismiss her abrupt invitation to Miss Blade to witness their exchange of vows: It had been a declaration of ownership.

A saber rattling, almost. A shot across the bow.

He observed her closely and listened not so much to her words as to her tone as she maintained an amusing, agreeable, if somewhat one-sided conversation.

Never a moment of awkward silence between the two of them—and certainly not now.

He walked her to the front door of her house and handed

her the music box. "Is there anything that bothers you, my dear?"

He was not at liberty to divulge the covert mission to Chinese Turkestan while he had been stationed in India, but he could truthfully say that he had met Miss Blade when he had traveled to China many years ago. And if Annabel pressed, he was prepared to admit having, at one point, harbored strong sentiments for Miss Blade.

The unease in Annabel's eyes barely existed before it was replaced by a look of seamless surprise—if he hadn't been looking for it, he would have noticed nothing unusual.

She rapped him on the arm. "No, silly, nothing bothers me. Well, except the prospect of Mother insisting on having pigeon pie at the wedding breakfast—you know how I feel about those dastardly birds."

He kissed her on the cheek. "Then tell her that I detest pigeon pie and would not stand for it to be served at my wedding."

They parted with every appearance of warmth and affection—and he walked away more than a little troubled.

*T*he clerk at the window shook his head.

Still nothing from Mrs. Robert Delany of San Francisco, then. Catherine hoped it was only because the woman had decided to reply via letter, which would take weeks to make its way across a continent and an ocean, and not because anything had happened to her.

The antique dealers of London could not help Catherine— of course not, if the other jade tablet remained in private hands. But Mrs. Delany could. Catherine had decided that Mrs. Delany must be Master Gordon's beloved's sister, and had acted as a liaison and facilitator of their forbidden affair. And he, in turn, had given her almost the entirety of his worldly possessions in a grand gesture of gratitude.

Catherine had a wishful notion, that of Mrs. Delany's eventual response containing not just the exact detail Catherine wanted—*the jade tablet he had once given my brother*—but a warm invitation to visit San Francisco at her earliest convenience. And of course this miraculous letter or cable would come in the nick of time, so that before her steamer sailed, she could reasonably send in her regrets for missing Leighton Atwood's wedding to Miss Chase.

"Thank you," she said to the clerk, and yielded her place at the window.

Outside the poste restante office, an unfamiliar sight greeted her: sunlight. When she had arrived at St. Martin's-le-Grand, it had still been overcast, and she'd had every expectation of yet another wet, grey day. But now suddenly London was in the fullness of spring, the sun shining, the sky blue, and the trees so green their leaves glistened.

London as Master Gordon would have wanted her to see it. So she took herself to the green lungs of the city, the vast expanse that was the combined acreage of St. James's Park, Green Park, Hyde Park, and Kensington Gardens.

There were fine gardens and pleasure grounds in Peking, but those that did not belong to the emperor belonged to the nobility and the very rich—and they were always surrounded by high walls. There were no great parks allotted, free of charge, to the enjoyment of the commoner.

And such great parks, with broad lawns, wide avenues, fountains, and a fine lake. She would never love London as Master Gordon had, but for today at least, she saw it through his eyes and she was glad for it.

"Miss Blade! Miss Blade!"

She turned to see Mrs. Reynolds. "Why, hullo. How nice to run into you, ma'am."

"I had just called on you. I should have guessed that you would be out and about on a day like this."

"Like the rest of London."

Fashionable London was out in force: Rotten Row all but choked with smart, open carriages conveying sumptuously dressed women. Ordinary London was out, too—elderly ladies seeking the warmth of the sun on their creaky joints, men pale from months of overcast skies, and, of course, scores of rowdy, rambunctious children who had been too long cooped up inside.

Catherine's gaze lingered on two dark-haired little girls of about seven playing with a toy sailboat at the edge of the water. If her baby had lived, she would be the same age. Would she be more like the girl on the left, energetic and obviously in charge, or the one on the right, good-natured and happy to be led?

"Oh, how nice it is to look at trees and flowers for a change," said Mrs. Reynolds fervently, bringing Catherine's attention back her way. "Yesterday we spent five hours examining dozens of different kinds of lace for Annabel's bridal veil—my head quite spun at the end of it."

The color of an English wedding was that of a Chinese funeral. Catherine would be digging graves on that day, graves for dreams old and new. "Was Miss Chase able to make a choice?" she asked tightly.

"She narrowed it down to three candidates. Tomorrow she and her mother will be going back to confirm a final selection. But I'm glad today she has decided to have some fun instead. Ah, there she is."

Mrs. Reynolds waved.

The lovely bride-to-be, in a fetching violet-and-white striped frock, waved back from a rowboat on the Serpentine. Marland Atwood, on the same boat, also waved. A second man turned around to see who had caught his companion's attention. He had boyish good looks and a head of straight, ash blond hair.

"That is Mr. Madison," said Mrs. Reynolds. "His father and the late Mr. Chase were cousins."

Miss Chase held up both of her hands so that her thumbs and forefingers approximated the shape of a rectangle. Then she gestured toward Catherine.

"Good gracious, I almost forgot," said Mrs. Reynolds. "I had volunteered to hand deliver your invitation to the wedding."

The invitation was printed on heavy stock and vellum, with tiny seed pearls sewn into borders of wine and gold. Inside, rose petals had been worked into the paper, their subtle scent rising. Above the time and place was a quote from the Song of Solomon, printed in ornate letters: *I have found the one whom my soul loves.*

She lifted her head to see Leighton Atwood, on the opposite shore of the Serpentine, watching her. For a moment it felt as if they stood on two sides of the Milky Way, separated by all the stars in the sky, but without any flock of magpies to bridge the distance between them.

I am already yours. Forever.

She glanced away, but not before Miss Chase observed the look that had been exchanged.

Miss Chase gestured to her fiancé. The two young men in the boat began rowing toward the southern shore. Mrs. Reynolds ushered Catherine into a for-hire boat, and the oarsman ferried them across to join the others.

By the time Catherine was on solid ground again, Miss Chase already had her arm entwined with Leighton Atwood's. If Amah still lived, she would cuff Catherine on the back of her head for being so incompetent that she couldn't even kill a faithless lover properly. But that particular failure was something Catherine could not regret, no matter what.

"You have not met my cousin yet, have you, Miss Blade?" said Miss Chase, her smile just the tiniest bit tense. "Allow me to present Mr. Madison. Edwin, Miss Blade, who has returned from the Far East to start a brand-new life in England."

Up close, there was an odd familiarity to Mr. Madison's face. Yet Catherine didn't think she had come across him in either Peking or Shanghai, and she certainly had not encountered him during her voyage to England.

"A brand-new life, eh?" he said, his voice surprisingly rich. "What do you think of London, Miss Blade?"

"Never mind what she thinks of London," Marland Atwood interjected. "What can she think of it but that it is a dirty, noisy, and crowded place? The point is, Miss Blade, have you been having fun?"

Master Gordon had loved to entertain her by describing all the fun he saw in her future. When Leighton Atwood had made his promises, they, too, had been implicit in their guarantee of diversion and merriment: the endless bazaars of Delhi and Bombay, the fireworks of Diwali, the tropical atolls of the Maldives, lapped by the aquamarine waves of the Indian Ocean.

But fun, to this day, remained an alien concept.

"I'm afraid I have been busy settling in," she answered, holding her voice steady. "But now I am more than willing to devote myself to fun. Any suggestion on what I should do?"

"Ride a bicycle," Marland Atwood said immediately. "I ruined two pairs of good trousers and still have a bandage on my knee, but it is the most delicious fun I have had in a while."

"I do enjoy the theater, myself," said Mr. Madison.

"And of course you must come to the ball we are holding the day after tomorrow," added Miss Chase. "Mother said we must have a ball before the wedding."

Catherine almost wished she could tell the girl to relax: A man who wanted to stay could not be lured away. And as for a man who did not want to stay, nothing could keep him from leaving. "My, so many fun things to do, so little time."

"Here is another fun thing," said Marland Atwood. "There is a man selling kites. Let me buy one and let's fly it."

"You will have a difficult time of it," Mr. Madison pointed out.

There were several boys trying to fly kites, none succeeding. The day was calm, the breeze a bare whisper on the skin, not enough to sustain a kite in the air.

"Somebody managed quite well," Marland Atwood said. "See that?"

Catherine was about to look up to see for herself when

Mr. Madison pulled a pair of spectacles from his pockets. As he put them on, she realized exactly where she had come across him. It was the second time she had passed through Kashgar, during her desperate search for her Persian. She had spied his horse in the market and had rushed toward it, almost knocking over a display of melons. Somehow she had managed to restrain herself in time when she realized that another man was already inquiring after the horse. Mr. Madison had been the man, in stiff but passable Turkic, asking the trader where he had come across the steed.

It had been found on the caravan route without a rider, had been the trader's answer.

And Catherine, hidden behind a cart, had slowly crumpled to the ground.

Mr. Madison, too, had been a spy.

She glanced at Leighton Atwood. He gazed back at her, while those all around him had their eyes on the sky. A nameless emotion surged through her, an uprising of chaos.

Vaguely Mr. Madison's voice came again. "That can't be a kite—it's too high. Must be a hot air balloon."

"But I can see a string on it," argued Marland Atwood.

"On second thought, you are right," said Mr. Madison. "It is a kite. What do you think is the design on it? A snake?"

"That would be a bit horrid, wouldn't it?" said Mrs. Reynolds. "There are many people who do not care for the sight of a snake, real or painted. They are so . . . reptilian."

"I'm amazed you can make out that much detail, Edwin. I can't see the design at all," said Miss Chase. "What do you think it is, Leighton?"

Leighton Atwood at last turned his gaze up. Catherine did the same. Instantly her blood turned cold.

The design on the kite was a black centipede.

Lin's sigil.

CHAPTER 10

Choices

Chinese Turkestan
1883

*L*eighton woke up inexpressibly happy. Every single step that he had taken in his life, it seemed, had led to this place, this moment: the dawn of not just a new day, but a new age.

His beloved sat on the edge of the bed, draped in his robe, her back to him, her head bent. He pushed himself up, wrapped an arm around her, and kissed her on her hair. "Good morning."

"Morning," she answered, her voice strangely subdued.

Unease shot through him. Did she regret taking him for a lover? Was she again contemplating leaving?

"What's the matter?" he asked, struggling to keep his voice even.

She pulled the robe tighter about her person and said nothing. Nerve-racked, he lifted her hair to one side and kissed her on her ear. "It is going to be a long forever for us, if you refuse to discuss things that bother you with me."

"Will it still be forever?"

This girl and her doubts. "Elephants cannot drag me away

from you—the only thing worse than never making love to you at all would be to make love to you for only one night."

She was silent again.

He shook her shoulder gently. "Please tell me what's the matter."

Her brows drew together. Her lips tightened.

He sighed. "Do I have to beg?"

Her head drooped even more, her proud, beautiful neck oddly vulnerable looking. She muttered something, but he couldn't quite make out the syllables.

"I'm sorry. What did you say?"

"I said I didn't bleed last night."

He could not make heads or tails out of that answer. "But that's good, isn't it?" he asked, placing his hand over hers. "With so many injuries, why would you want to bleed?"

She pushed his hand away. "A virgin bleeds."

He had never thought of her in those terms. She had seemed to him entirely outside the narrow paradigm that defined women by the presence or absence of a hymen, and whether the loss of that hymen had taken place in a sanctified manner.

"You were a virgin?"

"Of course I was," she said indignantly. Then her lips quivered. "But now there is no proof."

"It doesn't matter to me." He sincerely could not think of anything that mattered less.

"It matters to *me*."

"Why?"

"Because . . . because . . ." She took a deep breath. "Have I ever told you that my amah and my friend died on the same night?"

"No."

"Well, they did. And it's a long, complicated story. But the events of that night were set off because I was unwilling to let my stepbrother touch me. If I had just given in, two people I love might still be alive today." She turned toward him at last. "It was all for my virginity, and now there isn't even any evidence of it."

He gathered her into his arms. "None of it was your fault. None of it, do you understand? Sometimes the forces of destiny intersect in unpredictable ways, forces that have been gathering momentum for years, perhaps even decades. You were only unfortunate enough to have been caught in the middle.

"And it wasn't your virginity you fought for, but your ability to control your own life. Why should you ever cede that? Why should such a choice be made by anyone except you? You had every right to repel him, and I am glad you did, for the principle of it."

She pulled back and stared at him. "I have never heard anyone talk like that."

"Maybe not, but that is how you have lived. And that is how those you loved would have wanted you to live."

She gazed at him another moment, then laid her head on his shoulder. "I wish they, too, had lived. They both had so much to live for. My amah had finally cured herself of an injury that had plagued her for years. And my friend had just received some wonderful news—his life was about to start anew."

He caressed her hair, feeling impossibly privileged by her trust. "The great poet Rumi once wrote, *When you lower me into my grave, bid me not farewell, for beyond the grave lies paradise. And there is no end while the moon sets and the sun yet rises.*"

"Do you believe in that?"

"Perhaps not always. But sometimes I recite the whole of the poem, to remind myself that it is possible to find extraordinary beauty in the circle of life, to believe that we neither live nor die in vain."

She was silent for a minute. "So instead of making love to girls, you read poetry."

He smiled. "Sometimes."

"What do you do other times?"

"I read books that aren't poetry. I walk. I write letters to my family."

"Will you tell them about me?"

"Of course."

"What will you tell them?"

"That I have met a girl with the strength of steel, the cunning of a desert fox, and the beauty of the sky."

"You *have* read a great deal of poetry."

"Well, I thought I had better educate myself, since I could never rival you in brute masculinity."

She laughed at that, and his heart floated like a sky lantern set aloft. He rose to his feet and held his hands out toward her. "Come, let's go eat breakfast outside. I believe it will be another glorious day."

The meadow was a carpet of wildflowers, the sky so bright a blue it almost hurt the eyes. In the distance, the shapely peaks of the Heavenly Mountains, a high wall against the outside world.

At the edge of the meadow, Leighton's beloved, flipping her knife in her hand, waded nearly thigh-deep in the grass. She must have heard him approaching on horseback, but she did not turn around. Instead, her attention seemed entirely taken by the furious blooms that surrounded her: She was picking flowers, the knife serving as her garden shears.

The sight made him smile: Those who lived by the sword played by the sword.

And then he noticed that she also had his slingshot with her. She returned the dagger to its sheath and tied the wildflowers she had gathered into a bouquet. He dismounted. Before he could call out a greeting, she catapulted the bouquet into the air with the slingshot.

She had her back to him, yet the bouquet came at him so

perfectly he barely needed to extend his hand to catch it. "You are showing off," he told her.

She turned around, a smug smile on her face. "You like it."

"I like an arrogant, intractable woman." He lifted the bouquet to his nose. It smelled exactly as wildflowers under the sun ought to, clean, sweet, and vibrant with life.

Something else sailed toward him. He caught it with just as much ease—she'd returned the pouch of gems. "Diamonds and flowers—are they both for me?"

She tossed a strand of her hair over her shoulder and said grandly, "You may keep them."

This girl . . . put her in a proper frock and she would enslave legions. "I don't know that I have anything so nice to give to you in return, unless you'd like some of this tobacco I bartered from the Xibes."

Her eyes lit with interest. "Well, don't just talk. Hand me a cigarette."

He did, after first rolling one. She was lightning swift with her tinderbox and in no time at all was puffing on her cigarette. He rolled one for himself. They sat down, shoulder deep in grass, and smoked in companionable silence.

"Can I have another?" she said, before she was even halfway done with her first.

"How long has it been since you last had one?" he asked, his words muffled as he clamped his cigarette between his lips, his hands busy with tobacco and paper.

"Months."

He licked the edge of the paper, sealed the new cigarette, and handed it to her. "Hardship indeed."

She stuck the new cigarette inside her robe. "Why don't you frown upon my smoking?"

"The day I quit smoking myself," he answered, "is the day I start lecturing you on *your* filthy habit."

She threw her head back and laughed. He grinned at her, his heart full of sunshine and spring flowers. Smiling, she blew a jet of smoke his way. He grabbed the front of her robe, pulled her toward him, and planted a kiss on her cheek.

She laughed again and ran her fingers along his beard. Then her thumb was tracing along his lower lip. Her expression changed, from mirth to the beginning of desire. She glanced down at her cigarette, which still had a good inch left, and stubbed it out.

His heart beat hard all of a sudden.

She looked back at him. "Kiss me—and make sure I don't regret not waiting until I finished my cigarette."

He cupped her face. "You won't."

"Tell me your name," said the Persian afterward, as Ying-ying lay with her head in the crook of his shoulder.

Names were troublesome things. A name was never just a name, but an identity, a history, and sometimes an entire genealogy. If she gave her Chinese name, it would raise a whole field of questions. Did she come from the interior of China? Why? And why did she have slate-blue eyes?

Years ago, Master Gordon had told her that the unreadable note she had found among her mother's things gave the English name her father had wished her to have: Catherine. That, too, would be unhelpful here.

"You tell me your name first," she said.

"Hmm, come to India with me and I will."

"After we marry, maybe I will consider it."

He lifted himself up on one elbow. "You will marry me?"

She narrowed her eyes. "You think I will sleep with anyone I do not already consider my husband?"

An amazed smile spread across his face. "You already consider me your husband?"

"Of course." She bared her teeth at him. "You look at another woman and I will crush you where it hurts."

He laughed. "So how do we marry, as soon as possible?"

She inhaled. "We have to go to Kulja."

"Why Kulja?"

Kulja was the seat of the governor of Ili, where she was increasingly past due. Three days she had traveled west with her Persian, in the direction opposite her destination. Making up for that was another three days. And according to him, six days had passed since the bandits' ambush.

In her mind she had been making generous allowances for possible delays. It was quite reasonable, wasn't it, that she could have taken sick somewhere along the route and needed a few days to rest and recuperate? Also quite reasonable that she might have taken a detour, to investigate matters that might be of interest to Da-ren.

Even so, she should have been back in Kulja two days ago. To make matters worse, she usually returned several days early. So from Da-ren's perspective, by now she would have been missing for almost a week.

"I have family in Kulja," she said.

"Then of course we will go to Kulja." He suddenly looked anxious. "Do you think my gems would be enough of a bride price for you? I suppose my firearms are worth something, too—and my horse."

"Listen to yourself," she chided. "Are you planning to walk back to India?"

"I just want your family to know that a mountain of gold and a sea of wine is still too paltry a gift when I will have you in exchange."

Her eyes moistened. What were a mountain of gold and a sea of wine, next to such heartfelt esteem? She could almost imagine Da-ren's shock as he looked both Ying-ying and the Persian up and down, trying to imagine what this mad foreigner saw in his wayward stepdaughter.

One man's burden was another's treasure—that had ever been the case. Except Ying-ying had never dared hope it would be the case for *her*.

But now it was. Now she was this man's greatest treasure.

He was already sitting up. "Let's pack up and go. There are still five hours of daylight left and—"

"You shouldn't exert yourself so much."

She was almost entirely recovered, but the wound on his leg had not come along as well. It made her heart ache to think of how much work he had done, with an injury like that. The grass mattress hadn't made itself. Their sustenance required that he either hunt or ride out to find the nearest nomad yurts. And though the waterfall was not far, it was quite a steep climb from the cave, with the descent even more treacherous— she could only guess at the number of trips he'd had to make, to keep them supplied with water for drinking, cooking, bathing, and the washing of bandages.

He grinned and held out his hand. "I'll rest when we are married."

She took his hand. But instead of letting him help her up, she pulled him back down next to her.

He kissed her on her forehead. "Let's get on the road for now. After we stop for the night, I'll be all yours."

She tsked. "If I were starving, would you wait half a day to feed me?"

His gaze slid down to her lips. "Are you starving now?"

"Famished. And only you can satisfy my hunger."

He exhaled, a little unsteadily. "If you say it like that, then it becomes a moral obligation on my part, doesn't it?"

"It does."

He kissed her on her lips as he fitted her body to his. "I take my moral obligations seriously. Always."

*Y*ing-ying hummed to herself as she flitted around the cave, packing. She was alone, her husband-to-be having gone to hunt them something nice for supper. Husband-to-be, she winked at the kindly bodhisattvas on the wall. She never thought she'd have a husband-to-be. Or at least, she never thought she'd have one she liked.

Tonight, after supper, she would tell him who she was—and prepare him for the ordeal that awaited a nobody who thought he was good enough to marry the stepdaughter of the governor of Ili. Da-ren would disdain him. He would be outraged that she dared to bring back a man she had found on her own, without having gone through any of the proper channels of matrimony. And he would question Ying-ying's sanity and warn of dire fates in strange lands where she'd have no one to turn to, after the Persian had thrown her out of his household.

In other words, they would be on their knees begging for Da-ren's blessing and forgiveness—and would receive neither.

But that she would endure. She owed Da-ren this much, to let him know what would become of her, to absolve him of all further responsibilities, and to perform her three kowtows of gratitude and leave-taking. He was the closest thing she had to a father.

He *was* her father, in every sense that mattered.

And now she would depart his household in disgrace, never allowed to darken his doorstep again. In the euphoria of her unofficial engagement, she had not thought through to the inevitable conclusion: In gaining the Persian, she would lose Da-ren.

Not that she'd ever *had* Da-ren. And not that he'd ever spared a thought for her that wasn't tinged with impatience and disapproval. But he was fair: He held his own flesh-and-blood children to no less stringent standards and meted out just as few words of praise. And he was—and probably always would be—the greatest man Ying-ying had ever known, incorruptible, farsighted, tireless, a man who thought only of his country and never of himself.

She had always dreamed that someday he would tell her

that he wished she had been his own. As long as she remained a member of his household, her dream, however foolish and improbable, was not completely impossible. But when she left with the Persian, that particular door would close and never open again.

And if the Persian were to prove faithless . . .

No, she must not think such thoughts. At every turn he had proved himself a man of the finest caliber. She would trust him, and they would be happy together.

The packing took no time at all. Most everything in the cave had come in their saddlebags and would leave in those saddlebags. The grass mattress would be left behind, alas, and the bucket. But she wanted to take the blankets he had acquired from the nomads—it would probably be very, very cold tackling the Karakoram Pass, even at the height of summer.

She examined the strips of clean bandages that hung on the makeshift rack he'd built and decided that it would be good to have some of those on hand. Now if she wrapped the bigger blanket around her bedroll, she might be able to stuff the thinner one into her saddlebag. Which meant that the bandaging would have to go into his saddlebag.

She gathered and folded several of the longest pieces of bandaging. Then she opened his saddlebag and pushed them in. As she withdrew her hand, it brushed against the side of the saddlebag and there came a curious sound, rather like a piece of paper crinkling under the leather—a sound so faint that a person with less sensitive ears might not even have heard.

She bent the leather of the saddlebag with some force. The sound came again. But her fingertips could not feel any loose flaps or openings of hidden pockets. Taking the saddlebag with her, she went outside for better light. Every seam of the saddlebag was perfectly in place. Perhaps it was just a bit of loose material that had been accidentally sewn into the—

She saw it—one particular seam, instead of ending in a perfectly cut knot, disappeared into a tiny pouch. When she pulled, a dowel came up, a smooth, flattened wooden stick with thread wrapped around. And when she unwound the thread, and pulled on the seam, a little space opened up, enough for her to see the piece of paper that had been hidden.

At that exact same moment she realized that she was snooping. Until then her curiosity had carried her along and she had not even thought that perhaps she was doing something she ought not to do.

Don't go around digging in other people's things, Amah had once warned her. *Dig long enough and you'll always find things you wish you hadn't.*

What if it were a letter from his wife? Wouldn't she want to know now, rather than after she had burned her bridges with Da-ren?

But then again, how would she know if it were a letter from his wife? Persian and Indian languages probably all looked like what Chinese called demon notations.

She stopped arguing with herself, extracted the paper, and opened it. It was no letter, but a map, a rather detailed one at that—the paper was as thin as the skin of an onion and opened to a far larger dimension than she had expected.

The places were indeed labeled in demon notations, so she could not immediately make out what she was looking at. The next moment, however, a chill went down her spine. Was this a map of Chinese Turkestan, with the mountains surrounding the Takla Makan Desert?

She had never used a map in her travels. Da-ren had maps at the governor's residence, but she found them fairly useless. This map, however, concurred beautifully with the directions and distances she carried in her head.

If this particular faint line marked the course of the Yarkand River, then the city at its southern end would be Yarkand. Going northwest lead them to Kashgar. Back east, around the northern rim of the Tarim Basin, the Heavenly Mountains. And farther to the north, the spines and ridges of the Altai, in the shadows of which was Kulja, the seat of the governor.

But there was so much more on the map, from the larger settlements she knew to little hamlets she had barely given a glance as she rode past, lakes, rivers, changing from solid line to dotted line to indicate that they were seasonal. The Buddha caves at Kizil were marked with a stylized icon of a Buddha head.

Underneath the map there were calculations done in Arabic numbers. She couldn't make out what the calculation was about until she remembered rumors of English mapping expeditions, boasting of members so skilled in the art of pacing, that simply by counting their steps, they could measure great distances with only minuscule discrepancy.

No, no, he was on horseback all the time she was with him. So he couldn't possibly have been on the ground, pacing. But before she could relax, she remembered that he had said that he had come through this area on an earlier part of his visit.

She had noticed nothing irregular about that comment then. If he was already up here in Chinese Turkestan, he might as well make a tour of Dzungaria—the region bound by the Heavenly Mountains to the south and the Altai Mountains to the north—even if Dzungaria didn't exactly hop with wealthy men eager for jewels.

What Dzungaria did hop with were men resentful of Ch'ing control, both Muslims of Chinese extraction and those of the various local ethnicities. A man fluent in Turkic could easily compile of list of warlords and chieftains who might be persuaded to rise up in arms.

The very thing that Da-ren, and she, by extension, was trying to prevent.

No, no, she was quite mad. Even if a man carried a better map than the governor of Ili possessed, that did not necessarily make him a spy.

But was he any more likely to be a gem merchant? What

kind of gem merchant went into a warlord's compound to rescue prisoners? What kind of gem merchant could get rid of a band of bandits in two minutes? What kind of gem merchant would want to travel with someone who had boasted of being a master thief?

Not to mention he had refused to give her his address, though he had been desperate for them to keep in touch. And she, the fool, had only thought in directions of wives and concubines, never in her remotest flight of fancy wondering whether his address would show his connection to the British Raj.

Slowly she refolded the map and put it back, making sure that everything in the saddlebag was exactly as she had found it.

She could present a lowly merchant to Da-ren, but not a spy for the British.

*Y*ing-ying sharpened her dagger.

What should she do?

The Persian was a spy. Why was she even asking the question? They had already agreed to head out for Kulja, two days of hard riding northwest. When they reached their destination, she would simply hand him over to Da-ren and let Da-ren deal with him.

But the Persian would not confess, if she knew anything of him. Da-ren would have him tortured. She'd hear his screams of agony in her mind even if she took herself a thousand *li* away.

It would be easier to kill him. A quick stab to the heart. A swift death.

How? How could she possibly harm the man she loved?

Or she could let him go. Just let him go. Leave in the morning as planned, except by herself. Or leave in the night, slipping away like a ghost, never to return.

But she would be derelict in her duty to Da-ren, the man who should have been her father.

"Looking to skin something?" came the Persian's voice. He held an armful of firewood; a brace of hares dangled from his hands.

"To cut your heart out and feed it to the dogs if you aren't good to me."

She sounded deranged to herself. But he only chuckled, set down the firewood, and took out his own knife, getting ready to prepare the hares for roasting. "Don't you know how to break a man's heart? It's much less messy that way."

"No, poisoning is less messy. I don't know anything about men's hearts."

He looked at her sidelong. "Not even mine?"

She wanted to weep and howl. She wanted to pound on the hard floor of the cave until her fists bled. It was colossally unjust, even by her jaundiced standards. She did know what was in his heart, but it meant nothing now. He was a spy for the British, someone seeking to undermine Greater Ch'ing's authority in the region. He worked against Da-ren. He worked against the interests of her country.

He was an enemy.

"Tell me again what's in your heart," she heard herself say.

He gazed at her. Then he came, sat down next to her, and draped an arm about her shoulder. "You," he murmured, kissing her hair. "Just you."

In the silence she could hear her heart breaking piece by piece. Why? Why must she give him up? Why must she turn him over to Da-ren?

She turned her face to his. Their lips met. He kissed her. She whimpered, choked by indecision. He leaned into her, his hands cupping her face, and kissed her deeper.

This was the perfect opportunity. He was defenseless. She had to but raise the dagger high. One great downward plunge and he'd be dead.

She shuddered. The dagger fell from her hand and hit the rocky floor with a bright, harsh clang. She wrapped her arms about him.

The opportunity was still ripe. A half dozen hard taps and he would not be able to reach for his gun. A half dozen more and he'd be as paralyzed as a ninety-year-old man after three strokes.

He kissed the tip of her chin, the sensations warm and pure. Tears rose underneath her tightly shut eyelids. How could she turn him over to the torturers? How could she live with herself knowing that he'd either die at their hands or lose his mind completely, spending the remaining days of his life wandering in the wilderness, muttering to himself, terrified of the least noise and human contact?

She went wild, kissing him, dragging his clothes up, her hands ravenous for him, for the feel of his muscles and sinews beneath the smoothness of his skin. It would be the last time. She would allow herself this one last time. To imprint him on herself, to savor the taste and scent and texture of him for the lonely eternity ahead.

But though he let her pull him down atop her, he would not cooperate with the frenzy she desperately wanted. Instead he cupped her face between his hands and kissed her gently, soothingly. When she clutched at him, he took her wrists in one hand and pinioned them behind her head.

"I am not going anywhere," he said as he kissed her jaw.

Maybe not, but she was. She was leaving as soon as he had his back turned. She caught his lower lip between hers and licked it. He sucked in a breath and kissed her more deeply.

"I think of you every minute of every day," he told her, his words hot and unsteady.

She whimpered again, then cried out sharply as he took her nipple into his mouth. He played with that sensitive tip, rolling it around his tongue, making her writhe and tremble.

He kissed her again. "You are so very beautiful. Your eyes,

your hair, your throat, your breasts—everything about you is beautiful."

Her nails dug hard into her palms. But a knife wound could not distract from the pain in her heart—or the dark, unbearable sweetness of his words.

He kissed her throat, her shoulders, her arms. He kissed her breasts, sending a fresh jolt of desire through her. Then at last he came into her, and she moaned with the pleasure of it, the sheer necessity of it.

She broke free of his restraint, wrapped her arms around him, and fastened her lips to his. She could not hold him close enough or kiss him deeply enough. Such pleasure, she could already feel the beginning of oblivion, that blessed state in which there were no harrowing choices, no forever sundering, no eternal regret.

"I love you," he whispered in her ear. "I will always, always love you."

And her oblivion descended like an avalanche.

When it was over, instead of letting go, she clung to him even more tightly. Despair swamped her, quicksand and sinking mud everywhere she turned. She knew then that she had embraced the unthinkable: She had thought she would leave him; instead she would *choose* him, above everyone and everything else.

"You will stay with me, always?" she asked in a small voice, shamed and disgusted by her frailty, loving him so much it hurt to breathe.

"Of course," he answered easily, in full sincerity. "Always."

She buried her face against his shoulder. "You promise?"

He didn't answer immediately. Her heart went cold, so cold.

"I am beginning to wonder how many promises you will need," he said. "But I am willing to promise as often as you'd like."

She exhaled weakly. He would honor his promise—she knew he would. She trusted him. "We are not going to Kulja."

"No?" He sat up halfway, surprised. "What about your family?"

"I changed my mind."

He smoothed his hand over her hair. "What's the matter? Please tell me."

She set her jaw. "I was too optimistic. We will find no blessing in Kulja."

"But don't you want to tell your family where you are going?"

"No. And I don't have any real family in Kulja, in any case, just someone I had hoped would be happy for me."

He opened his mouth to speak; she placed her finger over his lips. "Say no more. We head for India in the morning. Directly."

Sweet or bitter, she had sealed her fate.

*R*elief washed over Leighton.

Until he had come back to the cave, he had thought his biggest problem would be how to explain her presence to his colleagues. But the moment he saw her, a cold fear had overcome him: She was about to leave him.

All her things had been packed away, and she had sat there staring at her dagger, looking one moment as if she were at a funeral, the next as if she had killed someone by mistake.

Until she suddenly threw herself at him, all molten and urgent.

He was not convinced that all was well, but it only mattered now that she had not changed her mind about spending her life with him.

"You won't regret it," he said. "You'll like India."

She touched her palm to his cheek. "My amah killed the man who betrayed her. So you be very good to me. Make sure I do not regret my choice."

* * *

*T*here were eight Ch'ing soldiers outside the yurts, in dark tunics and broad-rimmed hats, their long queues reaching halfway down their backs. Leighton reined in his horse a respectable distance away, wondering what could have brought them to the Kazakh camp. He hoped it had nothing to do with Madison and Singh's rescue from the Tajik warlord's compound.

Two more Chinese soldiers came out of the largest yurt, one looking to be of higher rank than the rest. All the soldiers mounted. The officer spied Leighton and wheeled about.

When he came close enough, the officer said, in quite decent Turkic, "We are looking for someone who rides a fine red horse. Have you seen anyone like that?"

Leighton's hand tightened on the rein. Only two days before he had ridden this way on her blood-bay stallion, to give the steed some exercise. "No, I haven't."

"If you do, tell her to return to Kulja as fast as she can," the officer said curtly.

"She? It's a woman?"

The officer's lips curled in annoyance. "No, my mistake. Stupid language. It's a man, a young man."

The soldiers left. Leighton approached the yurts and dismounted. An old Kazakh woman from whom he had purchased food before lifted the tent flap and greeted him.

He returned the greeting. "Have they been giving you trouble?"

The old woman smiled, deepening the lines on the leathery skin of her face. "No, they only asked me if I'd seen anyone riding a red horse. Don't worry, I didn't tell them a thing. We don't help the Ch'ing."

He shook his head. "I doubt they were looking for me."

"They said a very pretty boy, no hair on the face." The old

woman's smile widened. "Not that I wouldn't call you pretty, but you are not exactly beardless."

"Do you know why they were looking for the boy? Is he a criminal?"

He didn't believe that. The Ch'ing officer was seeking one of his own. How else was Leighton to interpret *Tell her to return to Kulja as fast as she can*?

The old woman shook her head. "You know what I think? I think it's one of their girl spies. The Ch'ing governor in Kulja sends them out by the dozens, into the households of all the important men in the region."

He could only hope he didn't look too flabbergasted. "You think she is someone's escaped concubine?"

"Who's to say not?" The old woman nodded at her own sagacity. "Well, don't stand there. Come in, and see what you want today."

He did not remember purchasing the food, yet a sack of it swayed gently on his back. He could not recall getting on his horse, yet here he was, riding away.

Could she be someone's escaped concubine? It was possible, he supposed. And it was the best scenario under the circumstances. He did not mind that. If she had been forced into some warlord's household and then fled, so much the better for her.

But what if it wasn't so simple?

If he were the Ch'ing governor in Kulja, he would not be so stupid as to criminally under-use her by assigning her to be someone's bedchamber plaything. She spoke the language. She was deft with a sword. He would . . . he would . . .

God help him.

She had been spying on the Tajik warlord. She was not a Ch'ing girl spy. She was a Ch'ing spy, period.

How had he not seen it before?

He had never considered himself physically weak, but he had to slide off his horse and sink to his knees in the tall grass. He couldn't breathe.

She knew who he was. He was absolutely certain she did. The map. Dear God. Was that why she had shifted her stance so suddenly after her recovery? Had she been using her delectable body and her beautiful face to whip him into an insensate whirl of love and lust? He would be a perfect source for her, the enthralled, unsuspecting Englishman who'd willingly escort her back to his lair, where she could patiently and cunningly ferret out all she needed to know.

God help him.

He had already designed, in his mind, the house he'd build for her. And fretted over whether she'd like his Punjabi cook's dals and curries. And worried about her staying by herself when he went on his next mission. All while she'd plotted intricately and mercilessly to exploit him until he was of no more use to her.

He was fortune's fool.

*S*he was already waiting for him in the meadow beneath the cave, having loaded all their bags on her horse. He kept telling her not to exert herself too much, that her wounds and illness were too recent. But obviously she didn't need such hennish clucking from him.

She lay in the grass, her torso propped up on her elbows, beautiful as a summer sprite. He closed his eyes. To rip her out of his heart was to rip himself to shreds, never to be assembled quite whole again.

"You'll need to fashion a turban for me," she said as he drew near, patting her head. She had braided her hair and wound it about her head. "I lost my hat."

Without a word he dismounted, took the turban off his head—he was skillful enough in the matter that the turban came off holding perfect shape—and handed it to her.

She didn't accept the turban immediately. "What's the matter?" she asked, with that trace of anxiety that he had come to know all too well.

Except she wasn't worried for herself, but for her clever plans to spy upon the British Raj.

He leaned over and placed the turban on her head. She looked adorable in it. He wrenched his eyes away from her face and went to her horse to unload his saddlebags, his blanket, and his waterskins.

She came to stand near him as he began fastening everything to his saddle. As he tightened a strap, her hand combed through his hair. "Sometimes I think you hair is darker than mine," she murmured.

He caught her wrist and firmly, perhaps too firmly, removed her hand from his person. A small wince of pain crossed her features. She looked at him uncertainly, the beginning of doubt—or was it fear—in her eyes.

"What's the matter?" she said, her voice rising slightly.

"Nothing," he said. "Don't unwind the turban. Take if off before you lie down and you won't lose the shape."

She attempted a feeble laugh. "You can always remake it for me again if I accidentally squash it."

He kept his expression stony, dead. "I'm afraid that won't be the case."

Her face turned a waxen pallor. "You are . . . you are leaving me behind?"

"I think it would not be wise for us to travel together anymore."

"But I thought . . . but you said . . ."

If he didn't know better, he'd have believed her heartbroken.

He wavered. What if he was wrong? What if her connection with the Ch'ing was a more innocent one?

Did it matter, in the end, what kind of connection it was, when she was important enough for the local authority to send out soldiers because she had been delayed a few days by an injury? And how many such teams of soldiers were out there, searching for her?

He was a spy in a hostile country. He had friends who were also spies. Could he possibly risk everyone's life and freedom in the hope that the soldiers were looking for a different cross-dressing girl who rode a fine bay horse?

"You can't come with me," he said.

"Why not?" she asked, her voice breaking. "Why are you changing your mind all of a sudden? And at the last moment? Have you been telling me a pack of lies, just so that you could sleep with me for as long as you wanted?"

Each one of her accusations was a kick to his abdomen.

"You can't come with me because of what I am," he said in low growl. "And what you are. It simply cannot be. Nothing can come of this."

She staggered back as if he had slapped her. Every muscle in him strained to reach out to her, to hold her tight, to tell her to discard everything he had said. Because nothing else really mattered. Nothing mattered but her.

He kept himself rigidly in place, his lips clamped tight.

"Right," she mumbled. "Right. Of course nothing can come of this. Of course."

He turned away and fumbled with the straps and knots, cursing her, cursing himself, cursing the men who decided that Russia was an imminent threat to the British Raj and therefore Britain must contest every square inch of territory that lay between their frontiers.

But he was who he was and she was who she was. And nothing could ever come of an ill-fated love affair in the shadows of the Great Game.

*Y*ing-ying couldn't see. Everything was a blur.

Everything had been a lie—all the tender touches, all the sweet promises. She had trusted him. She had *depended* on him.

For him, she had turned her back on her country. She had

turned her back on Da-ren, on everything she ever knew, ever held dear. And it had all been a lie.

Anger surged, an explosion inside her, burning away the dejection, the self-pity, and the numbness that came before. Her heart pumped audibly. Blood rushed through her veins like a river in springtime, swollen mad with the release of an entire winter's pent-up detritus.

He had used her. He had taken advantage of her weakness, satisfied himself on her, and was now about to cast her aside as if she were no more than a pair of old boots. If Amah had been alive, she'd have seen to it that he never again saw another dawn. Amah would not have approved of her meekly standing aside, twisting her hands as if she had no more resources than those girls who hung themselves without first exacting any retribution from their heartless lovers.

He would not get away with it.

She walked, like an automaton, to her horse. Her fingers dug out the jar of salve, but left behind the pilules that must be taken while one used the salve. He was already mounted when she approached him.

A quartet of birds trilled raucously as she presented the jar to him. Perhaps they were trying to warn him. Or her.

"Here, a parting gift," she said softly. "Your wound is not yet healed. You must not neglect it. You should apply this for seven consecutive days without fail."

He looked at her, his eyes clouded. "I can't. You might need it also."

The slope rose behind him, a vivid backdrop that matched the verdure of his eyes. He looked so sincere, so decent. Bitterness swamped her. All false. False chivalry. False courtesy. False love.

Her eyelids drooped in a flutter of disappointment. "It's all right. If you do not wish to have it . . ."

Tears spilled out, hot and unruly. She turned her head aside. Crocodile tears, she reminded herself. They were crocodile tears. If only she could halt them the moment the act was over.

"I will accept it, with much gratitude," he said.

His hand closed over hers for a moment, comfortable, familiar warmth. The porcelain jar was gone, but something else was in her hand. She looked down. It was the pouch of jewels.

She immediately thrust it back at him, as if he had offered her a handful of scorpions. Did he think that a few baubles would soothe her? Did he think it was *payment* enough for her?

"No," she said. "Memories will have to suffice."

He stared at the pouch for a long minute before putting it inside his robe. "Yes, you are right. Memories will have to suffice."

Then he was riding away, as swiftly as his mount could carry him. Something quaked violently inside her. *Come back*, she wanted to scream. *Come back to me. You cannot go.*

But no words emerged.

Her fears fell unchecked. Mountain and meadow became one indistinct, watery blur. She turned and stumbled away, so she would not see him disappear forever from her life. But she knew the exact moment it happened, when she could no longer hear the hoof-falls of his horse.

Only the silence of his desertion.

CHAPTER 11

The Dagger

London
1891

*L*eighton had never seen Miss Blade afraid. But as she stared at the Centipede's kite, every breath he drew was icy with her fear.

"I can see the end of the line," he said, trying to nudge her out of her shock. "Looks like it got away from its owner."

"Ah, so we are agreed it is a kite." Marland sounded quite pleased. "Now let's buy one of our own and fly it."

"Let's do," seconded Annabel, looking at Leighton.

He ought not to pay so much attention to Miss Blade before Annabel, but he could no more turn away from Miss Blade's distress than he could stop a speeding train.

Gradually, Miss Blade's gaze lowered. She glanced at the members of their little group and then at all the revelers in Hyde Park on this first true spring day of the year. For them nothing had changed. Few noticed the distant kite. And those who did were already turning their attention to other things.

But *her* peace had been shattered.

"Did anyone see the design on the kite?" Madison's question was for everyone, but he looked at Leighton.

"I thought it looked rather like a map of Britain," Leighton answered. Madison didn't need to know yet—not this moment.

"Bit odd but why not, I say?" said Marland. "Are you also interested in flying kites, Miss Blade? Perhaps I will buy more than one if we have sufficient interest."

She was slow to answer, as if her brain still stuttered. "I would dearly love to fly kites, sir, but alas, I am afraid I must take leave of everyone. I need to be home to receive a delivery of new furnishings."

"Which reminds me of an appointment I have with my man of business," said Leighton. He turned to her. "Miss Blade, are you familiar enough with the park to find your way out?"

She frowned, then shook her head.

"In that case, will you allow me to walk you to the gate that is most convenient for your purpose?"

She looked at him a moment, as if he were a stranger. "Thank you, Captain. Terribly kind of you."

Annabel's hand tightened just perceptibly on Leighton's arm. "One can always rely on the Captain to be most considerate."

Leighton had the feeling that Annabel's words were meant less as praise than as a reminder of his obligation to her. She was entitled to the utmost consideration from him, of course. But she did not have a dreaded nemesis who had just returned from the bottom of the Atlantic, not only alive, but well enough to send up a signal meant to strike fear in the hearts of his enemies.

"I will call on you on the morrow," he told Annabel. Then, to Miss Blade. "Shall we?"

In her mind, Catherine heard Lin's laughter: He always laughed after he killed. A slightly maniacal laughter, almost awkward, as if he couldn't quite believe what he had done.

As if he had done something as silly as accidentally stepping on his victim's toes.

He was still alive.

Faintly she recalled the door that she had ripped off the hinges and thrown at him aboard the *Maria Augusta*. It had fallen into the waves after him and she had thought no more of it. But what she had believed to be his doom must have been his salvation, something for him to cling onto as the storm raged.

"Are you in immediate danger?" asked Leighton Atwood.

She turned her head, half surprised to find him walking beside her, a handsome man in a long, black overcoat, his walking stick gleaming darkly.

When she didn't respond, he pressed, "Do you have cause to fear for your safety?"

She raised her head. The kite still floated somewhere in the sky, though it had become even more distant, scarcely visible.

"No," she said.

Her fear had been instinctive and mindless. Lin was neither omnipotent nor omnipresent. He would not be waiting for her in her parlor—the kite all but proved as much: If he knew where to find her, he wouldn't be trying to intimidate her through such secondary means.

"Is there anything I can do to help?" Leighton Atwood said quietly.

Carriage wheels clacked, a hawker cried the virtues of his ginger beer, and somewhere to her right a boy begged his governess to buy a piece of boiled sweet. The park was crowded—so very crowded. London was so very crowded. Was that enough to offer Catherine a measure of safety?

"What help can you offer me?"

"That would depend on your aim. Do you wish to run, hide, or fight?"

She had wanted to disappear, to shrink to the size of a flea, barely visible even in plain sight. But as his question hung in the air, a grim determination began to displace her fear. "I am going to kill him."

"And what about what you came to England to do?"

"What about it?"

"You are only halfway done."

She stopped. "How do you know?"

"Keep walking—it is not good form for a lady and a gentleman to stop in the middle of an avenue to speak," he said. "And I have my means."

She resumed walking. "My task is my own concern."

He glanced at her and said nothing. Outside Hyde Park Corner he stopped. "I take my leave of you, Miss Blade. Do please let me know if you need anything."

She snorted. "And then what? You will drop everything and come to my aid?"

He bowed. "I will do what I can."

As it turned out, Mrs. Reynolds took Annabel's invitation to Miss Blade quite seriously. And when the latter protested that she did not have a ball gown suitable for the occasion, Mrs. Reynolds booked an appointment with her modiste to alter a ball gown of her own to fit Miss Blade.

This development pleased neither Annabel nor Mrs. Chase, but did give Leighton an opening: a time when he could be certain that Miss Blade would be out of her flat. He bypassed the landlady—no place that purported to provide respectable lodging for ladies would easily allow a man past the front door. Instead he knocked on the service door and greased the palm of a maid who was all too happy to look the other way.

Before Miss Blade's flat he first knocked. When no answer came, he picked the lock and let himself in.

On one side of the vestibule was a console table with slender, curved legs supporting a pot of orchids; on the other side, a coat tree and the umbrella stand that had borne the brunt of her anger when he'd last called. He stood before the curtain for a moment, sliding his palm along a few strands of cool, heavy beads, imagining her doing the same thing—and had to remind himself that it could not possibly be the same curtain she had spoken of, because that one had been cut up and used for her training.

The furniture in the parlor, four straight-backed chairs and a square tea table, had no upholstery or any hollow place to hide a secret cache. The fireplace did not have bricks that had been pried loose or shelves inside the flue where items could be concealed. Nor did the artwork she had hung mask any openings that had been cut into the walls.

He gazed around at the room. Had he made a different decision that long-ago morning in Chinese Turkestan, had he brought her back to India with him, would their home have looked like this, spare to the point of austerity? Or would the more high-spirited girl of yesteryear have settled on a more exuberant style?

More than once he'd dreamed of coming back to his quarters at the British garrison to find that it resembled exactly the interior of the Kashgar brothel, with her, in her dirty Kazakh tunic, lolling upon a sea of brilliantly colored pillows, grinning cheekily at him. In the dream he'd been completely flustered. Did she not know that his superiors were coming to dinner that night? They needed to present a respectable front for at least a few hours.

Bah, the dream-girl had waved a nonchalant hand. That most English of dinners—a boiled leg of lamb—had already been prepared. She would change in plenty of time to a prim-and-proper dress. And his superiors would enjoy dining in a slightly different set of surroundings for a change. Now, had he ever wondered what they would have done at the brothel if she had not left so precipitously?

He dreamed of her often, but this was the only dream in

which she'd come to India with him. He had loved it—if one could love something that broke the heart every time—for the glimpse of what could have been: a life with her.

Her mantel clock chimed the quarter hour. He shook his head and moved on.

The pantry had some baked goods, some tins, her supply of tea and chrysanthemum blossoms, a few bowls, a few spoons, and two pairs of chopsticks. If she cooked, there was no evidence of it.

He still remembered the savor of her fish stew—the broth, almost white, was one of the most delicious things he had ever tasted—and his astonishment that a woman deadly with a sword could be equally adept with a kitchen knife.

Her bedroom was almost as spare as her parlor. No mattress on the bed, only a few blankets acting as padding on the planks—almost as hard as sleeping on the floor.

On the wall opposite the bed were three paintings, colored ink on absorbent paper, which had been mounted on heavy silk. All three had for their subject the same lovely young woman: She fished from a dainty pavilion, read at a stone table by a peach tree in blossom, and stood on a garden path, her delicate, wistful face upturned to a rain of flower petals.

For a moment he wondered whether the young woman wasn't Miss Blade, until he remembered her mother.

You could look upon her all day long and there would not be a moment when she was less than perfect.

Sometimes events of a week ago were already blurred in his memory. But her, sitting on a pair of saddles in their cave, telling him about her beautiful but helpless mother—that was etched upon his mind.

He turned away and opened the wardrobe. On the lower levels were her clothes, in neatly folded stacks and containing no particular secrets. On the highest level were four vertical plaques, black with intaglio characters that had been painted with golden ink.

He could guess what those were: spirit plaques, dedicated to ancestors and other loved ones who had departed this realm of existence. One for her mother, one for the nanny who had been her master in martial arts, and a third for her great friend who had loved Darjeeling tea. But who was the fourth person?

Him?

The sensation in his heart was bittersweet.

He moved on to her trunk, which acted as something of a low table. He carefully removed the toiletries on top, arranging them on the floor in the same way as they had been on the trunk, before picking the lock of the trunk. There was also a single strand of hair wound around the opening, which he untangled and set aside.

Inside there were clothes meant for a night burglar, some Chinese garments, finely embroidered and smelling faintly of jasmine, and another spirit plaque—*this* one probably his, now no longer needed as he had proved himself still alive. Whose was the other one, then?

At the bottom of the trunk lay her sword, exactly as he remembered it. The cross guard, with its fish-scale pattern. The scabbard, plain except for a bas-relief carving of a branch of plum blossom, the golden ink that had once been painted on the petals worn off long ago, before he'd even met her, except in the deepest nooks and crannies. And, of course, the black tassels that dangled from the pommel of the sword, with the one missing strand that she had cut off and given to him, the strand with its decorative jade bead that was locked out of sight in the safest, most secret location that was still wholly his.

The sword had not changed, only everything else.

He took rubbings of all the spirit plaques, stowed the rubbings in an inside pocket of his coat, then restored the bedroom to the way it had been when he first stepped inside. It would seem he had checked everything in the flat, but the object of his search remained unseen.

He had not come for the jade tablet she had taken from the

house on Victoria Street, which he would wager was on her person, rather than in the flat—it was too important to be left behind in an unsecured location, with the Centipede on the prowl.

Instead his goal was something he had only inferred to exist: a second counterfeit copy, exactly like the one she used to swap out item 1880.18.06.05. It made sense for her to have brought two such copies, since she needed to steal two originals. And it also made sense that she would not cart around the copy with her all the time.

Ah, of course. The orchid in the vestibule: The pot was of a rectangular shape, perfect for the concealment of something like that. He walked back into the vestibule and, very carefully, felt inside the orchid pot. There it was, near the very bottom, a flat, hard package wrapped in paper.

He had brought a copy of the *Times* with him—one never knew when it might come in handy. Now he spread the paper open on the floor—to catch any smudge of soil—and set the entire pot of orchids on the newspaper before attempting to lift the package out.

Inside the paper wrapping was a silk pouch, and then another, and only then the imitation jade tablet, counterfeit but beautifully pristine. He took rubbings of all the sides, and made sure to do each edge three times.

When he had replaced everything, and was tipping the small smattering of dirt on the newspaper back into the orchid pot, he heard voices one floor down—an exchange of neighborly greetings—and one of the voices belonged to her.

The flat was too high up for him to leap out from a window. He could climb to the roof, but he could not be confident that he could leave the roof before she caught up with him. And in any case, she was now close enough to hear the movement of the bead curtain.

He passed through the bead curtain again, sat down in the parlor, and opened the *Times* to a piece on the latest parliamentary debates.

The door opened decisively. The bead curtain was swept aside with the tip of a dagger. She scowled as she saw him. The dagger in her hand changed directions. Her eyes, however, remained wary. "Captain Atwood, what an unexpected pleasure."

He rose and neatly folded his paper. "Likewise, Miss Blade. Are you already quite done at the modiste's?"

"Hardly. I have been sent back to fetch the pair of slippers I plan to wear with the ball gown." She crossed the parlor into her bedroom and re-emerged half a minute later with a cloth bag that presumably contained the intended footgear. "And dare I take it you have been guarding my flat while I'm out?"

There was no mistaking the sarcasm in her tone.

"No, indeed not. I have been searching through your belongings."

"There is nothing here that isn't rightfully mine."

Her lips slanted, as if she had belatedly understood the implication of her own words. He was here. Was he also rightfully hers?

"You will have no disputes from me on that account," he said.

Her gaze swept over him. "What exactly are you looking for?"

A place for me, but I do not see one here.

He brushed aside the answer that had arisen from nowhere. "I thought you had disavowed any further dealings with the Tang Dynasty jade tablets."

Her expression hardened. "You of all people should know, Captain, that what people say often has little bearing on what they do."

He had not looked after her, as he had promised, but in his heart there had never been anyone else.

"Does the Centipede know why you are here?" he asked.

"What does that have to do with anything?"

"He is a wanted man in England—he once left his sigil on Her Majesty's nightstand, with the queen sleeping in the same room. Such a man does not advertise his presence simply in the hope of intimidating an adversary. He knew that agents of the crown would be alerted, that they will hunt down any clues as to his whereabouts or his intentions."

"And?"

"And that could lead them to you."

If the enmity between the Centipede and Miss Blade was indeed as profound as Leighton suspected, then he must consider the possibility that the Centipede's action had been undertaken with vengeance in mind.

"How?"

"I am not sure yet. But if the Centipede has any inkling as to your intentions . . . I would not leave anything lying about that might cast suspicion on you in the eyes of the authorities. Such as, for example, a copy of a jade tablet."

To her credit she did not glance toward the pot of orchids. "As I have said before, everything here is mine."

"All the same, remove everything that would put the lie to your story of being a simple expatriate," he said. He had already issued his warning; at the moment there was little else he could do. "I will see myself out."

She had been on the other side of the room, standing before the door to her bedroom. All at once she was next to him, her dagger against his neck. "So you were the drunk in the fog."

She wore a narrow-brimmed hat of grey felt trimmed with a dark blue ribbon. Beneath the hat, her eyes were as cold as her blade. His gaze lowered to her lips, wine-red lips that he had wished to kiss from the very beginning.

The pressure on the dagger increased, almost to the point of brutality. "Have you been following me about?"

He looked back into her eyes. Somehow, having her dagger at his throat made it possible to reconcile memories of the girl from Chinese Turkestan with the woman before him. They had been two related but separate entities; now they were one. "I lack the necessary skills for such a pursuit," he said.

She considered his answer. "Of course, I should have realized sooner: You know where the other jade tablet is."

He issued neither denial nor confirmation.

"If I tell you I will leave England as soon as I have it, will you tell me where it is? You do want me gone, don't you?"

His gaze dropped to her lips again—the only thing worse than making love to her for only one night was making love to her for only two nights and day. He should want her gone, but he had no idea anymore how to want the things he should. "You won't leave England, not while the Centipede roams free."

The dagger wedged even harder against his jugular. "I can force the answer from you."

Her hand remained as steady as ever. But the pulse at the base of her throat was quick and irregular—their prolonged proximity affected her, too. "You could," he told her, "but you won't. You are not the kind to hurt anyone, unless absolutely necessary."

At times he had been furious with her for the murder she had intended. But he had ever only blamed himself for the agony that could be directly attributed to her salve. Perhaps it was warped of him to think so, but he had always regarded the pain as just punishment for breaking his repeated promises to her.

Slowly she lowered the dagger, but the pulse at her throat grew ever more agitated. Her gaze landed on his lips. He held his breath, his heartbeat wild. He remembered the taste of her skin, the texture of her hair, the lithe shape of her body pressed into his. He remembered the whimpers of pleasure that escaped her, the glazed look in her eyes, the way she writhed and clung and took him ever deeper inside herself.

The parlor echoed with the sounds of their breaths.

She pivoted and walked out.

Behind her, the bead curtain shook and swayed, as restless as the desires of his heart.

CHAPTER 12

The Confession

"What do you make of it, gentlemen?" Windham glanced at Leighton and Edwin Madison.

Forty-eight hours after Leighton had sent a note to Windham, alerting him to the Centipede's surfacing, the kite had at last been found and brought back. The credit for locating the kite, however, could not go to Windham's runners. A boy had spotted it in the branches of a tree two miles north of Hampstead Heath. As it had been intact and looked impressive from the ground, the boy had climbed up the tree with the hope of retrieving the kite, only to prick his fingers on the needles that had been embedded.

His parents had found him at the foot of the tree, unconscious, his hand swollen to ridiculous proportions. After they had fetched a physician, the boy's father did not hesitate in bringing the matter to the attention of the local constable. And that was how Windham had learned of the matter, with the story spreading among members of the metropolitan police.

"Will the child be all right?" asked Leighton.

"That seems to be the consensus," said Windham. "Took

my men half an hour to extract all the needles from the body of the kite."

There had been four helium balloons attached to the top of the kite—that had been the reason it had been able to soar aloft on a day of little wind. The balloons were now flaccid white shreds, long since burst.

The needles, which had been gathered in a metal jar, had a blackish look to them. Madison picked one up with a pair of tweezers and turned it in the light. "Poisoned?"

When Leighton had dispatched the note to Windham, he had also sent one to Madison's house, confessing that when he had viewed the kite from a different angle, he realized he had made a mistake concerning the design.

"I believe so," said Windham. "They were stuck into a mound—a pincushion, if you will—made of strips of silk. And when we removed all the needles and unwound the cloth, this is what we found."

He slid over a glass plate on which rested a claim ticket.

"But this is for luggage claim, at Paddington station." Madison looked up, a gleam of excitement in his eyes. "Any chance the Centipede is trying to contact someone?"

This was exactly the conclusion Leighton had not wanted anyone to draw.

"You read my mind, sir," said Windham.

"The Centipede had penetrated into the queen's bedroom and left his sigil on her nightstand," said Leighton. "What can anyone do for him that he cannot do better himself?"

"But what if he has a task that requires help?" asked Madison.

What if he is only using his notoriety among a select set to catch your attention?

Leighton turned to Windham. "Did your men see anyone loitering about when they retrieved the kite?"

Windham grimaced. "No, I do not believe they observed

their surroundings with as much care as perhaps they ought to have."

"You think the one the Centipede was trying to contact was on the scene?" asked Madison.

Leighton was more worried about the Centipede himself having been on the scene. "How did your men come here?"

"They did not," answered Windham. "I met them at the house in Lambeth, which they reached via tunnel. And I did not come here directly, either, but from the tunnel underneath the Hopkins house."

"Why the concern, Captain?" asked Madison.

"I do not believe the Centipede has friends in England. So I wonder whether he means to strike at those who have been looking for him—who else would take the trouble of cutting down his kite and bringing it back but us?"

Both Windham and Madison were taken aback. But it was a plausible enough theory that they did not dismiss it out of hand.

Windham tapped at the edge of the plate that contained the claim ticket. "In that case, we will be sure to be very careful while retrieving the luggage."

Good, as Leighton did not want the Centipede to be able to easily identify—and follow—Windham's men.

"Indeed," said Leighton. "Take all the care in the world."

*C*atherine moved slowly, deliberately, imagining the fireplace poker in her hand as an extension of her arm, so that her energy flowed through into the cold iron, imbuing it with a power that mere metal could not hope to possess.

This was what Amah had always emphasized. A woman was unlikely to rival a man in brute strength. But her inner force, the energy generated by the skillful harnessing and amplification of chi through the pathways of her body, needed not be inferior to a man's.

That was what allowed a woman to defeat a man—that and the dexterity and cleverness to turn his strength against him.

But had she really defeated Lin aboard the *Maria Augusta*, or had there simply been a confluence of factors in her favor, a stroke of pure luck? And would she be as lucky the next time?

At the thought of her nemesis, her injury throbbed, a cold, dark pain. It had always struck her as strange, twisted almost, that she and Lin had ended up such bitter foes, when they had so much in common. The European fathers that neither had known, the Chinese upbringing, the secret martial arts training, the long years in Da-ren's household, and their mutual loathing of Shao-ye, Da-ren's eldest son.

Yet there it was, an enmity sown by fate and nurtured by spilled blood and ruined lives.

She wished she could come upon him without warning, as it had been on the steamer. There had been no time for fear or second-guessing of her abilities, only the intensity of battle that swept away any useless thoughts. Much better than this slow, simmering dread, this sensation of being meticulously stalked.

And yet for all that Lin had declared himself still very much alive and still very much a menace, life had been oddly normal since she'd sighted the kite. If one defined normal as having been pulled into the hurly-burly of getting ready for a ball.

Slowly she sank into a split. Just as slowly she pulled herself straight again, without using her hands to help. The poker she thrust toward an imaginary enemy, if the enemy moved with the speed of a glacier. A kick, executed with just as much leisure and control.

She had not wanted anything to do with the ball. She even told Mrs. Reynolds outright that she could not dance—Master Gordon had offered to teach her, but the idea of holding the hand of a man who was not related to her, or, in the case of the waltz, standing in his arms, had quite scandalized her, and so she had never learned.

But Mrs. Reynolds would not be gainsaid. She saw the occasion as Catherine's social debut, an occasion for her to meet all kinds of suitable men.

If only those poor men knew just what sort of unsuitable woman they would be meeting.

How impossibly complicated everything had become. She hadn't anticipated that her mission would be easy, but she had supposed it would be more or less straightforward. But now she was caught in a tangled web, her lover on one side, her enemy on the other, her still unfinished task in the middle.

She lowered into a crouch, then leaped up atop the table, balanced upon an upside-down teacup. A twist of her torso and she was on the floor again, the landing silent, the poker and her other hand both pulling toward the middle, and then sinking to her abdomen.

She was done with this suite of exercises.

She returned the poker to its stand and walked into her bedroom—it was time to change for the ball. The ball gown that Mrs. Reynolds had more or less forced on her was already spread out on her bed, ready to be donned. But instead of getting on with her next task, she stopped to light a stick of incense before the spirit plaques of all those she had loved and lost.

Her fingers traced over the characters of her daughter's name. Such a beautiful baby she had been, full of brightness and joy. Catherine had held her every moment of her life. And when she had slept, Catherine had gazed upon her sweet little face; the pink, chubby cheeks; the long, upcurled eyelashes; and those strong, winged brows that were exactly like her father's.

Now all she had left of the child was a lock of soft, dark hair.

"Forgive me," she said to the girl's spirit. "I did not mean to fail you. Never again."

* * *

*L*eighton danced.

Herb had told him, ages ago, that a gentleman at a ball should dance every set, as there were always ladies in want of partners. So after he had accompanied Mrs. Reynolds for the quadrille to open the ball and spun around on a waltz with Annabel, he danced with young ladies who did not have sufficient gentlemen clamoring for their attention, so that they would not be wallflowers all night long.

But his attention, as always, was on Miss Blade, who looked quite extraordinary in her silver blue ball gown. People whispered about her, Mrs. Reynolds's former-expatriate friend. Gentleman lined up to be introduced.

Put her in a proper frock and she would enslave legions, he'd once thought. He had been right.

She was not the girl he had known in Chinese Turkestan, but neither was she the dowdy, faded woman who had reentered his life on the platform of Waterloo station. Something had changed—or revived—in her. She was beauty and mystery, her seeming fragility belied by a heart of blade.

Annabel, who had issued the invitation in the first place, was not pleased. Of course she was more than generous with her praise of Miss Blade's appearance and related the story of Miss Blade's rescue of Mrs. Chase with apparent relish. But Leighton could not help but feel her frustration: It was in the set of her jaw, the grip of her hand on her fan, and the way she seemed to show too many teeth when she smiled.

He tried to make up for the fact that she was at risk of being eclipsed at her own ball. It would have been better form had he not danced with her at all—it was frowned upon for an engaged couple to pay too much attention to each other at public functions—but that would have seemed like abandonment on his part.

Unfortunately he did not think his solicitude helped, or the fact that he spoke three times as much as was normal. Annabel was too clever; she understood that such a heaping serving of courtesy and consideration meant that a man was concealing a guilty conscience.

But they played along, he fetching her glasses of punch and champagne between sets, and she reacting with every ostensible pleasure, all the while the center of the storm stood fifteen feet away, a force of nature with black hair and beautiful shoulders who smiled and made small talk.

Leighton had just reached the punch table again when Madison took him by the arm. "Windham wants us."

"Now?"

"He is outside."

They found Windham inside a large brougham with all its drapes drawn. He looked quite grave.

"We have retrieved a traveling case from Paddington station."

"Did you—" Leighton began.

"We took every care. Put out word that there was an Anarchist bomb. The station was closed. It swarmed with police. All kinds of baggage were carried out. Ten of the Centipede would not have seen us smuggling out the traveling case in question."

Windham was good at what he did, but he did have the occasional tendency toward overconfidence.

"I take it you found something quite interesting in that traveling case," said Madison.

"We did. We found the jeweled clock taken from Her Majesty's nightstand."

Madison whistled. Leighton felt as if he had been pushed off a bridge: This was exactly what he had feared.

"And we found a note. It was written in code, but Sanders was able to decipher it without too much trouble."

The deciphered text read:

Dear Miss Blade,

Welcome to London. I hope your trip from China was enjoyable. Please accept this gift fit for a queen. I look forward to serving as your right hand.

Yours truly,
The Centipede

"And Tomlinson found this in the *Times* right before I left to come here."

Windham handed them a copy of the paper, opened to a page of small advertisements, with one circled in red. *Blade, did you watch the sky? Did you find your present?*

Now Leighton felt as if he had fallen through ice to the frigid water below.

"My God," Madison cried. "Captain Atwood, you don't suppose he means the Miss Blade we know?"

Leighton took a deep breath. "I do suppose that. I believe the Centipede is trying to frame Miss Blade."

"What do you mean?" asked Windham. "And who is this Miss Blade?"

"Miss Blade is an English expatriate my fiancée's mother and aunt met in Bombay." Leighton went on to give a brief account of her action on the *Maria Augusta* against the Centipede.

"But how would you know that was the Centipede?" asked Madison.

"And was there any eyewitness to her actually shoving this man overboard?" Windham frowned. "If not, we have only her word that it had been any kind of a combat at all."

"I began to suspect that the man might be the Centipede when I heard that before Mrs. Chase described him as Chinese, she had thought him a Frenchman," Leighton answered, holding on to his calm. "It has been the rumor that the Centipede is of mixed race and that he lives in France. As for how we know he truly went into the Atlantic, I checked the passenger list and picked up the luggage belonging to a man who boarded the *Maria Augusta* in Gibraltar but never claimed his things in Southampton. And inside the luggage I found brush-and-ink drawings of the Centipede exactly like those he leaves behind. I don't think the Centipede, unless he truly had been pitched overboard, would leave his luggage for someone else to discover."

Windham frowned even more. "Why did you not bring this to my attention? The Centipede's movements are always a matter of concern."

Windham was right. Leighton should have reported his findings as soon as he had them. Yet he had deliberately kept the news to himself. He had wanted to protect her from any association with the Centipede and from the notice of anyone, such as Windham, who might turn an unfriendly eye toward her.

"It seemed less important when I was convinced that the Centipede was dead," he said.

"Well, he is not. And, Captain, as much as I appreciate your gallantry, we cannot blithely assume that this Miss Blade and the Centipede feel any enmity toward each other. It could be all for show. Now, where can this Miss Blade be found?"

Madison laughed a little. "Funny you should ask, sir."

*M*aster Gordon had once shown Catherine an image of a ballroom of magnificent size and grandeur. She had pored over every detail of the picture: the floor, as smooth and shiny as a mirror; the pillars, surely wrapped in an abundance of gold leaf; and the overhanging gallery—a balcony on the inside!—a concept that had turned her understanding of architecture upside down.

Miss Chase's ball was a far cry from what she had imagined a real ball to look like.

Mrs. Reynolds's house overflowed with guests, unable to move two steps sideways; the drawing room, emptied of furniture, was crammed to a rather alarming density with spinning dancers.

Almost invariably, those dancers included Leighton Atwood, light on his feet and quite something to behold with his beautiful carriage and expertly tailored evening coat.

Tonight he was perhaps the furthest he had ever been from her Persian. But yesterday, in her parlor, the way he'd watched her, as if the dagger at his throat was a caress . . .

She had come so close to kissing him, the very thought of it still made her lips tingle.

"What a wanton tragedy, Miss Blade," said a very dashing Marland Atwood, stopping by her side. "An entire roomful of gentlemen delirious to waltz with you, thwarted by the fact that you have never learned to dance!"

She smiled at him. "The gentlemen seem to have no trouble finding substitute partners, but alas, it is a bit ridiculous to be at a ball when I cannot dance."

"Well, that will not do, will it? Come to Starling Manor and I'll teach you."

"Starling Manor?"

"Leighton's house in the country."

Many gentlemen had houses in the country—it was practically a requirement. But for some reason, she had always thought the pouch of gems and his horse the entirety of her Persian's fortune—and had liked his lack of worldly goods.

"We are going down the day after tomorrow and you should join us," continued Marland Atwood. "The English experience is not complete unless you have trudged through ten miles of mud and then have had your picnic eaten by ants."

The English experience. He said it almost as if he were also a foreigner.

"If you don't mind my curiosity, sir, why is it that you are Captain Atwood's brother but you speak more like an American?"

"I don't mind at all. After my father passed away, Leighton remained in England under the guardianship of our uncle, but my mother and I emigrated to the States."

When my father died, my uncle, whom we all despised, told her that if she did not give me to him, he would take both me and my younger brother from her. I convinced her to go away with my brother where my uncle could not reach them—and she did.

"Were you separated for long?"

"Quite a few years. We finally reunited when I was ten—in the Sandwich Islands, of all places."

"Hawaii?"

"Yes, on the island of Oahu. I remember waiting for his steamer to come into port, so many leis around my neck I almost couldn't see anything. The moment the smokestacks became visible on the horizon, I started to cry—definitely one of the happiest days of my life." Marland Atwood grinned. "You should visit there someday, Miss Blade. I, for one, never understood the term 'perfumed air' until I stepped onto those shores."

The important thing was that we protected my brother, her Persian had said. The brother certainly seem to be happy and well adjusted.

It was a moment before she remembered to ask, "But why were you meeting in the middle of the Pacific Ocean, of all places?"

"Oh, because Leighton sailed from Shanghai," said Marland Atwood, as if it was the most natural thing. "Oh, goodness, the music is starting again. I had better go find Miss Chase. I believe I am her partner for the next set."

Catherine blinked. Leighton Atwood had been to China's eastern seaboard?

Before she could decide whether that boyhood journey to the Far East meant anything, Mr. Madison took Marland Atwood's place. "Are you enjoying yourself, Miss Blade?"

"I am." With Mrs. Reynolds two steps away, Catherine could scarcely give any other kind of answer.

"The day we met, I asked you what you thought of London."

There was something odd in Mr. Madison's expression: an intensity of interest that had been wholly absent earlier. Catherine became wary. "And you never got an answer, because Mr. Atwood gave everyone's opinion of London."

"Precisely. But then I realized I had asked the wrong question. Instead of your opinion on London, I should have asked for what you thought of China. For there you are the expert, are you not?"

"That would make everyone in London an expert on England, wouldn't it? And that is hardly the case."

"Well put. Be that as it may, you have far more experience with China than any of us."

Why did Mr. Madison suddenly want to know what she thought of China? Did it have something to do with the Centipede's schemes? "Greater experience actually renders it more difficult to have a decisive opinion, at least for me. It is such a large country, of such varied geography and people, any sweeping judgment must come with a staggering number of caveats."

"And yet it is one country, under a centralized government."

"You do realize, sir, that many Han Chinese consider their country to be under foreign rule, since the Manchus originate from outside the Great Wall."

"Then let me ask you, what do you think of the decline of China?" asked Mr. Madison. "While the European Age of Exploration was barely under way, great fleets from China had already sailed to the Middle East and Africa. They could have colonized; they could have developed trade monopolies. But the Chinese instead decided every bit of the outside world was inferior, so they went home and closed their doors—until one day men they deem to be savages forced those doors open. Surely, sentiments must run quite strong against foreigners."

It was a nuanced view, for an Englishman. But Catherine only grew more convinced that he was asking her leading questions. "Yet hordes of foreigners live unmolested in China."

"But while many of them are but passing through, you lived a very different life. To you China was home. Did you ever find yourself considering matters from the Chinese point of view?"

"It would be strange if I never did, wouldn't it? Everyone should be able to consider matters from someone else's perspective."

Mr. Madison opened his mouth to say something more but was interrupted by Mrs. Reynolds's arrival. The latter took hold of Catherine to present to her yet another cluster of gentlemen. Catherine smiled and chatted until she could stand it no more. With the excuse of using the cloakroom, she escaped to the garden behind the house, the one from which she had spied on Leighton Atwood her first night in England.

Somehow it did not surprise her to find him by the fountain, a cigarette in hand. He glanced at her, his eyes grave.

"What is it?"

He exhaled a stream of smoke. "It is as I feared. The Centipede is coming for you."

As he spoke of the Centipede's machinations, cold sank into Catherine's very marrow.

"They believe him?"

"They don't dare not believe him."

"What are they going to do? Arrest me?"

"No, they will use you. Earlier I was able to persuade them to act with caution, to not bring the Centipede's gaze upon themselves. But now I believe they will do the exact opposite: They will draw the Centipede's attention and lead him to you—and see if they can, with you as a lure, get him into the open."

"They will do his work for him," she murmured.

"I'm afraid so."

She turned to him. "And you, why are you telling me this? Aren't you worried that I also want to slit Her Majesty's throat?"

"If that were what you wanted, we would have already had a state funeral." He pulled on his cigarette and stubbed it out against the edge of the fountain, his motions unnecessarily rough. "You had better leave England. Go far away. He cannot find you so easily."

"Leave? No. This is the murderer of my—" She took a deep breath. "No. Either he dies or I do."

"Most likely it will be you."

He had spoken her exact fear aloud. She clenched her fists. "That would be good for you, wouldn't it?"

All at once his fingers dug into her wrist. "Do not say that."

They both wore gloves, yet his grip was like a burning brand upon her skin. "Why shouldn't I, when the first thing you suggest is that I make myself scarce?"

The brightly lit windows of Mrs. Reynolds's house were pinpricks of light in his eyes, eyes with just a hint of wildness to them. "I went back for you," he said.

A tremor went through her. "What do you mean?"

"I went back to Chinese Turkestan to look for you. I went as far as Kulja, knocking on the governor of Ili's door. But it was a different governor by then and no one could tell me anything about you. I left a letter in the cave, in *our* cave, telling you how you could find me."

"When was that?"

"In eighty-five—and eighty-eight."

She felt her lips tremble, her throat constrict. He'd gone back *twice*? "You must not have realized that I caused your occasional disability."

"I have known it for years. The poison in your salve was extraordinarily powerful."

She could scarcely believe it. The backs of her eyes prickled. "And still you looked for me?"

He exhaled. "And still I looked for you."

Something hot and wet rolled down her cheek. "I left Chinese Turkestan in the winter of eighty-three. I never went back."

He closed his eyes for a moment and let go of her. "I guess some things are not meant to be."

Neither of them said anything more. And then the silence became that of his absence, a silence that she had come to know all too well.

CHAPTER 13

The Years

Chinese Turkestan
1883

What did you say?" asked Da-ren, his voice quiet. Too quiet.

"I am . . . I am . . ." Shame swamped Ying-ying. If she had any fortitude, she would have already killed herself. "I am with child."

She was six months along, but on her knees, in the thick, loose Kazakh robe, it was not yet completely obvious.

Da-ren slammed down his teacup, rattling its lid. "Who did this to you? I'll empty the garrisons, hunt him down, and tear him from limb to limb."

She pressed her forehead into the hard floor. She wanted to disappear, never to be seen again. "I was not violated, sir."

A long, lacerating silence.

"My men searched for you for months," he said slowly. "Every night I kneel before your mother's spirit plaque, begging her forgiveness. The departure to Peking I have delayed again and again, in the hope you might yet return. But all this time you have been playing at love."

She trembled, but dared not contradict him. She, too, had been searching. The mountains, the deserts, the dusty settlements of this harsh land. If anything, after learning that his horse had been found without a rider, she had redoubled her efforts, going as far as the Karakoram Pass, her heart shaking at the sight of the bones strewn along the barren path, from all the pack animals that had not survived the crossing.

As she stood in the saddle of the pass, gazing down at the desolate plain on the other side, she realized that there had never been any reason for her to climb so high she could scarcely breathe. But she had run out of places to search, and if she stopped, she would have to accept that her Persian had died.

That she had killed him.

"Where is this man?" Da-ren demanded, rising to his feet. "Bring him to me. He will not dare refuse to marry you."

She could no more bring the Persian than she could conjure rain. After seven days of daily application, the poison in the salve she'd given him would have manifested on the ninth day. He'd have keeled over by sunset three days later, his flesh rotting from the inside out.

"He has passed beyond the borders of this land."

Into the underworld, shadows and phantoms. When remorse had come, hot as tears, thick as blood, overwhelming her pain, overwhelming even her fury, she had ridden frantically after him. But she could not find him in time to save him. Nor could she locate his body for burial.

"Who is he? A nomad? A *Russian*?"

Worse. A spy. She could not speak for the magnitude of her disgrace.

"Have you no respect for yourself? Have we taught you nothing of right and wrong?! How could you, after all that your mother—"

Da-ren broke off, at a loss for words. Her mother had been the love of his life. How Ying-ying had dishonored her memory.

"I had planned to find you a husband when we returned to Peking," Da-ren said coldly. "A good man, not too old, who would tolerate your pride and your wildness."

She knocked her forehead against the hard floor, hollow, abject iterations of apology and contrition. "I dare not beg Da-ren for forgiveness—never in this life or the next will I deserve any. I wish only to thank Da-ren for his generosity all these years and then to take my banishment."

Da-ren sighed wearily. "Then go and bother me no more."

Hot streaks of tears ran down her face. She kowtowed three times. "Da-ren, please take care."

She rose to leave, to ride out into a world where she had absolutely no one.

"Stop," said Da-ren.

Numbly she obeyed and turned back, her head bowed. He came to stand before her, but she could scarcely see him through her tears.

The impact of his palm on her face nearly knocked her sideways. "Fool!" he shouted, losing his temper at last. "Are you so proud that you are not capable of sense? Have you forgotten the man who wants you dead? How will you protect yourself in this state?"

She sank to her knees again, bewildered at the implication of his words. "I have dishonored Da-ren. I have dishonored my mother. I do not deserve any better."

"You do not, but your mother would have wanted better for you." Da-ren returned to his chair and sat down heavily. "It is late. Eat and get some rest. We will speak of what needs to be done tomorrow."

She kowtowed again, speechless with gratitude.

With the relief of not having lost everything.

Shandong Province
Four months later

The baby was two weeks old and Ying-ying still could not stop watching in amazement at everything she did: the fierce concentration as she latched on and nursed, the big, adorable yawns afterward, the peacefulness as she slept, with occasional smacks of her lips as if she dreamed of her next feed.

"When you are old enough," Ying-ying told her, "Mama will take you to the western territories, so you can see the Heavenly Mountains."

She'd had to leave Chinese Turkestan, of course. Da-ren had been called back to the imperial court and did not want her to remain behind. But it had been a difficult departure. She hated to think of the ghost of her Persian all alone, without anyone for company.

"And maybe I will take you to the Buddha cave, if I can still find it." She wondered how long it would take for the grass mattress to turn to dust, for the last vestige of their few days together to disappear into the stream of time.

The child slept on, heart-meltingly content. Ying-ying traced her finger over her daughter's brows. "Maybe you are the wonderful thing your father saw for me. Many, many wonderful things, he said. But you are enough by yourself."

Auntie Lu, the local woman hired to look after Ying-ying during the first month after giving birth, entered with a covered bowl. "Eight-treasure porridge for you, Bai Tai-tai. Have it while it's hot."

Bai was Ying-ying's family name; tai-tai was how one addressed a respectable married woman—Ying-ying pretended to be a young wife traveling north to join her husband, one who had to stop for a bit to give birth. Auntie Lu did not question the story too closely, even though sometimes Bao-shun, Da-ren's trusted guard who had accompanied Ying-ying from

Chinese Turkestan, still made the mistake of calling her gu-niang, the term used for an unmarried girl.

She thanked Auntie Lu and accepted the bowl. Auntie Lu adjusted Ying-ying's covers—women who had just given birth were to leave their bed as little as possible during the first month. Ying-ying had thought she would be driven stark mad from the inactivity, but her daughter had proved to be such lovely company that she had not felt a moment of boredom or restlessness.

Auntie Lu chatted as Ying-ying drank the porridge. Spring Festival was around the corner, and Auntie Lu's sister would make her annual dish of "pulling silk" sweet potato—the "silk" being threads of caramelized sugar. "I will have her come and make some for tai-tai also. It will give you tastier milk—and baby will drink more and grow up fast."

She patted the baby's cheek fondly. "Such a beautiful girl. The matchmakers, so many of them will come, they will flatten your threshold!"

"I don't want her to grow up too fast," said Ying-ying. She wanted her baby to remain in a state of happy ignorance for as long as she could, insensible of the tragedy of her background.

There would be no matchmakers for this girl of irregular birth and parentage, just as there had never been any for Ying-ying. But that was fine. Ying-ying would not die of illness like Mother or recklessness like Amah. She would survive and protect this child, who would be the bright pearl in her palm, as the saying went—her greatest treasure.

"Oh, they always grow up too fast," said Auntie Lu. "Keep eating, tai-tai, don't let the porridge get cold or—"

Ying-ying held out a hand. "Shhh."

Auntie Lu blinked in incomprehension, but Ying-ying had heard something: the sound of a body slumping over.

They had rented two rooms from a prosperous landlord, one for Ying-ying, one for Bao-shun, who acted as her bodyguard. Today was the landlord's aunt's seventieth birthday;

the entire family had gone to the next village for the birthday feast, and the servants had taken the opportunities to visit home—there was no body to fall over inside the walled estate, except for that of Bao-shun.

She shoved the bowl of porridge into Auntie Lu's hand, swept aside the thick, pink silk-covered comforter, and leaped off the bed.

Auntie Lu gaped, scandalized—a woman who stepped on the cold floor in her bare feet in the month following childbirth risked all kinds of terrible aftereffects to her person. Ying-ying made another shushing sound and grabbed her sword.

A shadow crossed before the windows. The window panes were small, translucent squares of mother-of-pearl—they let in sufficient light but did not allow her to see out properly. But Ying-ying was already trembling: She had seen the shadow but she had not heard any footsteps.

This was not Bao-shun coming to check on her.

The double door opened quietly. A cold blast of air rushed in. Just beyond the threshold stood the man who blamed Ying-ying for the deaths of both his master and his beloved.

"Bai Gu-niang, it has been a long time," he said softly, politely, his eyes viciously hard.

His master's death had been a fluke. The death of the woman he loved had not, but he believed that if only Ying-ying had willingly submitted to Shao-ye, Da-ren's wastrel son, then Shao-ye would not have beaten his concubine in frustration, causing her to miscarry and then to take her own life.

And nothing Ying-ying could say would change his mind.

"Take her and go," Ying-ying told Auntie Lu. "Now."

Auntie Lu set down the bowl of porridge she still held and reached for the baby. But Lin raised his hand and Auntie Lu slumped over, half on the bed, half off—he had hit her major acupuncture points with his hidden weapons.

"I have come to see Bai Gu-niang's thousand-gold," he

said as he walked into the room, using the most courteous
term for referring to someone else's daughter. "Surely Bai
Gu-niang would not deny me the privilege."

Ying-ying's heart froze. She had not thought that he would
seek to harm an infant. She'd been such a fool.

Her sword left its scabbard. He casually picked up the
wooden bar used for locking the doors at night. She swallowed. It was said that in a state of true, sublime mastery, a
practitioner of martial arts could counter steel with cloth. Had
he reached such a stage?

She lunged at him. He blocked her blade. The wooden bar
promptly broke in two. Ying-ying heartened—no mythical
mastery for him yet. She lunged again, aiming to force him
outside. The more distance she put between him and her baby,
the safer her baby would be.

He stepped backward and dodged one thrust. Stepped
backward and dodged another thrust. One more and he would
be on the other side of the threshold.

Ying-ying charged. He pushed back. This time, the pieces
of wooden bar did not further splinter. She, on the other hand,
felt the block all the way into her armpit. She was still weakened from childbirth and two weeks of utter inactivity, and
he was incredibly strong, incredibly powerful.

She kept driving her blade at him. But he seemed to antici-
pate her every move. Her mind clouded with fear; her moves
were too obvious and imprecise. He countered and thrust
aside her attacks, easily holding his ground.

Every block from him was like a boulder hurling her way.
Already she was tiring, the sword growing heavy in her hand.
Her heart pounded, her concentration slipping while panic
surged. How long could she last? Could she hold him off long
enough for Bao-shun to recover his mobility and come to whisk
the baby away?

At last, a mistake on his part that left his right shoulder
exposed. She jabbed toward that point of weakness. He

stumbled back a step. She pressed her advantage. He stumbled back another step, almost tripping over the threshold.

She leaped up, desperate to disable him. But the man who a moment ago had seemed completely out of balance shot up like a cobra emerging from a field of grass and used Ying-ying's own forward momentum to send her nearly to the middle of the courtyard.

Even while she was still airborne she understood that she had been bested: She had been tricked and now nothing stood between Lin and her greatest treasure. She landed screaming, rolled, came to a stop, pivoted around, and charged back into the room. Everything together probably took only a second or two. But it might as well have been a year and a half, for Lin already had his hand on her baby.

He did not strike her, but seemed to pat her gently, like a fond uncle. Yet the baby shuddered and woke up gasping. Lin lifted his hand and laughed, that same surprised, awkward laugh that already haunted Ying-ying's nightmares.

She reached for the baby with shaking hands and gripped her tiny wrist. The pulse was that of someone on the verge of death: Everything inside her baby was broken, so broken that the little one could not even cry, but only tremble in agony.

Ying-ying barely hearing Lin as he said, "Now Bai Gu-niang also knows what it is like to lose the one she loves most. Bai Gu-niang, please take care."

She set her hand on the baby's abdomen and forced her own chi into the baby's body. The baby jerked, her breath rasping in her throat. Ying-ying hated herself for causing her daughter even greater pain, but she must keep trying. It was the only way.

Her energy poured into her daughter—a trickle, a stream, then a flood. Her baby stilled and quieted. For a moment hope rose bright and searing in Ying-ying's heart, until she realized that the baby had not fallen asleep. She gripped her tiny wrist once more. Her pulse was gone. Ying-ying grabbed her baby's other wrist. She held her hand under the baby's nostrils. She listened with her ear on the baby's heart.

A muffled wail broke the silence, the sound of a desperately injured beast. It came from Ying-ying, who could not quite scream, as if part of her still believed her baby asleep and did not want to disturb her with loud, ugly noises.

There would be no bright pearl in her palms. No trip to see the Heavenly Mountains. No hope of redeeming herself by giving her child a wonderful life.

She screamed at last. For a long time, it seemed she would never stop screaming. Then tears came, burning her eyes as they fell and fell.

She had lost everything after all.

* * *

My beloved,

I write to you from Rawalpindi, with the help of a Turkic-speaking imam, a kind man with a twinkle in his eyes and a soft spot for lovers. Now two years after I left Chinese Turkestan, I am about to embark on a solo journey there to find you, and my heart shakes with both hope and dread.

If I do not find you, then I will leave this letter in our cave, and pray that God willing, someday, as you ride by, you will be moved by an inexplicable urge to see the place where we had been so happy.

I was a fool to leave. If you can forgive me, please come and find me in Rawalpindi. Ask for Arvand the gem dealer at the British garrison, and they will know where to direct you.

I enclose a bar of chocolate, a packet of tea from Darjeeling, and all my fervent wishes for your well-being and happiness.

The one who loves you, always

Peking
1886

Da-ren did not recognize Ying-ying.

When he'd last seen her, she had still been a pretty girl. Now she was no longer pretty, and no longer a girl. It was a hard, grim woman who lowered herself to one knee before him.

This, she had realized some time ago, was the doom that Mother, Amah, and Da-ren had always feared for her—that her pride, impulsiveness, and obduracy would lead to great misfortunes. And make her the kind of woman who could never again lead a safe, normal life.

She didn't care anymore.

"Da-ren wished to see me?" she said by way of greeting.

He pushed aside his tea. "Three years we have had no news of you and this is all you have to say?"

She did not answer.

She had ridden to Peking to bury her child, wrapped in fabric from the turban her Persian had left with her, next to the grave of her mother. And then, without a word to anyone, she had left to hunt down Lin. Several times she'd had good leads, but she had yet to come close.

Her failures only fueled her. It had taken him five years to exact his revenge upon her. She had plenty of time.

Da-ren's hand tightened around the armrest of his chair. "Bao-shun, how long did it take you to find her?"

From behind her, Bao-shun answered, "Four and half months, Da-ren. And it took us three weeks to return to Peking."

Three weeks she could have used to locate Lin. But she had come—one did not refuse a direct summons from Da-ren.

He, too, was older and grimmer. She had heard what happened to Shao-ye, his eldest son who had been the source of so much trouble to everyone: Not long after she and Da-ren had departed for Chinese Turkestan, Lin had laid waste to him, breaking every bone in his body, savaging all the tendons and ligaments. Shao-ye had been bedridden ever since. But while Da-ren had remained in Chinese Turkestan, the news had been concealed from him, for fear it would upset him too much.

"Lin is dead," said Da-ren. "The one who killed your child and maimed mine has been beheaded."

She stared at him in incomprehension. How? Lin was almost untouchable.

"They found him in Tienjin, in a drunken stupor. The magistrate was an old subordinate of mine and had his head specially delivered to Peking."

Two servants brought in a basket filled with salt. She could see something black at the top: a long queue of hair.

"See for yourself," said Da-ren.

She gritted her teeth and yanked out the head by the queue. The preservation in salt had come too late; the head was largely rotted. She dropped it back into the basket. "Da-ren is sure that is him?"

Da-ren's hand slammed down on the tea table beside him. "Do you think if that were not him, I would not keep looking?"

Tears stung Ying-ying's eyes. She had not wept since she buried her daughter—the search for Lin had consumed her. But now that he was dead, all the grief that had been packed away threatened to overwhelm her control.

And what was she going to do with herself, with no child, no husband, and not even an enemy she could pursue?

Da-ren sighed. "I have ordered your mother's old home prepared for your use—you have been on your own for so long, I doubt you can live under someone else's roof and someone else's rules. Go there and take rest. When you are ready, come back and see me. I can always use someone like you."

She had not seen her childhood home in a dozen years—she hadn't even known Da-ren still kept it.

"Da-ren's generosity I will never forget," she answered, now down on both knees.

Da-ren sighed again. He waved his hand, indicating that she was now to be off. She kowtowed once, rose, and walked out into a bright Peking October day.

Into a life she did not know anymore.

* * *

My beloved,

I write to you from our cave. Did you know I have learned to read and write in Turkic? At times it feels like the only worthwhile thing I have done in the five years since we parted.

The chocolate and tea I'd left for you last time are gone. My letter remained, a little trampled but largely intact—whoever took the other things had been considerate and did not use the letter to start a fire. I will leave another bar of chocolate and another packet of tea in the hope that this time it will be you who come upon them.

I dream of you often, for which I am glad, for in my waking hours I can no longer recall every detail of your appearance. But in my dreams everything is precise and clear, as if you are right here before me, firelight glowing upon your skin.

I still live in India and still occasionally journey to other places. Please come to Rawalpindi and ask for Arvand the gem dealer at the British garrison.

Come find me while we are still young.

The one who loves you, always

P.S. I have cleaned the mural as best as I could. It is amazingly beautiful. I hope you will see it.

CHAPTER 14

The Connection

England
1891

It wasn't until Catherine had pulled herself together enough to go back into Mrs. Reynolds's house that she realized Leighton Atwood had left a folded note in the palm of her kidskin-gloved hand.

The note was composed on Mrs. Reynolds's stationery, the handwriting hurried.

> *Do not return to your flat. Proceed to 12 Royal Street in St. John's Wood. The key is in the window box on the south side of the house.*
>
> *I repeat: Do not return to your flat.*

Catherine hesitated. Half of her wanted to return to her flat—so what if Lin found her there? Sooner or later she would meet him head-on.

But perhaps in this case, later would be more prudent, given her injury from their last encounter. And she was curious about 12 Royal Street in St. John's Wood.

Half an hour later, she turned the key in the door and let

herself into her temporary lair. It was a small, pleasant house, quite feminine in its decor, and it did not belong to Leighton Atwood—the estate agent's placard still leaned against the wall just inside the door.

The kitchen was in the basement, and several bags of provisions sat atop the worn and pitted kitchen table. One bag was filled with fruits and vegetables; another contained a loaf of bread, eggs, and what she suspected to be a meat pie; and a third held such things as cooking oil, herbs, and salt and pepper.

The last bag had only a tin of Darjeeling tea and half a dozen bars of chocolate.

He remembered.

She found a kettle and a spirit lamp—the kitchen was supplied with woodchips and coal, but she didn't feel like taking the trouble to light the cold stove. While the water heated, she inspected the rest of the house, which was furnished but empty of personal items—until she reached the bedroom upstairs.

There she found not only toiletries but clothes—a tailor-made jacket-and-skirt set, a nightgown, petticoats, stockings—and a pair of walking boots. On the nightstand was another note, one with much neater handwriting.

I hope you will not be reading this. But if you are, forgive me for the liberties I took in purchasing the garments: It seemed prudent to have a change on hand.

There is food in the kitchen and some money in the nightstand drawer. I have established credit for a Mrs. Westfield at Madame Dumas's on Regent Street, should you need more clothes.

In case this location becomes compromised, take the train to Brighton and then the coastal line for the village of Claymore. From the village anyone will be able to direct you to Starling Manor, where there is an unoccupied cottage you can use. On the back of this note I have drawn a map of the cottage's approximate location on the estate.

    To avoid becoming an unwitting tool for the Centipede, I will not come again to this address. If you can, telegraph me as Mrs. Westfield to let me know you are safe. After the ball I will be going down to Starling Manor for a few days, so send your cables to Claymore in Sussex County, if you would.

    Look after yourself.

The last line on the note was written in a language she could not decipher but readily recognized: Turkic. Did he forget that she was illiterate in Turkic or had he written something he did not want her to understand?

The kettle whistled. She returned to the kitchen, made a cup of tea, and tasted chocolate for the first time in eight years. Then she slept very, very well, in the nightgown he had bought for her.

ave you ever seen the ocean?" he asked her.
    It was the night before he left her, but he did not know it yet. He was planning for a lifetime together.

    She shook her head and snuggled closer to him, as if she were cold.

    "There is a chain of tropical coral islands not far from the southern tip of India. And all around them the water is the exact color of the sky, and so clear you can see the fish swim. I want to take you there."

    "Will you also take me to meet your family?"

    "Yes, of course."

    "What if your mother does not like me?"

    "I daresay she will pretend to, just so you don't stab one of your daggers into her table."

This made her smile a little. "Do we need to live with her if she doesn't like me?"

"No, I have enough money to support a wife. And if I become a poorer man, well, you are a master thief, aren't you?"

Her smile widened. "You want to live on my criminal proceeds?"

"Nothing would make me prouder. And I will disdain other men who aren't clever enough to marry girls capable of robbing the neighbors blind."

Leighton opened his eyes in the predawn darkness. The past lived and breathed, a phantom within. Sometimes, a monster within.

Fifteen minutes later, he was in a hansom cab, being driven in the direction of St. John's Wood. He had managed, the night before, to return home and not leave again. But the compulsion had become too strong this morning.

He made sure to get off the hansom cab well away from Royal Street. He made sure that he walked nearly the entirety of the district before stepping onto her street. And he made sure that he did not stop, or even slow down, as he passed her house.

A light shone gently from behind the curtains of an upstairs window.

He exhaled. That would have to be enough reassurance of her safety.

For now.

*I*n the morning, after Catherine made sure she was not being followed, she wired a short message—*Safe. Thank you.*—to Leighton Atwood's address in the country. Then, as had become her habit, she went to the poste restante office on St. Martin's-le-Grand and asked if anything had come for her.

"Yes, ma'am," said the clerk, "a cable from America."

Mrs. Delany, at long last. Catherine yielded her place before the clerk's window and opened the telegram.

Dear Miss Blade,

My apologies—I was away on a short holiday and only read your cable today. I did not know Mr. Herbert Gordon very well. But he was a great friend to both my late husband and my son, Captain Leighton Atwood. Captain Atwood is in London for the Season and I am sure he would be delighted to hear from you. His address is 15 Cambury Lane in Belgravia, the house left to him by Mr. Gordon, in fact.

Yours,
Anne Delany

Catherine gripped the paper, nearly tearing it, as she read the words again and again.

For a while, but then I ran away to find a friend, her Persian had told her once, as if he had simply ridden from one town to the next.

And what had Master Gordon said, on the last day of his life? *I cannot believe it. It is a journey of more than ten thousand miles. I cannot believe he came all this way to see me.*

How excited Master Gordon had been, at the prospect of meeting his young friend from England, how stunned and happy. He had wanted to introduce her to this boy who had traveled halfway across the world. But he had died too soon and she would not meet the boy until years later, at the edge of the Takla Makan.

Some things are not meant to be, Leighton Atwood had said the night before.

But if they were not meant to be, then why did the forces of destiny keep bringing them together?

* * *

I stayed near her until she went to the cloakroom," said Madison. "Captain Atwood volunteered to guard the garden, so she could not slip out."

There was a faint note of accusation in Madison's voice.

"She came out to the garden and spoke to me for some time," Leighton said calmly. "But then I noticed Miss Chase observing us from inside the house. I could not very well remain in the garden with Miss Blade and lead my fiancée to suspect that there might be something untoward between us."

He could not be sure, however, that Annabel hadn't seen his hand on Miss Blade's.

"That's when she must have left. And that's when I came to alert you," said Madison to Windham.

Windham braced his hands on the edge of his desk. "Well, the fortunate thing is that my men searching her flat were not interrupted."

"That is fortunate indeed," said Leighton. "Did you find anything interesting among her belongings?"

"Nothing at all, I'm afraid, unless one considers two pairs of metal chopsticks to be of interest."

Leighton exhaled. So she had heeded his advice and removed items from her flat accordingly. "You said the fortunate thing was that your men weren't interrupted in their search. Is there something unfortunate that you are about to tell us?"

"I wouldn't call it unfortunate—interesting, perhaps. Miss Blade never came home last night."

"You are sure?" asked Madison.

"I had men watching the building from all sides and angles, plus two stationed in the empty flat next to hers. No one saw her."

Leighton rose from his chair—a sudden pain had zigzagged down his left thigh. He did not want it to be the seven-day agony returning, but he had no hope that it wasn't. "Your men, did they *hear* anything?"

Windham hesitated. "There is a bead curtain in her flat. According to one of the men in the next flat, around four o'clock in the morning, he heard a sound that could have been that bead curtain in her flat moving. But when he and his partner went to check, they saw no one at all."

"Was the curtain still moving when they got in?"

"Slightly, according to him, but he could not be sure whether it had already been swaying, or whether the draft from the opening of the door was responsible for it."

"You think Miss Blade came back to the flat in the middle of the night, then disappeared as soon as she got in?" demanded Madison.

The pain in Leighton's leg had turned atrocious. He gripped the handle of his walking stick and willed himself to not collapse against the wall. "Did anyone check the roof?"

The question was for Windham, who frowned. "The pitch of the roof is steep. Without mountaineering gear a man would slip off in three steps and crash to his death."

"Not every man," said Leighton. He turned to Madison. "And no, I do not believe it was Miss Blade the men heard. I believe it was the Centipede."

After I left Windham last night, I returned to the ball," said Madison. "It was already past time for carriages and Mrs. Reynolds had gone to bed. But Annabel and Mrs. Chase were still up, so I spoke to them."

He and Leighton were in the underground tunnel that led from the house that served as Windham's office to the house several streets away that his agents used for access.

Light from the lantern in Madison's hand swung on the brick walls of the tunnel, lighting their way ten feet at a time. "I believed—and Windham concurred—that they should be warned about the Centipede," Madison continued. "And Miss

Blade's possible connection to him, since she is on such friendly terms with Mrs. Reynolds."

Leighton barely managed not to stumble at the next spike of pain. "What did they say?"

"Mrs. Chase did not say much of anything, except along the lines of 'oh my' and 'goodness gracious.' Annabel, on the other hand, refused to believe that Miss Blade could be in league with the Centipede. She said that she had seen Miss Blade's face that day at the park, when the Centipede's kite was sighted—and Miss Blade had looked petrified."

Annabel would have seen that, wouldn't she, she who had taken to observing Miss Blade minutely, whenever they were all thrown together?

"So Mrs. Reynolds, too, will know by now?" Leighton would hate for Miss Blade to lose her only friend in England.

"Annabel promised to tell her aunt."

Only a matter of time, then.

From the house at the other end of the tunnel, Leighton headed for Victoria station. Windham badly wanted to see the contents of the Centipede's luggage. He had asked Leighton to go down the night before; using his fiancée's ball as an excuse, Leighton had flatly refused.

But now one of Windham's runners was already at Claymore, waiting for Leighton to hand over the Centipede's belongings. He met the man at the village station. They drove to Starling Manor together and the runner departed with the trunk and the satchel, as well as the miscellaneous objects the luggage had ejected in anticipation of unauthorized openings.

Without bothering to change, except into a pair of boots more suitable for hiking, Leighton set out for the downs—the hours in the train had been sheer agony. Walking was also sheer agony, but one he preferred. As he left the house, a footman had chased after him to give him the latest mail from his mother.

Without looking, Leighton had stuffed the letter into his pocket. Two hours later, when he finally allowed himself to sit down and rest, he took out the mail and realized it wasn't a letter, but a telegram, which she rarely sent.

My dearest Leighton,

A lady recently cabled me. She has known the late Mr. Gordon in China and is eager to find some of his friends in England. I gave her your address in town. I know how much you valued Mr. Gordon and I hope you will welcome a call from Miss Catherine Blade.

Love,
Mother

Leighton closed his eyes.

At long last he knew where he had first seen her: from his room at the British Legation in Peking, so drained by quinine that he hadn't quite known whether he was asleep or awake. She had stood on the opposite side of the street below, tears falling down her face. What he had not seen at the time, but could now guess, was that she had escorted Herb's body to the legation.

Leighton would not be informed of Herb's passing until the next day. As a result, he had never made the connection between the weeping girl and the death of his friend. And yet years later, when she walked back into his life, some part of him had instinctively recognized her importance.

I have made a friend here, a lovely young lady of mixed blood who studies English with me and teaches me Chinese, Herb had told him during their brief visit. *Perhaps I can obtain permission for you to visit my patron's residence, and you will be able to meet her.*

He had envied Herb's new friend, for having had Herb's companionship all these years. Little had he realized how difficult her life had been, always trying to evade the unwelcome attention of her stepbrother, trapped behind walls she could not escape.

Some things are not meant to be, he had told her less than twenty-four hours ago.

Did he still believe it, faced with this fateful connection?

Had he believed it even at the moment he'd spoken those very words?

*T*he Sussex countryside was beautiful. Gentle rolling hills, green woods, fields blooming with bright yellow flowers, pastures dotted with content flocks of sheep.

A neatly trimmed hedge now ran alongside the road. After a while the carriage slowed and passed through a wrought iron gate. "Here we are," said the driver of the hansom cab Catherine had hired at the village railway station. "Starling Manor."

The gravel drive, lined with mature chestnut trees, meandered. The land rose and fell. They crossed two streams— or was it the same stream twice?—a small meadow, and what Catherine almost thought of as a stretch of woodland before she realized there was nothing wild about it—the trees had been carefully planted, almost equidistant, while between them ran clear paths with herbaceous borders.

They rounded a turn and came before a lake. Two black swans glided on its smooth surface. A white gazebo grazed the edge of the water. On the far shore rose the manor, a large house dominated by a three-story central section flanked on either side by an octagonal tower. Beyond the east tower, the house ended, and the land gave way to orchards and small buildings. Beyond the west tower, the house continued, two stories, one story, at last ending in what looked to be a walled garden.

Despite its asymmetrical shape, the entire structure had been built with the same almond-colored bricks, its numerous windows evenly spaced, their trims white and the slats of their shutters a deep, calm green. The whole house sat on a raised terrace. Peacocks—peacocks!—roamed the wide front lawn.

He had come back for her. He had wanted to share all this with her. Catherine was completely unconvinced that she was suited to a life in an English manor, but it was the gesture that counted.

A butler who heroically concealed his surprise at the sight of an unaccompanied female caller told her that the master of the house was out on the downs. The downs—she had once asked Master Gordon why English made so little sense; shouldn't an area of undulating land be called the ups, if anything?

She declined the butler's offer to wait inside, but instead walked the grounds. Behind the house, a wide stone terrace gave way to a formal rose garden. The garden path exited under an arched gate. Beyond the gate extended an avenue of laburnums in bloom. The branches had been trained to form a leafy pergola. Long racemes of canary yellow flowers hung from the branches, like palmfuls of confetti waiting to flutter down.

It was quiet here, the quiet of breezes and an occasional birdsong. The air smelled heart-stoppingly pure, of sun-warmed stone, clean soil, and spring subtly expanding into summer.

She sensed him before she saw him. He appeared at the far end of the path and stopped. They gazed at each other. For a moment she felt precariously balanced: The forces that would hold them apart and the affinities that would draw them together in a perfect yet dangerous equilibrium.

But as he began to advance, she forgot about the larger forces: He was in pain again, pain that she had caused.

She pointed at a wooden bench. "Sit down. I will see to your limb."

A flare of hope lit in his eyes, before he shook his head. "It must be too late for anything to be done."

"It's never too late. Sit down."

He did not put up more argument, but did as she ordered, grimacing only slightly.

She felt along his leg. Her fingers recoiled. He had not been gentle on himself. This seemingly fluid walk of his was a product of brutal will. His natural chi paths had become a jumble of knots and dead ends.

She lowered herself cross-legged to the ground, took a deep breath, and raised her hand, index finger and middle finger tight together, the other digits held down at the center of the palm. Gently, she tapped at his leg along a circuit of chi nodes.

His sinews stiffened in resistance to the inpouring of her energy.

"Relax," she commanded. "Breathe deeply and don't speak. I won't injure you."

She didn't actually know that. Chi healing was intricate and potentially dangerous. A powerful infusion at the right places could aid his own chi in reconnecting its natural paths. But one wrong move . . .

This was not the best time or place for it. Impulse had overcome her. She had started too hastily, without adequate explanation to him. But now she also could no longer speak, for fear of breaking her concentration. Any interruption would be detrimental to them both and could even lead to permanent paralysis for him.

Three times she quick-tapped the circuit of chi nodes, using short bursts of chi to reopen sealed pathways. Then her rhythm slowed. Her chi streamed in a steady flow, smoothing the pathways, pushing, oftentimes forcing his own chi along, guiding it into the proper pattern of circulation.

Beads of perspiration rolled off the tip of her nose. Her chemise adhered damply to her skin. This must hurt him, like a swarm of angry bees inside his flesh. But he remained quiet and breathed as she had instructed.

On the final round, she placed her entire palm against him, passing along torrents of her chi to fill his empty reservoirs. Exhaustion mauled her, as if she had given him half of her blood.

When she at last finished, she had to put her hands down on the ground so that she wouldn't topple over. Now it was he who caught her and sat her down on the bench.

"How is your limb feeling?" she panted.

"Much better," he said. "Thank you."

"You should know that the relief is temporary."

For the healing to be permanent, they would need such a session daily, for fourteen—perhaps twenty-eight—consecutive days.

"I did not expect it to be anything but," he answered quietly.

Since Lin's return, she'd carried the salve and the pilules on her person, in case of injury. Now she dug out the jar of pilules and handed it to Leighton Atwood. "This was what I did not give you last time. Take one every morning and night, without fail, for seven days, and that should expel the remaining poison. Once the poison is gone, further repairs will be much easier."

Now she closed her eyes and moved into the beginning of a long set of breathing exercises. She must circulate and replenish her own chi—or risk severe damage to herself.

She had no idea how long she remained in place, but when she opened her eyes, he was there, waiting for her.

CHAPTER 15

The Pledge

Catherine had thought he meant to take her to the cottage he had mentioned, but instead, he led her to an outbuilding that he called a lavender house, pushed aside a straw mat on the floor, and pulled up a hidden trapdoor. The trapdoor led to a tunnel. He lit a lantern and helped her down.

"I still don't understand how you survived," she said, even though her words set off detonations of afterfright. "After seven days of the salve . . ."

"I stopped on the sixth day," he answered calmly, his profile beautiful in the dim, swaying light.

"Why?"

He hesitated. "I wanted to preserve the remainder of the salve as a souvenir."

He'd lived because he'd loved her. She swallowed the lump in her throat. "Did you ever find your friends? I came across Mr. Madison in Kashgar, looking for you."

He shook his head. "I reached Rawalpindi October of that year, well after their return."

"I searched for you," she said. It sounded quite inadequate, her action. But she'd sought him until she no longer dared to be abroad, with her advancing pregnancy.

"Thank you," he said, after a moment.

She had no idea how to respond to that. Fortunately she didn't need to. They had reached the end of the tunnel, where a flight of stairs led up to another trapdoor. They emerged in what looked to be a study, with dark, masculine-looking furnishings and bookshelves lining one entire wall.

He peered out of the door of the study, then led her down a wide, carpeted corridor to the library, two stories tall, with a wraparound gallery that was accessed via a spiral staircase.

She studied him every step of the way, not sure whether the sensation in her chest was her heart breaking or her heart healing.

He slid aside one of the shelves that lined the gallery, revealing another secret passage.

"What kind of house is this?" she couldn't help asking, even with the distraction of all the revelations of the past twenty-four hours.

"A house built by a man who imagined he had many enemies," he answered.

This passage, so narrow they could only fit through sideways, gave out to a room he called the solarium. And from the solarium, it was a very short walk to the mistress's apartment. There he drew her a bath. And when she had washed off her perspiration, she found clean clothes and a tray of tea waiting for her.

Her Persian, she thought as she dressed, her Persian who had always looked after her as if she were a princess.

The door opened and in walked Leighton with an armful of framed photographs, every one of them of Master Gordon, often together with a young Leighton and a man who must have been the late Mr. Atwood.

Master Gordon with one arm around Mr. Atwood, the other around a young Leighton. Master Gordon at a picnic with his beloved. Master Gordon and Leighton seated on the same bench, their eyes closed, their features soft with contentment and relaxation.

The photos were black-and-white, but it was easy for her to see the clear, unclouded sky, the thick foliage on the trees, and the opened collars and rolled-up sleeves on the men. She blinked back tears: This was what Master Gordon had remembered, his eternal English summer in the countryside, bright with laughter and affection.

Leighton, who had slipped out while she was looking at the photographs, came again, this time with a number of small containers. He laid them out on the table before her.

"I claimed the Centipede's luggage from Southampton. That luggage I've had to surrender, but I kept a portion of each of the salves he carried, in case they might prove useful to you."

She opened the containers, which were made of a dark, smooth wood, and gingerly sniffed their contents. She was not as much of an expert in the study of poisons and their antidotes as Amah had been, but she had absorbed a good bit of knowledge. "This is a poison. This one, too, I think. My goodness, this is the one with which his palm is poisoned."

"Does he not need an antidote for it himself?"

"Yes, he does. Can you bring me five glasses and a pitcher of water?"

When he had done so, she poured water into the glasses and to each glass added a small amount of the palm poison. Immediately all the water in all the glasses turned black.

"The correct antidote will turn the water clear," she explained to him.

But none of the other five salves managed to do that.

She frowned. "Perhaps two of the salves need to be combined for the proper effect."

He brought more glasses and more water. He also labeled the salves and the glasses, so that they would know what combination had been put into which glass.

Still no luck. They repeated everything, this time combining three salves together. At last, one of the combinations changed the glass of water it was dropped into a lighter color, grey instead of black.

She experimented further and found out that three parts of one salve, two parts of another, and one part of a third turned the water perfectly clear.

"Do you mind if I pass on the method of how to arrive at an antidote to one of the Centipede's poisons?" he asked. "There is a child whose suffering might be relieved sooner for it."

"Of course I don't mind," she answered.

The glass of clear water in hand, he led her out of the house via another secret tunnel, this one leading directly to the unoccupied cottage he had talked about. Behind the cottage was a stream. He caught a minnow and a tadpole and dropped them into the glass.

"So the Centipede killed Mr. Gordon," he said, from where he knelt by the bank of the stream.

She sighed, reluctant to relive the memories. "I don't think he meant to take Master Gordon's life—Master Gordon taught him the French language. It was a heated combat and Master Gordon was trying to stop everyone. The Centipede shoved Master Gordon aside. He fell, but it wasn't until later that we realized the fall had led to a fatal head injury."

Leighton was silent for a moment. "But the Centipede did mean to kill your amah."

"In retaliation for the death of his master."

"Do you know how he left China and became the Centipede?"

She plucked a leaf from a branch overhead. "Before my journey to England, the last I had heard of him was in 1886. He was supposedly arrested and beheaded in the summer of that year. It is quite possible that someone at court decided that a man such as he, who spoke French and could pass for a European, was more useful alive than dead."

He swirled the water inside the glass, then looked up at her, his gaze level. "Why have you come to England?"

While she had been in the bath, he had also washed and changed. Now he wore a suit of country tweeds, about as English as could be, and about as un-Persian. But all she saw was the man who believed in wonderful things for her.

It was a few seconds before she realized that she was only staring at him, and not answering his question. "My stepfather is in need of funds," she hastened to say, her cheeks warming. "He has been tasked with the revitalization of the Ch'ing navy, but little of the silver budgeted for him ever arrives—the amount of graft, corruption, and mismanagement at court is staggering. His last best hope is the treasure laid down by the Buddhist monks from long ago, and for that he needs the two jade tablets he doesn't yet have."

Now it was Leighton who looked at her a little too long before he asked, "So he has the third tablet that your amah once stole?"

"He'd had it for many years. It was from him that my amah stole the tablet. I gave it back after she died."

"And he is father to the stepbrother who tried to molest you?"

"That is the tragedy of great men—theirs sons are often wanting in every aspect. And he didn't know. He was busy and seldom home."

Leighton examined the water inside the glass. The tadpole and the minnow swam happily, showing no hints of succumbing to poison. "You have probably guessed by now that I have the other jade tablet that you are looking for. If you want, I will give it to you."

Her breath caught. The jade tablet, inherited from his father, must hold a special place in his heart. "What's the catch?"

"That you take it and go to your stepfather. Don't risk your life for vengeance." He looked down the stream, toward a small, arched stone bridge. "For years I waited for you to come and find me in India. The idea of harm befalling you, now, after everything . . ."

She almost crushed the leaf in her hand. If only he'd asked her to give up anything else . . .

It occurred to her that she could tell him—that maybe she *should* tell him—about their daughter. Then he would understand why she could not suffer Lin to live.

But then he would also have to know the ravages of losing a child. And she did not want to expose him to that torment. Let him continue to believe that all he'd lost was her. Let him not even conceive of this other, irreversible devastation.

"I will not flee, so don't give me the jade tablet," she told him. "I'll just have to rob you blind."

His lips curved into something that was half grimace, half smile. He poured out the contents of the glass into the stream, then he straightened and turned to her. "Come with me."

He did not speak much as they walked, except to point out places around the estate that would be of interest to someone who had loved Herbert Gordon.

My father enjoyed fishing, but Herb didn't have that kind of patience. We used to all come together, but he and I would play card games or climb trees. My father used to have to tell us to be quiet—we were too loud for the fish.

He liked to go for an afternoon gallop when he visited. Sometimes, I would look out my window, and see him crest that knoll, the setting sun behind him.

He had a camera with tapered bellows and he often brought it with him to Starling Manor. That was in the days before dry plates, and the wet plates that were used had to be processed immediately. So he would bring a portable darkroom as well. The two of us would go around the estate with everything on a dogcart, and I would be the one responsible for setting up and taking down the darkroom as he took pictures.

She listened hungrily to those details of Master Gordon's life—and his. And she was just beginning to fear he might eventually run out of places to show her when they reached the top of an incline and she found herself standing before a small, well-tended cemetery. He stopped at a slab of dark granite that read, *Nigel Richard John Atwood, beloved husband and father.* "This is where Mr. Gordon's ashes are scattered. He and my father are together in death, as they could not be in life."

She plucked a wildflower that grew at the head of the grave and wrapped it in her handkerchief. "I'm glad he made it home. He was happiest here."

He lowered himself to one knee and cleared some flower petals that had fallen into the chiseled letters of his father's name. "Where were *you* happiest?"

When I was with you. "In Chinese Turkestan."

Her memories of the place had become dreamlike: the impossibly blue sky, the gleaming white mountains, the sometimes abrupt change from brown wasteland to lush green meadows, dotted by the nomads' yurts and their grazing horses. Sometimes she could not believe that she had ever lived anywhere so wide-open and rugged. Sometimes she could not believe that she had ever been that fierce and untamed girl.

He pulled a few weeds from the edge of the tombstone. "When did you realize that I wasn't a Persian gem dealer?"

She exhaled. "I didn't know you weren't Persian until I met you at Waterloo station. As for when I learned you weren't a gem dealer—I found the map hidden in your saddlebag the evening before you left. "

He looked up sharply. "Why didn't you say something?"

She shrugged and looked away, at the lovely panoramic view that the dead in this most considerately situated resting place would never again enjoy. "Why say anything? I chose to not turn you in as a spy."

He rose slowly to his feet. "The morning we were supposed to leave, I came across Ch'ing soldiers looking for you, for a girl who might be dressed as a man. They were seeking one of their own."

She stared at him: He had also never said anything. "Of course they were seeking one of their own. My stepfather was the governor of Ili."

"I thought you were an agent of the Ch'ing. I thought I could not possibly bring you back to India with me, not when I had the safety of colleagues to consider. Not when we were all acting on behalf of the British Raj."

You can't come with me because of what I am. And what you are. It simply cannot be. Nothing can come of this.

Now she finally understood what he had meant. "You were mistaken. I was not an agent for the state. I never have been. I have only ever acted at my stepfather's behest, and he was—and is—hardly in favor at court."

They fell silent. In the games that empires played, no one counted losses such as theirs.

"But you said you came back for me," she heard herself speak. "Did our incompatible allegiances no longer matter then?"

He walked a few steps to a smooth-barked tree in full bloom and set his hand against the trunk. "I thought if I could find you again, we could run away to someplace like Hawaii, too far for the other Ch'ing agents to come after you."

Hawaii, where the air was perfumed. Where his brother had stood weeping on the dock, as the steamer from Shanghai at last pulled into port. "And you? The British would have just let you go?"

A breeze fluttered. Tiny pink blossoms fell upon his shoulders. "I'm a man of property. Gentlemen are not expected to spy for the country, in any case."

She bit the inside of her lip. "Why are you telling me this?"

Why do you want me to think that there could be a future for us?

He looked at her. She gazed back and saw neither the fearless young Persian nor the wary, wounded Englishman, but simply a man who had never forgotten her, not for a moment.

They both turned at the same time—someone was coming. He walked to the edge of the cemetery.

"Leighton, there you are," came Miss Chase's voice. "Ponds thought you might be here. Trust a good butler to know everything."

"Annabel," he said, almost curtly, "I didn't expect you until tomorrow."

"Mother and I were quite ready to get out of London after the ball—I hope you don't mind our being a day early." Miss Chase was all smiles. "How do you do, Miss Blade? Mr. Marland Atwood told my aunt that he had invited you, and she remained behind in London specifically so she could be sure to bring you along—but here you are."

Catherine smiled back. "Actually I came in search of the final resting place of a friend of mine. As it turned out, he was a close friend of the Atwood family and his ashes are scattered here. Captain Atwood was kind enough to show me the exact spot."

"Oh, what a nice coincidence. Now that you are here, do please stay for a few days."

Strangely enough, there seemed nothing insincere about her desire for Catherine to remain.

"It is beautiful here," she replied. "But I didn't pack anything for a stay."

"That will present no difficulties at all—I packed too many things. You can wear my dresses—my maid will see to it."

The conversation continued in that vein for a while, with Miss Chase pressing Catherine to remain and Catherine cautiously demurring, until Catherine said, "Since you insist, Miss Chase, I will, as I'm already here."

And she didn't need Miss Chase's dresses; Leighton had a supply of his mother's clothes that suited Catherine just fine.

At her acceptance, Miss Chase's smile faltered briefly, before she began to speak effusively of all the fun games they could play after dinner.

They started for the house, Miss Chase with her hand on Leighton's arm, Catherine walking a few steps to the side. At some point, they needed to climb over a low wall. He helped Miss Chase over. When he came back to lend a hand to Catherine, he said, his voice barely audible, "She and her mother have been told."

R̲ather than sit for hours at the same table with Miss Chase and Mrs. Chase, Catherine pleaded a headache and asked for a tray to be sent up to her room. And then, with everyone else at dinner, she slipped out to the cottage, where she could be sure of remaining undisturbed, to administer to herself the antidote that would counter the poison from Lin's palm.

The antidote went down like a swallow of flames. Within a half hour she felt the thick, cold knot at her side warming, the poison becoming neutralized. She settled into a long set of breathing exercises, nudging matters along, encouraging the healing of any chi paths that had been blocked.

When she opened her eyes, Leighton stood by the mantel, watching her.

"How long have you been here?" she asked.

He stoked the fire that she had built to make sure that the parlor of the cottage remained warm. "Twenty minutes or so."

"What time is it?"

"Almost midnight. I went to check on you in your room, since I thought this might be what you were doing this evening. And when I saw that you weren't there, it followed you had to be here."

She smiled at him. He almost smiled back, but then his gaze slipped lower and turned taut. She realized that she had on only her chemise, her stockings, and her petticoats, with the petticoats pushed up almost to midthigh by her cross-legged pose—a rather scandalous state of dishabille.

Not that he hadn't seen her in less, but it had been many years.

Too long.

He was still in his dinner attire. And if she were to remove that perfectly fitted jacket—and the waistcoat and the snow-white shirt underneath—would she see the same wide, strong shoulders she remembered so well? He had been beautifully sinewed from all those months on horseback, the corded arms, the hard abdomen, the—

"Would you like me to step into the next room so you can dress or would you prefer a blanket?" he asked, his voice just perceptibly strained.

"The blanket, for now." She didn't want him to go anywhere.

He spread open a blanket that he must have found else-where in the cottage and draped it around her, carefully—or so it felt—not touching her as he did so. "I brought you some food, since you didn't seem to have taken anything from the plate that was sent up to your room."

She had been in too much of a hurry to come to the cot-tage. "Thank you for always remembering my stomach."

This time he did smile slightly. "My pleasure."

He moved about as she ate, fetching water from the small kitchen, putting a kettle in the grate, picking up her clothes from where she had tossed them rather carelessly. She was reminded of the first morning she'd awakened in their cave; he'd also kept himself busy for a good long time while she devoured the food he'd brought. Then she simply thought that he was the kind who couldn't sit still as long as there remained any chores to be done; now she understood that it was his way of keeping nerves at bay.

When she was finished with her supper and had accepted a cup of tea, he sat down at the table and brought out a stack of paper from his pocket, sheets upon sheets of rubbings. She recognized them as those of the marks on the edges of the jade tablets.

She flashed him a look of mock severity. "And here I thought you came only to see me."

"I came only to see you," he answered quietly. "But I thought you might like to start on deciphering the clues from the jade tablets. If the treasure still exists, then the sooner you learn of its location, the better."

Considerate as ever, her lover. "Thank you, I would like that. Do you have a pair of scissors?"

He found a pair. She cut the rubbings and assembled them. The physical cipher was a simple one: It was as if someone had taken a vertical line of characters, sliced each line in three from top to bottom, and etched each third onto the edges of one jade tablet.

"What do they say?" he asked, looking impressed.

"They are gibberish. Or rather, individually they are perfectly legitimate Chinese characters, but together they make no sense at all."

He glanced at her. "Why are you not more disappointed?"

Perceptive as ever, her lover. "The tablet in my stepfather's hand is the middle panel of the three. With the strokes and shapes visible on the edges of that tablet, one can reasonably guess at the full characters, provided one has some familiarity with classical calligraphy."

"As you do."

She cleared her throat, a little flustered at being thought of as knowledgeable in that particular arena. "I am embarrassingly uncultured, compared to my mother. But she was a wonderful calligrapher, so just by growing up in her household, some of it rubbed off on me."

"I am still shocked that you are not actually illiterate," he said dryly.

She chortled. He was as capable of tickling her mirth as ever, her lover.

He watched her, his features softening with the hint of a smile. "If you already know what characters are likely to be seen on the edges of the jade tablets, when all three are put together, why did you still make the trip?"

"Because we couldn't make sense of them. And my stepfather thought that perhaps, if we had all three of them together, we could glean something more."

"Do you think so?"

"Probably not. But he wants them so I came here to find them."

"I'm glad he wants them," said Leighton, his eyes on the strips of characters.

Because that had brought them back together. And even if she had never met Mrs. Reynolds and Mrs. Chase in Bombay, in her search she would still have come across Mrs. Delany's name, and would have still been led to him.

Fate, it seemed, was determined that they not miss each other this time.

She was almost about to reach out and touch his hair when he asked, "Can you read the characters aloud for me?"

Sighing inwardly, she said. "Of course."

His brow furrowed as he listened to her. "I wonder if this might be a foreign language being rendered phonetically in Chinese."

The possibility had never occurred to her. Like everything else in China, the practice of Buddhism was in a state of decline and decay. Many monks joined temples not because they were men of faith but because they could not succeed at any other endeavor. Their spiritual practice consisted of reciting the sutras by rote and burning a great deal of incense—precious little piety and nothing at all of scholarship.

But it hadn't always been like that. During the Tang Dynasty, when the jade tablets had been made, the monks had been both devoted and erudite. And there had been great enlightened masters from central Asia, Persia, and India who had made the arduous journey into China to help translate the Buddhist canon into Chinese.

If one took the historical context into consideration, then Leighton's suggestion made a great deal sense. Of course some sort of code must have been used; and of course the monks would have wanted that code to be understood only by other learned monks.

She gripped the edge of the table, excited for the first time about the possibility of the treasure. "You mean, something like Sanskrit?"

"I was thinking of Pali, which is the language of many of the earliest Buddhist texts that still exist today."

She had never heard of the language. "And what I read sounded like Pali?"

"Alas, not quite."

She looked at the characters on the table before her, sorted into four lines, each representing one side of the combined tablets. She rearranged the order of the lines and read them out again. He jotted down the sounds on a piece of paper. "Does Chinese have no consonant clusters?"

"Like the 'cl' at the beginning of 'clusters'? No. We also do not have consonant sounds at the end of a syllable, unless they are those of 'n' or 'ng.'"

"Then it is ill suited to phonetically representing an alphabetic language," he said.

"But it is absolutely tremendous for poetry. English poems, no matter how well metered and rhymed, always look—and sound—messy when you are accustomed to the elegance of Chinese poetry."

He smiled. "Thus speaks the abominably uncultured brute."

She smiled back at him. "That's right. And if you don't agree with me, you can argue with my fist."

Something warm and wonderful bloomed in her heart. For a moment, it was as if no time had passed at all, and nothing stood between them.

He took a strand of hair that had fallen loose from her chignon between his fingers. The gesture shocked her, not because his self-control seemed to have snapped, but the exact opposite—it felt like a deliberate choice on his part.

He let go of her hair. "I have cabled Mrs. Reynolds to let her know that you are already here. As soon as she arrives tomorrow, I intend to speak to Miss Chase about ending our engagement—Mrs. Chase is useless, but I hope that Mrs. Reynolds would be a source of comfort to her niece."

For a long second, she was capable of neither thought nor movement. Then her hand was on his shoulder, her other hand curved around his cheek. But he stopped her when she would have kissed him.

"Let's wait a day," he said, his eyes again that impossible clarity she remembered so well. "I am still engaged. And I would like to come to you only when I am a free man."

She smoothed his brow, her hand shaking only a little. Sometimes hopeless hopes did come true. He had returned to her, just as she had dreamed in her bleakest hours. "Yes, I can wait."

What was a few more hours after all these years?

He took her hand in his and kissed her on her forehead. "I will look after you, for as long as we both live. And there will never be anyone else but you."

CHAPTER 16

Yuan-jiang

*L*eighton woke up early, went down to the library, and pulled a half dozen dictionaries and treatises of the Pali language from the shelves. The presence of the jade tablet in his life had instilled in him a deep interest in the history and the propagation of the teachings of the Buddha. And during his years in India, he had learned both Sanskrit and Pali to better educate himself on the subject.

With the dictionaries open before him, he kept trying to pronounce the sequence of sounds that he'd recorded the night before in a more fluid manner, all the while wondering whether the language the Chinese characters were approximating was actually Sanskrit or Parsi.

A knock came on the door. Ponds, his butler, entered with a cup of tea and the early post. Leighton looked through the letters absently, until his attention was caught by one from Professor Wade of Cambridge University. He had sent the rubbings he had made of the spirit plaques to the sinologist for translation. The professor had returned the rubbings, along with his detailed annotations.

The first three plaques each had a heading—*Compassionate Mother, Beneficent Master, Noble Friend*—followed by a name. The fourth plaque, the one he had found in her trunk, read only, *The Nameless Beloved*.

He traced his fingers over the beautiful pictograms that he could not yet read but whose shapes would now forever be imprinted on his mind. *The Nameless Beloved*.

It was only as an afterthought that he went on to the next sheet, the annotation for the fifth spirit plaque, the one he couldn't quite guess whom for.

Immediately he reeled. *Cherished Daughter*, it read.

Cherished Daughter Bai Yuan-jiang. Bai, wrote Professor Wade, *is the family name. Yuan-jiang together means "far territory," most likely referencing Sinkiang, also known as Chinese Turkestan.*

The words shook before his eyes. Or were those his hands shaking?

A child. He'd had a child. A child he had never seen and would never meet.

He was the father of a girl who had drawn her last breath before he'd even learned of her existence.

*T*he mother of his child, still in her nightgown, was already up, a cup of hot cocoa in her hand. She smiled at him. "You sounded like a herd of water buffalo coming down the passage."

Her smile disappeared the moment she perceived his distress. "What's the matter?" she asked as he shut the door.

He almost couldn't speak for his grief—and hers. How long had she carried this loss? How many years had she mourned, with no one to share her sorrow? "Why didn't you tell me? Why didn't you tell me that we had a child?"

The cup of hot cocoa clattered on its saucer. Slowly she set it aside, her expression a careful blankness. "How did you know?"

"The words on your spirit plaques. I had them translated. The translations came this morning."

She was silent for several seconds. Then she shrugged. "What would have been the point of saying anything? She is no more."

He gripped the door handle behind him. "I know she is no more. But she was my child and I want to know everything about her."

Her face seemed to have turned to stone. "She lived for all of two weeks. There is hardly anything to tell."

Two weeks. So little time. His throat constricted. "Was she happy?"

A tear rolled down her exquisite face, shattering her stoic façade. "Yes, she was a happy baby. Very beautiful." Her voice caught and she swallowed. "She nursed well and slept well and loved the sound of the stone mill in the courtyard, grinding fresh flour for Chinese New Year."

A premonition chilled him. She had described a healthy, vigorous child. One who'd had no reason to perish at two weeks of age. "How did she die?"

The mother of his child closed her hand into a fist. Her eyes turned hard. "Why? Why do you need to know? Can you bring her back?"

He crossed the room and set his hands on her arms, his premonition becoming darker with each passing second. "Please, tell me. I need to know."

"Very well, then," she said calmly. Too calmly. "The Centipede killed her."

The words pierced him like arrows. "No," he said numbly. "*No.*"

He could not even comprehend it, his beautiful daughter, murdered in cold blood.

She hit him, hard. Not the kind of punches that would send a man flying backward with cracked ribs, but those of a woman who had too long borne her grief all alone. "She could have been safe in India. But you left me. You left me and he found me. And I could not defend her. I trained my entire life and I could never save anyone I loved."

Her face was wet and splotchy. His own tears fell, stinging his eyes as they left. He stood rooted in place and let her hit him again and again, wishing only that she would unleash the sort of violence that did true damage. Broken bones and punctured organs, that was what he wanted—the pain of the body always, always preferable to the despair of the soul.

All at once, without even thinking about it, he kissed her. She was stunned into stillness. Then she was kissing him back, with fury and something that was almost brutality.

Then, just as suddenly, the kiss was no longer fueled with anger, but with longing, the kind that had driven him to scale the Himalayas repeatedly, in the hope of finding her again. So much had happened—too much—but he had never, not for a moment, stopped loving her.

And he never would.

He kissed her face and her throat. Lifting off her night-gown, he kissed her shoulder and her collarbone. She cupped his face and gazed upon him, tears still in her eyes, but amazement and tenderness, too.

"*When you lower me into my grave,*" he told her, again borrowing those words from the great Rumi, "*bid me not farewell, for beyond the grave lies paradise. And there is no end while the moon sets and the sun yet rises.*"

And as she had all those ago, she asked, "Do you believe in that?"

"I do," he said, smoothing his finger over her brows. "I believe enough for the two of us."

They made love with infinite care, because they were fragile. But they also made love with infinite ferocity, because they were indomitable.

And together they were stronger yet.

* * *

*I*t snowed on the day she was born—we were in the last month of the Chinese calendar, so by the western calendar it was probably sometime in January," said Catherine. She lay with her head on Leighton's shoulder, their fingers laced. "I was really afraid of childbirth; both my mother and my amah had died too early to tell me anything about it. But I had a nice woman, Auntie Lu, and she had this round, generous face. She took one look at me and said I would be just fine, that I was young and strong and built for easy deliveries.

"And she was right. My pain started sometime in the middle of the night, and by dawn she was already born. Auntie Lu had a bowl of noodles ready for me, and I was so hungry, but I couldn't bear to hand the baby to her long enough to eat—Yuan-jiang was so, so beautiful. And I thought, maybe, if I did everything right by her, your ghost would not be so angry with me in the afterworld."

He caressed her arm. "I could never be angry with you. Not for long, in any case."

"And I thought, when she was older, I would take her to Chinese Turkestan, so she could see where we had met—and been happy."

"And maybe if you had gone," he said wistfully, "you would have seen the letters I left behind for you. And perhaps even some very old chocolate and Darjeeling tea."

She turned toward him. "That reminds me. Thank you for the refuge in London—and the tea and chocolate you left."

He tucked a strand of her hair behind her ear. "I like doing things for you. It makes me happy."

"I will put my feet up and make you do everything for me then."

"Ah, but then I might come to bed exhausted, without the strength to make love to you."

She smiled. "Somehow I don't think so."

He pulled her closer, his expression turning serious. "Would you like to have more children someday?"

She had never thought of it before—she had believed him dead and she had never met another man who inspired any romantic yearning in her. "Another child can never replace Yuan-jiang."

He laced their fingers together. "I know. All the same, would you like to have more children?"

She looked upon the face of the man who had waited long years for her, who had forgiven her long before she forgave herself. "With you, yes."

Then she made love to him again, because there was no better way to tell him how much she had missed him and how much she loved him still.

*H*e was helping her dress, afterward, when he stopped in mid-motion.

"What is it?" she asked. "Did you hear something?"

"No, I was having the greatest trouble earlier, trying to find a way to make sense of the Chinese characters on the jade tablet. But now suddenly it occurred to me that a certain series of sounds in there could mean 'tranquil summer' in Pali."

"Tranquil summer," she echoed, rather doubtfully. Then the realization dawned. She grabbed his arm in excitement. "Yes! There is a Chinese province the name of which could be translated as 'tranquil summer.' And it was part of the Tang Dynasty's territory."

He threw on his waistcoat and jacket. "Then we are on the right track after all."

She stepped hurriedly into her shoes, eager to make more progress deciphering the meaning of the characters. "And it's a small province, relatively speaking. Smaller than Scotland, I think."

"Scotland is still too big if you are looking for a single treasure cave. We had better narrow the area down much further."

She shook her head in amazement. "Have I told you? Last night was the first time I considered that perhaps there is a treasure to be had after all."

"Me, too. First time since I turned twelve, at least."

They grinned at each other.

"I'll leave first," he said. "Come join me in the library in a few minutes."

She watched him leave, glad he was only going downstairs. After making sure that her hair was properly coiffed and all the buttons and hooks on her clothes in place, she walked out herself. As she did so, she saw Mrs. Chase, at the other end of the corridor, peering out from her door.

Had she seen Leighton leaving earlier?

Catherine decided she didn't care about Mrs. Chase's suspicions. She nodded coolly and started for the stairs. On the bottom step, she stopped to orient herself. The day before she had been to the library with Leighton, but had done so walking from the direction of the study, which they had accessed via a secret tunnel. From where she stood, she wasn't exactly sure where the library was.

To her left was the front door. A hansom cab was parked outside. Had Mrs. Reynolds arrived, or Marland Atwood, perhaps?

"Miss Blade."

The voice belonged to Miss Chase. Catherine felt a stirring of guilt: It was far from the best form to make love to a man who was still another woman's fiancé.

She turned. "Good morning, Miss Chase."

She had expected to detect a measure of unhappiness beneath Miss Chase's sugar-and-spice demeanor: The girl was clever;

she had to understand that her fiancé was slipping out of her grasp. But she could sense no particular dejection in Miss Chase's features. In fact, Miss Chase's eyes glittered.

"Would you mind coming here for a moment?" said Miss Chase.

Her voice gave Catherine the impression of being strenuously modulated, just on the edge of an excitement too strong to control.

What was going on? But Catherine had no reasonable cause to refuse her request. "Of course."

Miss Chase indicated a set of double doors. Catherine walked through to a drawing room, its walls and curtains shades of light, minty green that were quite refreshing to the eyes.

There was a dark-haired man in the room, standing before a large seascape, his back to her—the guest who had arrived in the hansom cab?

But even before he turned around, alarm already raced along Catherine's nerve endings. Then he did, and she looked into the face of her mortal enemy.

CHAPTER 17

The Nemesis

"Mademoiselle Blade," said Lin.

He was and had always been handsome, his bone structure extremely fortuitous. Dressed in the style of a western gentleman, he cut quite a striking figure.

All Catherine saw was the monster who had murdered her child in cold blood.

She didn't know how he had found her here, but it didn't matter. In China there was a saying, *Those with unfinished business will meet on narrow paths.*

"Draw your sword," she demanded in Chinese.

"Bai Gu-niang should step into the modern age," he answered in the same language. "What sword? These days a man of action carries a firearm instead."

His hands had been clasped behind his back, but now he showed the revolver in his right hand. The sight staggered Catherine. The playing field had just tilted decisively in his favor. A blade was a deadly weapon, but a blade could be parried and dodged. How did one dodge a bullet at point-blank range?

"You should have left well enough alone—the slate was

wiped clean between us. But you had to cast me into the Atlantic." He shook his head. "My life will be more peaceful without you."

"Annabel, there you are!" cried Mrs. Chase from the door of the drawing room.

Lin's expression changed—revulsion mixed with glee.

"Mother!" Miss Chase's voice turned fearful—Catherine had not realized that she was still nearby. "I told you to stay in your room this entire day. Go back now."

"But you don't understand. I saw Captain Atwood come out of that woman's room. If you are not careful, she is going to get him to cry off the engagement. Then when your Aunt Reynolds is no more, we'll be out on the streets! You must do—"

Mrs. Chase gasped.

Lin moved the aim of his revolver a few degrees. "*Ma chère Madame Chase, nous nous réunissons de nouveau.*"

My dear Mrs. Chase, we meet again.

Catherine did not speak much French, but she had spent enough time in the French concession in Shanghai to understand his words.

Mrs. Chase only whimpered.

The relish in Lin's voice was evident. "I wondered why this young lady looked familiar. She is your daughter, is she not?"

A warning bell clanged in Catherine's head. "Leave her alone," she said from between gritted teeth. "Leave them both alone."

Lin turned to her and switched back to Chinese. "Why? The fat one believes that people of mixed race—like you and me—are abominations. As for the daughter . . . someone sent me a message via the newspaper, telling me to come here. Any guess as to whom?"

Catherine did not want to take her eyes off Lin, but she couldn't help glancing toward Miss Chase. Before Miss Chase had found Catherine and Leighton at the private cemetery, she could have already learned from the butler that an unaccompanied woman had come to call on the master of the manor. That would have given her enough time to send a cable to someone in London, in order to purchase an advertisement in the morning paper before it went to print.

Had Miss Chase done that?

Catherine turned back to Lin—she was hardly in a position to judge another woman for what she did in the name of love. "Leave them both alone," she repeated.

"I won't kill the girl," said Lin, again in French. "She needs just a nice, long cut on her face, then her mother will have an abomination of a daughter."

The very idea made Catherine ill.

The fingers of Lin's left hand moved. Catherine heard the fall of two bodies. He must have locked their major acupuncture points so that they could neither run nor call for help.

He smiled. "I'll have enough time for her after I'm done with you."

The muzzle of the revolver was pointed at her again. And she had not a single weapon with her—lovemaking made one forget that the world was a dangerous place. She had, however, grabbed a small clock from the table next to her, when Lin had dispatched his hidden weapons against the Chase women.

If she could launch it and knock his aim off by a few degrees, she might be able to dive behind the settee before he got off a second shot. And if—

A gunshot went off.

She was stunned for a moment, all her muscles rigid, expecting to feel the pain of a bullet digging into her flesh and puncturing a major organ—only to see the revolver fall to the floor.

Someone had shot it out of Lin's hand.

From the mirror opposite, she saw Leighton at one of the room's open windows. Had she not stood in the way, he could have had a clean shot at Lin.

She dove for the revolver. Lin, on the other hand, leaped

over to where Miss Chase lay, pulled her to a standing position, and set a knife at her throat.

"Drop your weapons, or she is dead," he said in French.

Miss Chase trembled in fright.

Reluctantly, Leighton set down his rifle. Catherine did likewise, though in her case, it was likely no great loss; the revolving mechanism had been bent enough that a bullet might get stuck.

Lin shifted his weight slightly. Instinctively, Catherine sensed that he had changed his mind about what to do first. Since now there was more uncertainty surrounding his killing of her, he was going to mar Miss Chase's beautiful face while he had her in his grip.

She hurled the ormolu clock toward the major acupuncture point on his right shoulder. He brought up his knife to knock the projectile aside. She grabbed the next thing on the table by her side, a cut-glass candelabra, ripped off a handful of glass drops, and fired them in Miss Chase's direction, hoping to unblock her mobility.

But Lin had ripped a small painting off the wall behind him and used it to block the glass drops. She launched the rest of the candelabra at him. He deflected it with his knife, the impact metallic and loud.

She lifted a chair and swung it at him. He let go of Miss Chase and, with a snarl, lunged at Catherine. The chair broke apart into several pieces as his palm met the seat.

Catherine somersaulted backward. "Get the Chases out of here," she shouted to Leighton.

Lin's knife came at her throat all too rapidly. She reached for a pair of bronze candlesticks on the mantel and barely managed to block him. Lin aimed a kick at her. She stepped back—only to realize that he meant to move her out of the way so he could pick up the revolver from where she had set it down on the floor.

She dove behind the grand piano as a shot rang out.

Lin leaped up, revolver in hand. In desperation, she yanked at the curtain behind her and sent thirty yards of fabric whooshing toward him. The fabric caught him head-on, enclosing him in green floral velvet. She shoved the piano in his direction.

The moment he landed, the piano, careening on its caster wheels, knocked him down.

She had already run to the fireplace and grabbed a heavy poker. With all her strength and all her training, she hurtled it at him just as he was about to get up.

The poker met his skull with a most satisfying crack. He stilled. She grabbed a coal shovel and tried to decide how to proceed. He was still covered by the curtain and lay half under the piano, which made it easier for him, if he remained conscious, to disguise his movements. By pretending to be unconscious—or dead—he could lure her in and ambush her.

Someone tapped her on her shoulder. Leighton—he had moved the Chases to a safer spot and was back. He raised his double-barrel rifle, aimed, and signaled her to pull the trigger. An excellent solution. Now she no longer needed to risk her person to find out whether Lin had been incapacitated. She could make sure of it.

She stepped behind Leighton, reached around him, and pulled the trigger. Once. Twice.

It was more difficult for Catherine to believe that Lin was lying dead in front of her than at the bottom of the Atlantic—perhaps because he had been such an immutable force in her life, that only an ocean seemed powerful enough to destroy him. But dead he was, all his spite and all his skills evaporated into thin air.

Leighton had his arm around her. She leaned against his shoulder, overcome by exhaustion. "Are Miss and Mrs. Chase all right?"

"Still immobile, but unhurt. Are *you* all right?"

She nodded.

"Come with me," he said.

"And just leave his body there?"

"For now," said Leighton, pulling her out of the drawing room.

The butler stood outside, looking pale but composed. Leighton gave instruction for the rest of the staff to remain either in their quarters or in the servants' hall. "The police might come, as well as others. I trust the staff did not see anything?"

"No, sir," said the butler. "No, indeed."

Catherine could not be sure whether the servants had truly not seen anything or whether the butler planned to ensure such would be their testimonies. But either way it was a reassuring answer.

"Good," said Leighton. "And please send some whiskey—and some food suitable for traveling—to my room."

Catherine and Leighton climbed up the steps. He took her to his apartment.

"What about the Chase women?" she asked.

"What would happen to them if you don't see to them?"

"Nothing much. They would recover their mobility on their own, after some hours."

"Then see to them last. Don't forget British agents are also looking for you. If the Centipede saw the notice in the papers, others would have seen it, too. I am surprised they have not arrived yet."

He led her into his dressing room and opened a hidden safe. "Here's the jade tablet that Herb gave to my father. And this is the one you took from the house on Victoria Street."

She raised a brow. Before she had gone to the Chases' ball, she had stopped by his town house and hidden that jade tablet, along with all her other belongings that might come across as suspicious, in the mistress's room. She had thought it a good hiding place, but she supposed it must have been too obvious a choice to him.

"Your other things are still in my town house. You can retrieve them, but I would advise against it. Better go directly to Dover and get on the first ferry to Calais. You can stay in England and reason with the British agents, but they would prefer to err on the side of caution and hold you in custody until they are absolutely sure you pose no threat—and I don't think you want that."

"What about you? If they come and I've already left, won't they suspect you of being in league with me?"

He smiled. "But you overpowered me, as you overpowered the Centipede."

"What about the Chases? What would they say?"

"I will have a chat with Mrs. Chase—I do not believe she would wish her indiscretion with the Centipede to become known to our agents. And as for Miss Chase . . ." His expression hardened. "She will cooperate with my wishes."

Catherine placed a hand on his arm. "Don't be harsh to her. She loves you."

"She finds me agreeable, and my income even more agreeable. But let's speak no more of her." His eyes were gentle again as he looked upon Catherine. "Deliver the jade tablets to your stepfather. When things calm down here, I will come and find you. Now tell me your name."

Eight years ago, he had asked for her name. Then she had demurred, because there had been too many things she had held back from his knowledge. But now she could tell him everything, least of all her name.

"Bai Ying-hua," she said. "Ying is the word for England, and Hua for China—but you can call me Ying-ying."

She had not been addressed as such in years, perhaps not since Amah passed away. But when she had imagined her Persian, miraculously alive, coming to find her, this was the name he'd always used for her. *Ying-ying. Ying-ying.*

"Ying-ying," echoed the miraculously alive Leighton Atwood. "Am I pronouncing it correctly?"

She rubbed her thumb along his jaw. "You are saying it exactly right."

He pressed her palm to his lips. "And where do you live, Ying-ying?"

"Ask for me at Prince Fei's residence in Peking. They will know where to direct you."

He kissed her. "I will be there as soon as I can."

"I know you will." She laid a hand over his heart. "I know you will."

CHAPTER 18

The Treasure

China
1891

$\mathcal{D}$a-ren kowtowed before the spirit plaques of his ancestors, great conquerors and august emperors of yore. Ying-ying kowtowed, too, knocking her head on the floor until her forehead hurt. Silently, she beseeched Da-ren's ancestors to bless their search.

Da-ren touched down his forehead yet one more time. She watched his movement. He was stiffer than she remembered. His queue, so lustrous and thick in the years of her childhood, had turned white and sparse. She ached deep inside. No one escaped time's ravage, not even Da-ren.

He got up with some difficulty. He had been suffering from joint pains in the last several years. But despite his physical discomforts, he appeared to be in high spirits, his eyes bright and keen, his shoulders squared and confident.

They had left Peking ten days after her arrival. Fortunately they had been able to locate a Tibetan lama in Peking who had spent years studying Pali, as well as a scholar of ancient Chinese who specialized in how the pronunciation of words had shifted over the centuries. With the help of the two experts, they had been able to decipher the entire message.

Ning hsia Province. Ho-lan Mountains. Round Top Peak. Western Slope. Use heart in your search.

And they had been on the road since, finally arriving, dust bathed, at the nearest town to Round Top Peak the previous night. Da-ren, never particularly pious or superstitious, had forbidden his retinue of guards from drinking and carousing, and had sent them to all the temples and shrines in the surrounding areas.

As a further sign of respect, he had everyone dismount at the bottom of Round Top Peak and proceed on foot. The early September sun was still hot, though once above the denuded lower slopes, groves of elms, pines, and sophoras offered them some shade.

The hill was not particularly picturesque: no steep ravines, cliffs, or waterfalls to break the monotony of a steady climb. Neither did it host any major temples. Except for a few woodcutters and hunters, they did not come across any people.

Da-ren's optimism was buoyed by the place's relative isolation. "On the western side at the top?" he stopped and asked, when they were three fourths of the way up.

He knew as well as she what the jade tablets stated. "Yes, sir," she answered. "On the western side."

"We are almost there," he said.

She could hardly speak. And the sedate pace Da-ren set was far too slow for her. She wanted to rush forward and arrive at the peak this very second.

He stopped again, this time to catch his breath. Every sign of his old age pained her. She wanted him to forever remain the invincible figure he had been in her childhood, the confident, authoritative man who walked across an elegant courtyard to where her mother awaited him, with Ying-ying peering out at him from her window, bursting with admiration and longing.

He waved aside the two guards who came forward to help him but accepted her offer of a good stick. They continued, zigzagging and spiraling up to the top of the hill, a circular, flat peak that looked rather like a crumpled top hat.

Da-ren and Ying-ying inspected the weathered monolith, on the west-facing side, on all the sides. They found cracks, crevices and fissures, some seemingly more than a wingspan deep but none wide enough for her to fit through, even sideways.

She poked long sticks inside the fissures. Once a snake slithered out. Another time a pika scampered, annoyed to have been disturbed. The sticks did not come back with ropes of pearls. Nor did they activate any marvelous ancient mechanism that split open the hilltop to reveal a hollowed cave below, stuffed with gold ingots.

Da-ren's countenance darkened. "What are you doing standing around?" He frowned at the guards. "Spread out. Look carefully!"

"Look for anything out of the ordinary," Ying-ying added.

They had yet to tell anyone else what they sought.

*T*he guards found nothing. Lunchtime came and went. They ate the food they had brought and continued searching. Ying-ying tore her sleeves and scraped her elbows, but she could unearth nothing that had the remotest value. Still she went on, pulling out every blade of grass, overturning every rock, digging holes in the flinty soil alongside the guards, anything, anything at all, to keep at bay the rising sense of futility and defeat.

"Stop. We'll leave now," Da-ren ordered, late in the afternoon.

Ying-ying lowered her head. The day after Mother had died, Da-ren had sat in her rooms for endless hours, refusing both food and tea. When he'd finally emerged, he had looked exactly as he did now, in a daze, overwhelmed yet still disbelieving, not knowing what to do with himself.

They trudged down the way they came, the guards glancing at one another, deflated, bewildered, and still puzzled. The restoration of China had never been Ying-ying's ambition, yet Da-ren's sorrow enveloped her. She felt her heart scraping the bottom of her stomach, an unrelenting heaviness that threatened to drag her whole body to the ground.

She looked back at the top of the hill. They were some one hundred feet down from the summit, at the spot where they had first had an unobstructed view of it. As her gaze traveled lower, she saw something in a vine-covered face of rock that she had not noticed when she passed it on the way up, all her attention drawn up toward the unusual peak.

The rock face was some ten paces from the path, obscured not only by thick vines but also by shrubs and a few straggly trees. But now that she saw bits and pieces of characters incised into the rock, she couldn't understand how she had overlooked it the first time.

"Da-ren, look. Look!" She pointed and shouted, unable to contain her excitement. "And it faces the west."

He did not see. She ran to the rock face and tore away armfuls of wrist-thick creepers. "Look! It's the *Heart Sutra*. Remember what the jade tablets said. 'Search with your *heart*.' "

The guards rushed over and cleared the vines, exposing a huge tablet of rock, inscribed with the entirety of the *Heart Sutra*. At its bottom, a four-inch-thick, eight-foot-tall slab of stone bearing an image that was a close replica of the goddess found on the jade tablets.

Da-ren briefly closed his eyes. "Move the slab," he commanded.

Ying-ying anticipated a great deal of difficulty. But the guards pushed aside the slab with surprising ease, revealing a dark tunnel behind. Everyone took a few steps back, waiting for Da-ren to enter.

"Make torches," he said, thinking ahead as always.

Torches were made. He bade Ying-ying to take one. "Light the way for me."

Firelight flickered on the walls of the tunnel, illuminating more lines of Buddhist texts chiseled into the stone. The air was stale but not malodorous, the scent that of rock, soil, and a millennium of stillness. Ying-ying advanced carefully, trying to peer into the darkness ahead. Her heart thumped. Was there really a great treasure? Could Da-ren's dream come true, after all?

The cave opened.

But there were gold statues of Buddha, no life-size jade bodhisattvas. Not even a mundane stash of silver ingots. There were only stacks upon stacks of stone tablets, each the size of a small tabletop.

High up on the walls, there were thousands of tiny alcoves, each containing a stone statuette of a seated Buddha. Beneath the alcoves, thick as swarms of bees, were chiseled characters.

Most were sutras. But the text at the center of the far wall of the cave gave its story. Much of the tale was as Da-ren had told her long ago, of the monks' fear of imperial persecution and their decision to put their greatest treasure into hiding.

Except, she now realized, their greatest treasure was not any worldly wealth, but the words of Dharma. The monks had chiseled the entire known Buddhist canon into stone, set the stone tablets in a safe location, and left clues in the jade tablets for posterity to find, so that the teachings would never perish.

To be mistaken a second time should have been a crueler blow. But somehow, Ying-ying's disappointment paled next to her amazement. She shook her head, mostly in incredulity—that anyone should take all this trouble, years and years of thankless labor, to preserve something that had never come close to extinction.

She glanced surreptitiously at Da-ren. He walked slowly

amid the stacks of stone tablets, his face grim. "What a waste," he spat contemptuously. "All this work, all for naught. Do you not think it the height of stupidity?"

His anger took her aback, until she realized he wasn't speaking so much of the futility of the monks' work as his own. All the shame and humiliation of watching China become ever more impotent, the frustrations of being a man ahead of his time, the fruitless struggles against the obdurate Old Guard. And now, the one sole hope he had nursed, that he had clung to beyond reason, lay in shards at his feet.

She fell to one knee. "I do not think their work was in vain, sir."

She had never been a religious person, but the monks' undertaking moved her deeply. Just as Da-ren moved her with his selfless advocacy for reform and modernization. "They did all they could against the threats of their time. There will come a day when their valor is remembered and commended."

"And what good will it be to them, to their ghosts?" Da-ren asked bitterly.

"None." She could give him only brutal honesty. "Those who plant trees for others do not ask to sit under the shade."

Da-ren stood without speaking for the time of an incense stick. Ying-ying's knee throbbed from the cold that seeped up from the ground. But she dared not move.

At last he sighed. "Your mother would have known how to comfort me. But you . . ."

He did not finish. "We will leave now."

They took fourteen days to return to the capital. Ying-ying winced as she dismounted—she was no longer accustomed to riding day in and day out. She had to put a hand on one of the stone griffins that guarded Da-ren's residence to climb up the few shallow steps leading up to the red-and-gold gate. On stiff legs she made her way to the middle hall, so that Da-ren could dismiss her until he needed her again.

The middle hall, like the rest of Da-ren's residence, had not been kept up quite as it should have been—for years Da-ren had been digging into his own coffer to supplement his official budget. It was still imposing, but austere to a point of almost bareness. There were two chairs and a table on a slightly raised dais in the front of the room, two rows of lesser chairs along the sides, a large painted wooden screen, and not much else.

Still in his travel clothes, Da-ren arrived and took his seat at the front, the majordomo following closely in his wake to serve tea and refreshments. Ying-ying stood a little straighter and bent her head a little lower.

"Sit," Da-ren said.

Ying-ying made no move. She was certain she had heard wrong.

"Do you need an old man to ask you twice to sit?"

She raised her head. "Me, Da-ren?"

"Is there anyone else here?" he said impatiently.

She eyed the chairs lined up on either side of the hall and gingerly set her bottom at the edge of the chair farthest away from Da-ren.

"What is this? Now I must shout to be heard."

She moved one chair up. Da-ren sighed and signaled at the majordomo. The majordomo brought to her a cup of tea and a tray of candied apricots and candied papayas.

She jumped up. The majordomo himself, serving *her*.

"Sit!" Da-ren thundered. "Do you not know how to sit?"

She didn't. Not before him. She had stood, she had knelt, she had never sat down.

Now Da-ren called for distilled spirits. And when the

majordomo had brought the decanter, Da-ren rose from his seat, walked to Ying-ying, and poured for her himself.

She had never known such honors. She came out of her seat again and sank to one knee, completely flustered. "I am sure I do not deserve such privilege, Da-ren."

He raised her from the floor with his own hands.

"You deserve much more than I have given you," he said gently. "When you were young, I had hoped to keep you from the outside world, from all danger and cruelty, as your mother wished she could have been protected. But not for you the sheltered life; you were meant to test your wings against the height and the breadth of the sky.

"I have watched you fall—too many times to count, it seems at times. But always you take flight again." He set a hand on her shoulder, the barest of sheen of tears in his eyes. "Would that I had a son like you. Your mother might have known how to comfort me. But you know how to put the fight back into an old man's soul."

CHAPTER 19

The Last Line of the Note

Ying-ying was more than a little drunk when she left Da-ren's residence. She had a good head for liquor, and she hadn't really imbibed that much—they had partaken of a meal together and had spent most of the time reminiscing about her mother—so she suspected she was simply intoxicated by, well, by being someone to the man she had always wished were her father.

Usually she departed Da-ren's residence on horseback. This time, Da-ren sent her home in a fine palanquin like the one Mother used to ride, accompanied by a small cavalcade of footmen.

Would that I had a son like you.

She had waited her entire life to hear those words. How proud her mother would have been, if only she could have been there. For the first part of the journey home Ying-ying had to stuff her handkerchief into her mouth, so the sedan carriers wouldn't hear her laughing and laughing. Then the tears came, falling unchecked.

Would that I had been a better daughter to you.

* * *

*I*t was dusk when she arrived home, a few flame-colored clouds crisscrossing the edge of the sky. Before she dismissed Da-ren's servants, she gave each one a flask of fine spirits and a handful of coins. They left delighted, full of praise for Bai Gu-niang's generosity and good wishes for her health and well-being. To the pair of slightly elderly servants who looked after the property, she was equally lavish with gifts, thanking them for having taken good care of her home during her long absence.

The typical Peking residence was a courtyard surrounded by buildings on all four sides. But Ying-ying's childhood home was a suite of three such courtyards, its spaciousness and luxury a token of Da-ren's utmost regard for her mother, his beloved concubine.

When Mother had lived, there had been songbirds in cages beneath the eaves. She had also kept dozens of fancy goldfish in large, glazed crocks in the courtyards. The goldfish had been each as large as Ying-ying's hand, their tales fine as gossamer, their scales gleaming like dearly held dreams.

Now there were no more songbirds or goldfish—Ying-ying was away too often and too long. Besides, she didn't have much interest in such elegant pursuits—she *was* embarrassingly uncultured, as she had told Leighton.

Where was he now? Had he left England yet? Was he on a steamer sailing over rough seas at this very moment?

Sometimes a dark doubt would slip into her mind. He had broken his promise to her before. What if he had gone ahead and married Miss Chase?

She walked into Mother's rooms in the innermost courtyard and lit three sticks of incense before her spirit plaque. The one she had taken to England had been a copy. This one was much more elaborate. Da-ren still came regularly to offer sticks of incense, and sit or walk in her suite of rooms while the incense burned.

Bring him to me safely, she asked her mother's spirit.

Unlike her mother, she didn't need a man to protect her. But she wanted Leighton by her side. She wanted to take him to sweep their daughter's grave, see the rooms where Master Gordon had lived, and revisit Chinese Turkestan, retracing their route from the edge of the desert to the Heavenly Mountains.

From there they could make the trip that they had wanted to, all those years ago, over the eighteen-thousand-foot Karakoram Pass into India. Now more than ever, she wanted to see the great wall of Himalayan peaks that, as the day faded, turned the color of the setting sun.

Her own rooms were in the same courtyard as her mother's, along a different wall. As she crossed the courtyard, her ears pricked at the sound of footsteps. Her heart skipped. But then she remembered that the majordomo had told her that as soon as they were ready, he would send some "rolling donkeys"—a complicated pastry made from glutinous rice flour and red bean paste.

Still she went to open the front gate herself—and made sure that her smile betrayed nothing of her disappointment as she bade the two footmen to come into the kitchen. She offered them tea and some of the pastries while she moved the rest onto her own plates. Despite her encouragement, the footmen only dared each accept a tiny bite, declaring that the majordomo would flay them alive if he knew that they had practiced their gluttony on delicacies meant for Bai Gu-niang.

Did she hear the front gate open again? She had shut it earlier, but not put the wooden locking bar into place.

She saw off the footmen with good tips and, this time, made sure to bar the door. Then she slowly turned around, a dagger in her hand. Mother had arranged her home in the style of the scholarly household in which she had grown up, and at first glance, there would appear to be nothing of value in these courtyards. But Da-ren had acquired for Mother some noteworthy pieces of calligraphy over the years, and an art thief could find items well worth his time.

Night had fallen. Now that the footmen and their red lanterns were gone, the only illumination came from a flickering light in the caretakers' room. But as she scanned the courtyard, she managed to distinguish the silhouette of a man in the shadows.

She flipped the knife in her hand, holding it blade out.

"Well," said the man softly, in Turkic, "this is how you'll always greet me, isn't it?"

*I*t was difficult to suppress her own laughter while at the same time telling him to hush. She took hold of him—such a warm, secure sensation to have his hand in hers. They stole past the moon gate, across the dark, silent middle courtyard, and into her rooms in the innermost courtyard.

She closed and barred her door. Then she lit two candles that were on a pair of elephant-shaped jade candlesticks and turned around to have a good look at him. Good thing that she had put so much distance between herself and the caretakers, for she emitted a short scream: He wore a full beard, as luxuriant as the one he'd sported in Chinese Turkestan, and his hair was almost as long as it had been then.

He laughed as she reached for his face with both hands. "I thought I'd save myself the trouble of shaving while I traveled. And if you don't like it, you can always put your blade to good use and try your hand at barbering, as you said you were willing to."

She remembered that long-ago conversation in their cave and gave his beard a slight tug. "So you are calling yourself one of the bravest men in the world?"

"Absolutely," he said, grinning. "It's time I gave myself a little credit."

She touched the tender skin on the inside of her wrist to that dark and much beloved beard, at once soft and bristly. "Well, we won't find out immediately, because I want you to keep this for a while.

"And this, too." Her hands threaded into his hair, caressing the curls she had miss desperately, during those long years when she had thought them forever sundered.

"I'm glad you like how I look." He kissed her, a slow, languid kiss, a greeting of gladness. Then he stepped back a few feet and took her in. "You look altogether different again. Without your dagger I might not have recognized you."

She was in a Chinese woman's long blouse that reached to mid-thigh, and a pair of trousers. The dull blue fabric was plain and hardy, intended for the rigors of the road. And the cut of the garment was meant for modesty, not for showing off the figure. She groaned, half in frustration, half in mirth. "Why is it that every time we are reunited, I am always in the ugliest clothes I own?"

"They are not ugly," he protested. "Besides, why would you ever want anything to distract from the beauty of your features?"

Certainly his gaze was fastened to her face, a gaze of admiration, hunger, and delight. Her heart thumped happily. "Well, if you put it like that."

She pulled him to the edge of the *kang*, a raised brick platform that could serve as both a sitting area and a bed—Amah, in fact, used to sleep on this very one. She kicked off her shoes and sat cross-legged on the *kang*. "Now tell me how long have you been in Peking and how did you know to find me here? I was just at my stepfather's residence and no one mentioned any foreigners asking after me."

He mirrored her action and situated himself so that they were knee-to-knee. "I arrived a week ago. And as for how I knew you were here . . . I used a matchmaker."

She blinked at the word she had never heard associated with herself. "You used a what?"

He lifted the hem of her blouse and felt the fabric between his fingers. "I didn't think a man—a foreigner at that—sniffing after you at Prince Fei's would be welcome. So I asked at the British Legation if there was a way I may inquire into your whereabouts without raising too many suspicions or besmirching your reputation. And one diplomat, who has been in China for twenty years, suggested using a matchmaker: Matchmakers are almost always women and it is their business to ask about the young women of a house.

"It wasn't until three days ago that we found a suitable matchmaker, a very clever one. Not only did she discover your address, but when she learned that you were not expected back for a few days, she greased the palm of someone to let her know as soon as you returned. And I came here the moment I received her message."

Ying-ying laughed, monumentally amused. "That would make her the first matchmaker to have ever come for me."

His eyes widened in disbelief. "Really?"

"Yes, really."

He shook his head, still incredulous. "Well, if I were her, I would be overwhelmed by the honor."

She leaned in and kissed him on his cheek. How wonderful to see herself as he did, as this rare, magnificent creature coveted by one and all. "Since you have sent a matchmaker after me, may I assume you are longer engaged to Miss Chase?"

He laid a hand on her knee. "That engagement was doomed from the moment I saw you at Waterloo station, even if Miss Chase never had any designs on your safety."

Ying-ying was accustomed to direct violence. But the idea of "killing with a borrowed knife"—as the Chinese called plots such as Miss Chase's—quite chilled her. She was glad of the warmth of his hand permeating through the cotton of her trousers.

"So you found evidence that it was indeed Miss Chase who alerted the Centipede to my whereabouts?"

A look of distaste crossed Leighton's face. "She dispatched a footman to give a cable to be sent from the village post office. And the clerk at the post office remembered the message, because it was unusual. His recollection of the message matched almost word for word the notice in the paper."

Ying-ying sighed. "She seemed so wonderful at first."

"For a while I was similarly deceived. I never loved her, but I thought her a lovely person. In fact, when Mrs. Reynolds would look at me with some anxiety, I interpreted it as concern that I was not good enough for her niece. Only later did I begin to understand she was afraid that *I* wouldn't be happy, married to Miss Chase, because at some point I might see through her."

"I hope Mrs. Reynolds's life hasn't been made too unpleasant—the Chase women might blame her for bringing me to your attention," said Ying-ying. She remained quite fond of Mrs. Reynolds.

"She can fend for herself. In fact, she called on me before I left and asked me to convey both her regards and her apologies. She hopes that she can still call on you when you are next in England."

Ying-ying was far happier than she had expected to be at the thought that Mrs. Reynolds still wished to remain friends. "Of course—except I probably can't ever go back to England."

"I wouldn't be so sure. Given that the Centipede is actually dead, those in charge of security matters have begun to come around to the view that perhaps you two were enemies after all. I'd guess that in a year or two you'd be able to take a stroll on the Embankment without anyone batting an eye."

She didn't have any burning desires to return to England, but the news quite gladdened her—he had properties and connections there and she didn't want them to be separated every time he visited his home country. "I must say you are that most welcome of visitors, one who comes bearing nothing but excellent news."

He lean forward. "Actually, I do have a piece of bad news."

"Oh?" she tensed.

He nodded rather ominously. "After much consideration, I have decided that you are right, and these are the most extraordinarily ugly clothes I have ever seen. We need to get rid of them as quickly as possible."

She stared at him a moment before bursting into laughter. "Well, then, what are we waiting for?"

*Much, much later, after they had made love several times, they tiptoed to the kitchen in the first courtyard and smuggled back some pastries, a pot of tea, and two buckets of warm water. They washed each other, flicking water playfully all the while. When she had dried herself, she put on some new clothes, so they could sit down at the table to drink tea and dine on pastries.

But all Leighton managed was to gawk at her, in her blouse and trousers of pale lavender silk, her person lovely beyond compare.

She tossed a pastry at him. "Don't just eat me with your eyes. Have some food, too."

The pastry was sticky and barely sweet—and delicious for all that.

Her childhood bed in the inner room was where they decided to sleep. It was also a *kang*, but had been padded with more blankets. As they undressed and lay down, she asked about his leg, which had hurt for two days while he was crossing the Indian Ocean but not since. He asked about the treasure; she recounted the trip to Ning-hsia Province.

At the end of her story, she told him, "You would have been

at home there, in that particular Buddha cave. It was the work of men who believed, when they had every reason to despair."

He stroked her hair. "You were always a good reason to believe."

She smiled, her eyes shining in the lambent candlelight. "So what do we do now?"

"I believe we have a preexisting agreement in place that requires us to marry as soon as possible. What must I do to make that happen and how many matchmakers must I hire?"

His determination pleased her—she nuzzled her lips against his beard. "If Master Gordon were alive, he could have spoken to my stepfather on your behalf. But since he is not, perhaps the head of the British Legation might do, if he can vouch that you are a man of character."

He chortled with glee. "I never thought I'd have to ask the envoy extraordinary and minister plenipotentiary to secure me a wife, but I will speak with him first thing in the morning."

"Will it be an embarrassing conversation?"

"No, it will be a delightful one, one of the most delightful conversations I will ever hold in my life—or he in his," he declared.

They chatted for some time about their future married life, what they would do and where they would live—and concluded that they needed not come to a decision any time soon. There were many places they wanted to visit again and for the first time—they would settle down when they came to the right place at the right time.

They had already said good night to each other when he remembered something. "By the way—and I've been meaning to ask this for a while—but is there really such a thing as the snow chrysanthemum of Kunlun Shan, or did you make it up, like the frost sheep of the Heavenly Mountains?"

She laughed softly. "Yes, there really is such a thing as the snow chrysanthemum of Kunlun Shan. And this reminds me, there is something I've also been meaning to ask you. Do you remember that house you hired for me in London, so I'd have a safe place to stay?"

"Yes, of course."

"You left a note for me in that house. The very last line of that note was written in Turkic—and you know I can't read in that language. What does it say?"

He thought for a moment. "Why don't you offer me a bribe for the answer?"

Her lips touched his. He tsked at the inadequacy of her gesture. She kissed him more fully, the tip of her tongue gliding along his teeth. Still he disapproved. She snorted, fitted her body to his, slipped her hand between his legs, and kissed him again.

Which led to a good, long while of intense pleasure and nothing else.

It was only afterward that she asked, her voice drowsy, "So what does it say, anyway?"

He drew the bedcover over her and held her secure in his arms. "It says, *The one who loves you, always.*"

AUTHOR'S NOTE

Da-ren is not a name, but an expression of respect, meaning "great personage," which is why Ying-ying uses the term both to refer to her stepfather and to address him directly as such.

The author has absolutely no experience with real-life martial arts. The martial arts elements in this book are depicted as they would be in *wuxia* novels, a genre of Chinese literature that centers on practitioners of martial arts who reach near mythical levels of power and agility.

If you would like to know more about Ying-ying and Leighton, *The Hidden Blade*, the prequel to *My Beautiful Enemy*, is available at your favorite vendor of e-books and by print-on-demand. *The Hidden Blade* narrates the events of Ying-ying's and Leighton's formative years that have made them who thcy are, events the repercussions of which are still very much felt in *My Beautiful Enemy*.

Read on for a special preview of another
irresistible romance from Sherry Thomas

Ravishing the Heiress

Available now from Berkley Sensation

$\mathcal{I}$t was love at first sight.

Not that there was anything wrong with love at first sight, but Millicent Graves had not been raised to fall in love at all, let alone hard and fast.

She was the only surviving child of a very prosperous man who manufactured tinned goods and other preserved edibles. It had been decided, long before she could comprehend such things, that she was going to Marry Well—that via her person, the family's fortune would be united with an ancient and illustrious title.

Millie's childhood had therefore consisted of endless lessons: music, drawing, penmanship, elocution, deportment, and, when there was time left, modern languages. At ten, she successfully floated down a long flight of stairs with three books on her head. By twelve, she could exchange hours of pleasantries in French, Italian, and German. And on the day of her fourteenth birthday, Millie, not at all a natural musician, at last conquered Listz's *Douze Grandes Études*, by dint of sheer effort and determination.

That same year, with her father coming to the conclusion that she would never be a great beauty, nor indeed a beauty of any kind, the search began for a highborn groom desperate enough to marry a girl whose family wealth derived from—heaven forbid—sardines.

The search came to an end twenty months later. Mr. Graves was not particularly thrilled with the choice, as the earl who agreed to take his daughter in exchange for his money had a title that was neither particularly ancient nor particularly illustrious. But the stigma attached to tinned sardines was such that even this earl demanded Mr. Graves's last penny.

And then, after months of haggling, after all the agreements had finally been drawn up and signed, the earl had the inconsideration to drop dead at the age of thirty-three. Or rather, Mr. Graves viewed his death a thoughtless affront. Millie, in the privacy of her room, wept.

She'd seen the earl only twice and had not been overjoyed with either his anemic looks or his dour temperament. But he, in his way, had had as little choice as she. The estate had come to him in terrible disrepair. His schemes of improvement had made little to no difference. And when he'd tried to land an heiress of a more exalted background, he'd failed resoundingly, likely because he'd been so unimpressive in both appearance and demeanor.

A more spirited girl might have rebelled against such an unprepossessing groom, seventeen years her elder. A more enterprising girl might have persuaded her parents to let her take her chances on the matrimonial mart. Millie was not either of those girls.

She was a quiet, serious child who understood instinctively that much was expected of her. And while it was desirable that she could play all twelve of the *Grandes Études* rather than just eleven, in the end her training was not about music—or languages, or deportment—but about discipline, control, and self-denial.

Love was never a consideration. Her opinions were never a consideration. Best that she remained detached from the process, for she was but a cog in the great machinery of Marrying Well.

That night, however, she sobbed for this man, who, like her, had no say in the direction of his own life.

But the great machinery of Marrying Well ground on. Two weeks after the late Earl Fitzhugh's funeral, the Graves hosted his distant cousin the new Earl Fitzhugh for dinner.

Millie knew very little of the late earl. She knew even less of the new one, except that he was only nineteen, still in his last year at Eton. His youth disturbed her somewhat—she'd been prepared to marry an older man, not someone close to her own age. But other than that, she dwelled on him not at all: Her marriage was a business transaction; the less personal involvement from her, the more smoothly things would run.

Unfortunately, her indifference—and her peace of mind— came to an abrupt end the moment the new earl walked in the door.

*M*illie was not without thoughts of her own. She very carefully watched what she said and did, but seldom censored her mind: It was the only freedom she had.

Sometimes, as she lay in bed at night, she thought of falling in love, in the ways of a Jane Austen novel—her mother did not allow her to read the Brontës. Love, it seemed to her, was a result born of careful, shrewd observation. Miss Elizabeth Bennet, for example, did not truly consider Mr. Darcy to have the makings of a fine husband until she had seen the majesty of Pemberley, which stood for Mr. Darcy's equally majestic character.

Millie imagined herself a wealthy, independent widow, inspecting the gentlemen available to her with wry but humane wit. And if she were fortunate enough, finding that one gentle-man of character, sense, and good humor.

That seemed to her the epitome of romantic love: the quiet satisfaction of two kindred souls brought together in gentle harmony.

She was, therefore, entirely unprepared for her internal upheaval, when the new Earl Fitzhugh was shown into the family drawing room. Like a visitation of angels, there flared a bright white light in the center of her vision. Haloed by this supernatural radiance stood a young man who must have folded his wings just that moment so as to bear a passing resemblance to a mortal.

An instinctive sense of self-preservation made her lower her face before she'd quite comprehended the geography of his features. But she was all agitation inside, a sensation that was equal parts glee and misery.

Surely a mistake had been made. The late earl could not possibly have a cousin who looked like this. Any moment now he'd be introduced as the new earl's schoolmate, or per-haps the guardian Colonel Clements's son.

"Millie," said her mother, "let me present Lord Fitzhugh. Lord Fitzhugh, my daughter."

Dear God, it was him. This mind-bogglingly handsome young man was the new Lord Fitzhugh.

She had to lift her eyes. Lord Fitzhugh returned a steady, blue gaze. They shook hands.

"Miss Graves," he said.

Her heart thrashed drunkenly. She was not accustomed to such complete and undiluted masculine attention. Her mother was attentive and solicitous. But her father only ever spoke to her with one eye still on his newspaper.

Lord Fitzhugh, however, was focused entirely on her, as if she were the most important person he'd ever met.

"My lord," she murmured, acutely aware of the warmth on her face and the old-master perfection of his cheekbones.

Dinner was announced on the heels of the introductions. The earl offered his arm to Mrs. Graves and it was with great envy that Millie took Colonel Clements's arm.

She glanced at the earl. He happened to be looking her way. Their eyes held for a moment.

Heat pumped through her veins. She was jittery, stunned almost.

What was the matter with her? Millicent Graves, milquetoast extraordinaire, through whose veins dripped the *lack* of passion, did not experience such strange flashes and flutters. She'd never even read a Brontë novel, for goodness' sake. Why did she suddenly feel like one of the younger Bennet girls, the ones who giggled and shrieked and had absolutely no control over themselves?

Distantly she realized that she knew nothing of the earl's character, sense, or temperament. That she was behaving in a shallow and foolish manner, putting the cart before the horse. But the chaos inside her had a life and a will of its own.

As they entered the dining room, Mrs. Clements said, "What a lovely table. Don't you agree, Fitz?"

"I do," said the earl.

His name was George Edward Arthur Granville Fitzhugh—the family name and the title were the same. But apparently those who knew him well called him Fitz.

Fitz, her lips and teeth played with the syllable. *Fitz*.

At dinner, the earl let Colonel Clements and Mrs. Graves carry the majority of the conversation. Was he shy? Did he still obey the tenet that children should be seen and not heard? Or was he using the opportunity to assess his possible future in-laws—and his possible future wife?

Except he didn't appear to be studying her. Not that he could do so easily: A three-tier, seven-branch silver epergne, sprouting orchids, lilies, and tulips from every appendage, blocked the direct line of sight between them.

Through petals and stalks, she could make out his

occasional smiles—each of which made her ears hot—directed at Mrs. Graves to his left. But he looked more often in her father's direction.

Her grandfather and her uncle had built the Graves fortune. Her father had been young enough, when the family coffer began to fill, to be sent to Harrow. He'd acquired the expected accent, but his natural temperament was too lackluster to quite emanate the gloss of sophistication his family had hoped for.

There he sat, at the head of the table, neither a ruthless risk taker like his late father, nor a charismatic, calculating entrepreneur like his late brother, but a bureaucrat, a caretaker of the riches and assets thrust upon him. Hardly the most exciting of men.

Yet he commanded the earl's attention this night.

Behind him on the wall hung a large mirror in an ornate frame, which faithfully reflected the company at table. Millie sometimes looked into that mirror and pretended she was an outside observer documenting the intimate particulars of a private meal. But tonight she had yet to give the mirror a glance, since the earl sat at the opposite end of the table, next to her mother.

She found him in the mirror. Their eyes met.

He had not been looking at her father. Via the mirror, he'd been looking at *her*.

Mrs. Graves had been forthcoming on the mysteries of marriage—she did not want Millie ambushed by the facts of life. The reality of what happened between a man and a woman behind closed doors usually had Millie regard members of the opposite sex with wariness. But his attention caused only fireworks inside her—detonations of thrill, blasts of full-fledged happiness.

If they were married, and if they were alone . . .

She flushed.

But she already knew: She would not mind it.

Not with him.

* * *

$\mathcal{T}$he gentlemen had barely rejoined the ladies in the drawing room when Mrs. Graves announced that Millie would play for the gathering.

"Millicent is splendidly accomplished at the pianoforte," she said.

For once, Millie was excited about the prospect of displaying her skills—she might lack true musicality, but she did possess an ironclad technique.

As Millie settled herself before the piano, Mrs. Graves turned to Lord Fitzhugh. "Do you enjoy music, sir?"

"I do, most assuredly," he answered. "May I be of some use to Miss Graves? Turn the pages for her perhaps?"

Millie braced her hand on the music rack. The bench was not very long. He'd be sitting right next to her.

"Please do," said Mrs. Graves.

And just like that, Lord Fitzhugh was at Millie's side, so close that his trousers brushed the flounces of her skirts. He smelled fresh and brisk, like an afternoon in the country. And the smile on his face as he murmured his gratitude distracted her so much that she forgot that she should be the one to thank him.

He looked away from her to the score on the music rack. "*Moonlight Sonata*. Do you have something lengthier?"

The question rattled—and pleased—her. "Usually one only hears the first movement of the sonata, the adagio sostenuto. But there are two additional movements. I can keep playing, if you'd like."

"I'd be much obliged."

A good thing she played mechanically and largely from memory, for she could not concentrate on the notes at all. The tips of his fingers rested lightly against a corner of the score sheet. He had lovely looking hands, strong and elegant. She imagined one of his hands gripped around a cricket ball—it had been mentioned at dinner that he played for the school team. The ball he bowled would be fast as lightning. It would knock over a wicket directly and dismiss the batsman, to the roar of the crowd's appreciation.

"I have a request, Miss Graves," he spoke very quietly.

With her playing, no one could hear him but her.

"Yes, my lord?"

"I'd like you to keep playing no matter what I say."

Her heart skipped a beat. Now it was beginning to make sense. He wanted to sit next to her so that they could hold a private conversation in a room full of their elders.

"All right. I'll keep going," she answered. "What is it that you want to say, sir?"

"I'd like to know, Miss Graves, are you being forced into marriage?"

Ten thousand hours before the pianoforte was the only thing that kept Millie from coming to an abrupt halt. Her fingers continued to pressure the correct keys; notes of various descriptions kept on sprouting. But it could have been someone in the next house playing, so dimly did the music register.

"Do I—do I give the impression of being forced, sir?" Even her voice didn't quite sound her own.

He hesitated slightly. "No, you do not."

"Why do you ask, then?"

"You are sixteen."

"It is far from unheard of for a girl to marry at sixteen."

"To a man more than twice her age?"

"You make the late earl sound decrepit. He was a man in his prime."

"I am sure there are thirty-three-year-old men who make sixteen-year-olds tremble in romantic yearning, but my cousin was not one of them."

They were coming to the end of the page; he turned it just in time. She chanced a quick glance at him. He did not look at her.

"May I ask you a question, my lord?" she heard herself say.

"Please."

"Are *you* being forced to marry me?"

The words left her in a spurt, like arterial bleeding. She was afraid of his answer. Only a man who was himself being forced would wonder whether she, too, was under the same duress.

He was silent for some time. "Do you not find this kind of arrangement exceptionally distasteful?"

Glee and misery—she'd been bouncing between the two wildly divergent emotions. But now there was only misery left, a sodden mass of it. His tone was courteous. Yet his question was an accusation of complicity: He would not be here if she hadn't agreed.

"I—" She was playing the adagio sostenuto much too fast— no moonlight in her sonata, only storm-driven branches whacking at shutters. "I suppose I've had time to become inured to it: I've known my whole life that I'd have no say in the matter."

"My cousin held out for years," said the earl. "He should have done it sooner: begotten an heir and left everything to his own son. We are barely related."

He did not want to marry her, she thought dazedly, not in the very least.

This was nothing new. His predecessor had not wanted to marry her, either; she had accepted his reluctance as par for the course. Had never expected anything else, in fact. But the unwillingness of the young man next to her on the piano bench—it was as if she'd been forced to hold a block of ice in her bare hands, the chill turning into a black, burning pain.

And the mortification of it, to be so eager for someone who reciprocated none of her sentiments, who was revolted by the mere thought of taking her as a wife.

He turned the next page. "Do you never think to yourself, *I won't do it*?"

"Of course I've *thought* of it," she said, suddenly bitter after all these years of placid obedience. But she kept her voice smooth and uninflected. "And then I think a little further. Do I run away? My skills as a lady are not exactly valuable beyond the walls of this house. Do I advertise my services as a governess? I know nothing of children—nothing at all. Do I simply refuse and see whether my father loves me enough to not disown me? I'm not sure I have the courage to find out."

He rubbed the corner of a page between his fingers. "How do you stand it?"

This time there was no undertone of accusation to his question. If she wanted to, she might even detect a bleak sympathy. Which only fed her misery, that foul beast with teeth like knives.

"I keep myself busy and do not think too deeply about it," she said, in as harsh a tone as she'd ever allowed herself.

There, she was a mindless automaton who did as others instructed: getting up, going to sleep, and earning heaps of disdain from prospective husbands in between.

They said nothing more to each other, except to exchange the usual civilities at the end of her performance. Everyone applauded. Mrs. Clements said very nice things about Millie's musicianship—which Millie barely heard.

The rest of the evening lasted the length of Elizabeth's reign.

Mr. Graves, usually so phlegmatic and taciturn, engaged the earl in a lively discussion of cricket. Millie and Mrs. Graves gave their attention to Colonel Clements's army stories. Had someone looked in from the window, the company in the drawing room would have appeared perfectly normal, jovial even.

And yet there was enough misery present to wilt flowers and curl wallpaper. Nobody noticed the earl's distress. And nobody—except Mrs. Graves, who stole anxious looks at Millie—noticed Millie's. Was unhappiness really so invisible? Or did people simply prefer to turn away, as if from lepers?

After the guests took their leave, Mr. Graves pronounced

the dinner a *succès énorme*. And he, who'd remained skeptical on the previous earl throughout, gave his ringing endorsement to the young successor. "I shall be pleased to have Lord Fitzhugh for a son-in-law."

"He hasn't proposed yet," Millie reminded him, "and he might not."

Or so she hoped. Let them find someone else for her. Anyone else.

"Oh, he will most assuredly propose," said Mr. Graves. "He has no choice."

*D*o you really have no other choices, then?" asked Isabelle.

Her eyes were bright with unshed tears. Futility burned inside Fitz. He could do nothing to halt this future that hurtled toward him like a derailed train, and even less to alleviate the pain of the girl he loved.

"If I do, it is only in the sense that I am free to go to London and see if a different heiress will have me."

She turned her face away and wiped her eyes with the heel of her hand. "What is she like, this Miss Graves?"

What did it matter? He could not recall her face. Nor did he want to. "Unobjectionable."

"Is she pretty?"

He shook his head. "I don't know—and I don't care."

She was not Isabelle—she could never be pretty enough.

It was unbearable to think of Miss Graves as a permanent fixture in his life. He felt violated. He raised the shotgun in his hands and pulled the trigger. Fifty feet away, a clay pigeon exploded. The ground was littered with shards: It had been an excruciating conversation.

"So, this time next year, you could have a child," said Isabelle, her voice breaking. "The Graveses would want their money's worth—and soon."

God, they would expect that of him, wouldn't they? Another clay pigeon burst apart; he scarcely felt the recoil in his shoulder.

It hadn't seemed quite so terrible at first, becoming an earl out of the blue. He realized almost immediately he'd have to give up his plan of a career in the military: An earl, even a poor one, was too valuable for the front line. The blow, although harsh, was far from fatal. He'd chosen the military for the demands it would place on him. Returning an estate from the brink of ruin was just as demanding and honorable an occupation. And he did not think Isabelle would at all mind becoming a ladyship: She would cut a dashing figure in Society.

But as he stepped into Henley Park, his new seat, his blood began to congeal. At nineteen, he had not become a poor earl, but a desperately destitute one.

The manor's decline was frightful. The oriental carpets were moth-eaten, the velvet curtains similarly so. Many of the flues drew not at all; walls and paintings were grimy with soot. And in every last upper-story room, the ceiling was green and grey with growth of mold, spreading like the contours of a distorted map.

Such a large house demanded fifty indoor servants and could limp by with thirty. But at Henley Park, the indoor staff had been reduced to fifteen, roughly divided between the too young—several of the maids were barely twelve—and the too old, retainers who had been with the family for their entire lives and had nowhere else to go.

Everything in his room creaked: the floor, the bed, the doors of the wardrobe. The plumbing was medieval—the long decline of the family's fortune had precluded any meaningful modernization of the interior. And for the three nights of his stay, he'd gone to sleep shivering with cold, listening to the congregation of rats in the walls.

It was a step above outright dilapidation, but only a very small step.

Isabelle's family was thoroughly respectable. The Pelhams, like the Fitzhughs, were related to several noble lineages and in general considered just the sort of solid, upstanding, God-fearing country gentry that did the squirearchy proud. But neither the Fitzhughs nor the Pelhams were wealthy; what funds they could scrape together would not keep Henley Park's roof from leaking, or her foundation from rotting.

But if it were only the house, they might still have some-how managed with various economies. Unfortunately, Fitz also inherited eighty thousand pounds in debt. And from that, there was no escape.

Were he ten years younger, he could bury his head in the sand and let Colonel Clements worry about his problems. But he was only two years short of majority, a man nearly grown. He could not run away from his troubles, which assuredly would only worsen during any period of inattention.

The only viable solution was the sale of his person, to exchange his cursed title for an heiress with a fortune large enough to pay his debts and repair his house.

But to do that, he would have to give up Isabelle.

"Please, let's not speak of it," he said, his teeth clenched.

He didn't want much in life. The path he'd delineated for himself had been simple and straightforward: officer training at Sandhurst, a commission to follow, and when he'd received his first promotion, Isabelle's hand in marriage. She was not only beautiful, but intelligent, hardy, and adventurous. They would have been deliriously happy together.

Tears rolled down her face. "But whether we speak of it or not, it's going to happen, isn't it?"

She raised her shotgun and blasted the last remaining clay pigeon to pieces. His heart was similarly shattered.

"No matter what happens . . ."

He could not continue. He was no longer in a position to declare his love for her. Whatever he said would only make things worse.

"Don't marry her," she implored, her voice hoarse, her eyes fervent. "Forget Henley Park. Let's run away together."

*I*f only they could. "Neither of us is of age. Our marriage wouldn't be valid without the consent of your father and my guardian. I don't know about your father, but Colonel Clements is dead set on my doing my duty. He'd rather see you ruined than allow our marriage to stand."

Overhead thunder rolled. "Isabelle, Lord Fitzhugh," cried her mother's voice from inside the house, "better come back. It's going to rain soon!"

Neither of them moved.

Drops of rain fell on his head, each as heavy as a pebble.

Isabelle gazed at him. "Do you remember the first time you came to visit?"

"Of course."

He'd been sixteen, she fifteen. It had been at the end of Michaelmas Half. And he'd arrived with Pelham, Hastings, and two other mates from Eton. She'd sprinted down the stairs to hug Pelham. Fitz had met her before, when she'd come to see Pelham at Eton. But on that day, suddenly, she was no longer the little girl she'd been, but a lovely young lady, full of life and verve. The afternoon sun, slanting into the hall, had lit her like a flame. And when she'd turned around and said, "Ah, Mr. Fitzhugh, I remember you," he was already in love.

"Do you remember the fight scene from *Romeo and Juliet*?" she asked softly.

He nodded. Would that time flowed backward, so he could leave the present behind and head toward those older, more joyous days instead.

"I remember everything so clearly: Gerry was Tybalt and you Mercutio. You had one of my father's walking sticks in one hand and a tea sandwich in the other. You took a bite of the sandwich, and sneered, 'Tybalt, you rat-catcher, will you walk?'" She smiled through her tears. "Then you laughed. My heart caught and I knew then and there that I wanted to spend my life with you."

His face was wet. "You'll find someone better," he forced himself to say.

"I don't want anyone else. I want only you."

And he wanted only her. But it was not to be. They were not to be.

Rain came down in sheets. It had been a miserable spring. Already he despaired of ever again walking under an unclouded sky.

"Isabelle, Lord Fitzhugh, you must come inside now," repeated Mrs. Pelham.

They ran. But as they reached the side of the house, she gripped his arm and pulled him toward her. "Kiss me."

"I mustn't. Even if I don't marry Miss Graves, I'm to marry someone else."

"Have you ever kissed anyone?"

"No." He'd been waiting for her.

"All the more reason you must kiss me now. So that no matter what happens, we will always be each other's first."

Lightning split the sky. He stared at the beautiful girl who would never be his. Was it so wrong?

It must not be, because the next moment he was kissing her, lost to everything else but this one last moment of freedom and joy.

And when they could no longer delay their return to the house, he held her tight and whispered what he'd promised himself he would not say.

"No matter what happens, I will always, always love you."

The Luckiest
Lady in London

❧❦❧

Louisa Cantwell must marry rich to support her sisters. But does she dare fall in love with a man who has as many dark and devastating secrets as the Marquess of Wrenworth?

"Thomas is known for a lush style…[and] transporting prose even as [she] delivers on heat and emotion and a well-earned happily ever after."
—*The New York Times Book Review*

"A masterpiece…A beautifully written, exquisitely seductive, powerfully romantic gem of a romance."
—*Kirkus Reviews* (starred review)

sherrythomas.com
facebook.com/AuthorSherryThomas
facebook.com/LoveAlwaysBooks
penguin.com

M1462T0314